ABOUT THE AUTHOR

Thorne Moore lives in a north Pembrokeshire farm cottage on the site of a medieval manor, with an excellent view of the stars, but she grew up in Luton and studied history at Aberystwyth. Nine years later, after a spell working in a library, she returned to Wales, to run a restaurant with her sister, and a craft business making miniature furniture.

She took a law degree through the Open University, and occasionally taught genealogy, but these days, she writes, as she had always intended, after retiring from 40 years of craft work.

Besides her psychological crime and historical mysteries, including 'A Time for Silence' (finalist for the People's Book Prize and Bookseller Top Ten best seller), she also writes science fiction.

For some years she ran the Narberth Book Fair with fellow author Judith Barrow, and she is a member of Crime Cymru.

Published in Great Britain in 2023
By Diamond Crime

ISBN 978–1-915649-22-5

Diamond Crime is an imprint of Diamond Books Ltd.

Many thanks to my patient readers, Becky, Judith and Catherine, for seeing me through this, and to Steve, Jeff and Phil at Diamond Crime for taking it on and for allowing me, however reluctantly, to win some of my battles. And. Of course, thank you to the Cardigan Otter.

Book design: jacksonbone.co.uk
Cover photograph: Levi Guzman/Unsplash

For information about Diamond Crime authors
and their books, visit:
www.diamondbooks.co.uk

For my Becky, the doctor at large.

BETHULIA

THORNE MOORE

It is the province of the tarot reader to move backwards,
forwards, even sideways in time.
Sasha Graham

PART ONE
THE MOON

Oxford, 11th October 2000

Three girls were huddled in a bay window, peering up into the night sky.

The fair-haired one stretched out to trace the moon's outline on the window pane. "The full moon's so beautiful."

The dark-haired one peered up, calculating. "It's not actually full for another two days, Alison. It's still gibbous."

"Gibbous! Trust Danny." The third one laughed. "Lovely word. Really creepy, isn't it?"

"The moon's never creepy," said Alison. "It's like it's watching over us."

"Like a mother?"

"Yes," said Alison quietly. The other two exchanged shame-faced glances.

Danny, the dark one, picked up her book. "We're supposed to be doing homework. Haven't you got any, Jude?"

"German. Done it. Easy. What about you, Ali?"

Alison hugged her knees. "I'm excused because of the piano exam."

"Which you passed, of course."

"He was a nice examiner."

"So in love with you, I bet."

"He was an old man. But very kind."

"Not Prince Charming then?"

"No, but I liked him."

"What would your Prince Charming be like?"

Alison gave it serious thought. "Kind."

"Kind? Not handsome?"

"Well yes, that too. And loving."

"Smart," said Danny. "And not into football."

"Funny," said Jude. "Sexy."

Alison laughed and drew a smiley face on the moon. "Yes, all right. But he must be kind."

Jude sprang up from the window seat and whirled round the room. "What if we found one, you know, a really cool man who was kind and handsome and smart and funny and sexy and hated football. Which one of us would get him?"

"We could draw straws," suggested Danny.

"Or share him," said Alison.

"And all live together in a huge house!"

"And have lots of babies."

"I want three," said Danny.

"I want six," said Alison.

"Do I have to?" asked Jude.

"Yes!" they roared.

"One then."

"I'd love that," said Alison. "Wouldn't you? If we three could stay together always."

"For ever and ever, amen," said Jude.

Amen

PART TWO
THE LOVERS

1. Jude, Heathrow, 20th June 2018

We were coming in over Kew. I could see it clearly, sunlight flashing on the panes of the Temperate House. Rampant greenery and damp earth – I could almost smell it, feel the humid heat. As the plane took another plunge, I plunged too, into a memory of a greenhouse in a suburban Oxford garden and three little girls…

Me and Danny, our hands dark with potting compost, nudging each other as Dr Rackman approaches, guiding a fair-haired girl with a pale face, tear streaks on her cheeks.

"Danny, Judith… girls, you were supposed to be putting that compost into the pots, not out of them. Never mind. This is Alison and I want you to be very nice to her." Mrs Doctor looks over the top of her glasses at us, reminding us what she has already told us, that Alison Greenold's mum has died and she's very unhappy. We grip our dirty hands together, agreeing.

"Alison, darling, this is my daughter Danielle – Danny – and Judith Carr, who comes to stay with us when her parents are abroad. Your dad wants you to stay with us too for a while, while he sorts things out, so I hope these

two rapscallions will look after you and you'll all be friends. Do you think you will?"

The pale girl gives a snivelling nod. Danny drops my hand and rushes forward to throw her arms around Alison. She is crying, thinking of dead mums, and I cry too as I join them, my arms weaving with theirs until we are one knot of little girl…

Hands were pressing against my seat. The passenger behind me, who has been silent the entire flight, was breathing heavily now, shuddering with nerves. The ground was coming up to meet us. It's odd that as a plane slows down to land, the sensation of speed increases. We were going to crash. Bump. We were going to crash. Bump, we were hurtling along the tarmac towards oblivion, and there was a bit of me that usually enjoyed the thrill, but not today. All I felt was a sense of inescapable doom.

It grew as the plane slowed and turned to taxi to its dock. I'd travelled in haste, but now I wanted to delay the end. Unlike the other passengers.

"Ladies and gentlemen, please remain in your seats until…" Why do they bother saying it? The moment my fellow travellers sensed the plane was stationary, they were unbuckling their belts and trampling over each other to haul down cabin luggage.

I sat motionless until the order of disembarkation had been sorted and the hordes had finally shuffled to the doors. I gathered up my one small case and walked out after them. Once I'd passed the stewardess's corporate smile, I slowed my saunter to a foot-dragging crawl. Why not just stop? Go no further, hear no news. But I was Jude. I didn't do prevarication. I faced things head-on.

I switched my phone back on and texts promptly piled up. There was only one that mattered - the text I had been anticipating. The text I didn't want. The chill in my stomach gnawed its way into my heart. I pocketed my phone and marched towards Arrivals.

They were there, two women stranded on their own private island of quicksand in a milling ocean of confusion. I saw them before they spotted me and one look confirmed the brief blunt text. Madeleine – Dr Rackman – face lined by grief, and my Danny, drawn, gaunt, desolate, arms wrapped round herself until she saw me. Her mouth opened in a silent tormented greeting, and she ran towards me, embracing me in a wave of desperation. I embraced her back. One knot of woman. Just the two of us.

"Jude, thank God you came." Her broken voice whispered in my ear.

"I've been in the air for twelve hours. Only just got your text. Please tell me it's not true."

She gasped a strangled scream.

I pushed her back, holding her so that I could see her eyes. "Say it."

"Yes! It's true." Her face seemed to disintegrate before me. "I shouldn't have told her. But I did, I told her and she's dead, Jude. Alison is dead."

I took a deep breath, found myself swaying, disorientated by solid ground. I faced Madeleine over Danny's shoulder. Eyes shut, she shook her head in confirmation.

"How?" I asked.

Danny hugged me again, tighter. "I don't care what they say about suicide. It was Simon, I know it. He killed her, Jude! I know he did! I told them but they wouldn't listen.

5

They've let him just walk away. How could they? He killed her!"

I winced, picturing Danny throwing herself around a police station, wild and nonsensical with grief. She was always the Emily of us Brontë sisters. I hugged her close again.

Madeleine smiled painfully. "Simon was in London, nowhere near. Danny can't accept that it was suicide. She accused him so they took him in for questioning, but of course they had nothing to hold him on."

"Poor Simon," I said.

Danny pushed herself away, staring at me with horror. "How can you say that?"

But I was looking at her with equal horror, seeing her afresh – her skeletal frame, her hollow cheeks, her sunken eyes. "Danny! Are you…? Oh my God, it's back, isn't it?"

She looked away.

Madeleine swallowed. "Yes. It was too good to be true. It's back and it's spread."

"Jesus," I whispered. "Have you started treatment?"

Danny shook her head fiercely. "I don't want it."

"Danny…" I paused. There was too much pent-up emotion here on a Heathrow concourse. Too many horrors piling up on top of each other. I needed to get out of there. "Come on. Let's get you home. Where's your car? I'll drive."

"After that long flight?" asked Madeleine.

"I got some sleep," I lied, taking the keys from her. I wanted mother and daughter sitting together in the back, supporting each other. While I'd been away, so much had come to crisis point for Danny as well as Alison. I should have been there, for both of them.

We travelled mostly in silence, holding in the flood for now. Danny began, "Alison…" once or twice and then cracked up. I met Madeleine's agonised eyes in the mirror. At the Rackmans' Oxford house, we hurried inside and I managed to steer Madeleine into the kitchen, while Danny collapsed on the sofa.

"You said it's spread. How bad is it?"

She shook her head. "My darling girl, everything's been too much – Simon, the cancer and now Alison. It's destroyed her."

"We can't let her just refuse treatment. I know it was awful last time, but…"

"She's adamant. You think I haven't tried to persuade her? I've done nothing but, since she told me."

I took a deep breath. "We can at least sort out a hospice or something."

"I don't want a hospice." Danny had caught up with us, her eyes shining with fierce defiance. "You know what I want."

"No, Danny. Please, no."

"Yes! I want to make that bastard pay."

I wept inside, understanding her desperate need for blame and justice to fix on a target and ease her own guilt. "Danny, leave it. You must. For everyone's sake, but especially your own. Think about yourself and forget Simon Delaney."

2. DC QUILLAN

DS Gray turned into Tork Lane from Soweridge High Street. "Cat got your tongue, girl? Not squeamish or something?"

"No, Sergeant." DC Rosanna Quillan was determined to remain calm and professional. This was what she'd wanted, to be out on a case. Most of her first ten days in the department had been spent at a desk, staring at a computer screen, the office junior, lumbered with anything tedious while suspicion wore off. It had given her time to get a feel for the unit, to grasp some of the undercurrents flowing between her fellow officers. The good, the bad and the DS Grays.

Gray was referred to, repeatedly, with a roll of the eyes, as "Old School," which apparently meant sexist, racist, homophobic, anti-Semitic, anti-Islamic... just about everything now judged unacceptable. He had adapted to changing times by following every inappropriate remark with a chuckle and "but I suppose I'm not allowed to say that anymore."

She found it easiest to block him out and keep her thoughts to herself. *Be objective. Observe. Take mental notes, stay calm.*

Soweridge: typical quaint Oxfordshire village.

Tork Lane: scattered houses hiding behind double gates and long drives of finely raked gravel. Half-acre gardens along here, not like the sandstone terraced cottages with backyards on the crooked High Street. Names, of course, instead of numbers. Shrubs and trees mature enough to deter prying eyes.

Which wasn't stopping eyes trying to pry. Rosanna glimpsed strips of bright light at front doors furtively ajar. The area bristled with so many Neighbourhood Watch signs and burglar alarms that any drama, even domestic contretemps, would add a welcome spice. Domestic death even better.

Suicide. Don't think back. Be objective. Observe.

The car turned a bend and slowed to a crawl. This was it then.

Three houses, two on one side of the lane, figures at windows watching, and the third, Summervale, opposite. Not difficult to identify it with the gates and the front door standing wide and its spectral shrubs dancing in blue flashing light. A sea of gravel was cluttered with vehicles, including an ambulance, its rear doors wide open.

DS Gray tucked their Mondeo in beside a grey Porsche. "Right. Here we go." He grunted as he released his seat belt and struggled out. "Get your gear on and let's get to it. So, you got here first, Morgan."

DC Ben Morgan greeted them. "Yes, Sarge." He gave a friendly nod to Rosanna.

She nodded back, surveying the house, making mental notes. Mock-Tudor, brick and half-timbering with mullioned windows and ornately twisted chimneys, ivy and Virginia creeper clipped in check but clearly well-established. Early twentieth century and mellowed with age. It should belong to a retired solicitor whose wife held bridge evenings. Was that what the dead woman had been? An elderly lady tired of bridge? Or tired of her solicitor. Finally ground down by her solicitor…

Gray belched as he squinted up at the house. "How the other half live, eh? All right, so what's the low-down then?"

"Apparent suicide, sir. Upstairs, back room on the left. Female, thirty-two. Alison Delaney. There's no sign of disturbance or forced entry to suggest anyone else was in the house at the time. Nothing except pills and booze. Husband found her and called 999. They've got him in the sitting room for now."

"So, let's not waste time." Gray turned to the DCs. "Come on then, girlie. Let's see if you know how to be useful. Morgan, got your notebook?"

They followed him into the house. No hint of Tudor inspiration inside. The present owners had opted for defiantly modern décor. Glass and steel. Rosanna followed her colleagues up to the open bedroom door at the rear of the house.

Irony dictated that her first fatality had to be a suicide. She fixed on details to keep at bay that growl of anger permanently swilling deep inside her. The bedroom was large, elegant, so immaculate it was utterly impersonal. No books half-read, no slippers, let alone the discarded bags, mugs, underwear littering Rosanna's own room. Fitted wardrobes. A clock-radio on one of the bedside tables but nothing else. En-suite bathroom, its door ajar. Curtains wide, the sky golden beyond the quaintly latticed windows.

Rosanna forced herself to turn to the bed, partly shielded by a paramedic gathering up his equipment. He stepped back and she could see the figure sprawled across the duvet. Arms and legs akimbo, long fair hair concealing most of the face, one hand clenched tight on the satin cover. Rucked skirt, rumpled blouse, no shoes. She got a whiff of vomit and worse.

Gray stood hoisting his trousers up over his bulging belly. "No sign of life?"

The paramedic shook his head. "Nope. The doctor can confirm it but I'd say she's been dead for hours. Husband found her when he got back from London. No foetal heartbeat, of course."

"She's pregnant?"

"Husband says four or five months."

Ben Morgan peered down at a gin bottle on the bed. Empty. "DIY abortion gone wrong, could it be?"

"No, this was suicide all right, with this amount of pills and booze."

"Right." Gray scratched his head then turned back to Rosanna, stepping aside to let her take a better look at the contorted body. It wasn't resting in peace. "Not a pleasant sight, eh, Quillan? Spoiled her pretty looks, silly girl."

Ben's eyes squeezed shut for a second. The paramedic winced.

"Not going to throw a wobbly at the sight of a corpse, are you?"

11

Rosanna kept calm. "No, sir."

"Well, you never know with… but I mustn't say that, must I? Doc's been yet?"

"On his way," said Ben, and whispered in Rosanna's ear. "Just ignore him."

She allowed herself a grateful smile, though she didn't need Ben Morgan's support. She'd handled far worse than DS Gray, long before she'd joined the force. She'd handled suicide long before. Suicide in a grimy noisy street, not in a luxury bedroom. Suicide… She shook her head and shut out the image, concentrating once more on the scene before her.

"Why here?"

"Eh?" Gray turned to her. "What you mean?"

"It's not her room, is it?" She flipped open a wardrobe door to confirm what she suspected. Empty except for a collection of hangers. She stepped into the bathroom. No toiletries except for an expensive handwash. The cabinet was open, nothing in it except an empty gin bottle and a crumpled pill packet. Much like the emptied packet and the bottles that surrounded the figure on the bed. "It's a guest room."

"Yeah, she and the husband shared a room at the front," said Ben.

"So why here?" repeated Rosanna.

Gray's eyebrows rose. "Didn't want to soil her own nest? Women are like that."

"No risk of neighbours looking in?" suggested Ben.

"Curtains would do that." Rosanna walked to the window. No other houses in sight, just a lawn and trees, their branches bobbing in the breeze, against a twilit backdrop of open fields. The promise of fresh air. Would it really hurt to clear the sickly smell of this room and open the window wide? She needed to breathe. "This was shut?" If the paramedic had already handled the latch, it couldn't hurt to touch it now.

"Won't open," the paramedic replied. "I tried. They're all locked. Can't find a key."

Gray wasn't interested in the windows. He was examining the packets on the bed. "Tofranil. What's that? Antidepressant. Any sign of a note?"

"Not that we've found."

"What did she have to feel depressed about, living the life of Riley? Some people don't know they're born." Gray gave another belch and rubbed his stomach.

"People can feel suicidal wherever they live," said Ben.

"Selfish anyway. Waste of life, grieving relatives and too much work for us." Gray moved to the door as a murmur of voices wafted up from below. "Good, the doc. Upstairs, Mike! Back room."

The doctor heaved himself upstairs. Same age as Gray and, by his looks, of a similar disposition. "Ah. Harry. Good. Caught up with you at last. What have you got for me, then?"

"Suicide. Stupid girl." Gray slapped the doctor on the back as he entered the bedroom. "No consideration, some people. So, when are we having that return game? Got anything on, this weekend?"

"I'll question the husband, shall I?" interrupted Ben.

"What? Oh, yes, and take girlie with you. He might respond to the woman's touch. Just don't let her start cosying up to him, eh?"

Without a word, Rosanna followed Ben out to the stairs. He gave a sympathetic smile. "Don't let him get to you. He's one month off retirement and he's making the most of goading everyone."

"I can deal with his sort. But he shouldn't be jumping to conclusions so soon, should he? We don't know for certain it's suicide."

Ben shrugged as he reached the hall. "Yes, I know, assume nothing, believe nothing, etcetera, but it's unlikely to be anything else. And Gray likes speedy solutions. So we'd best speak to the husband, if he's up to it. They'll have made him a cup of tea but I don't suppose that will have been much comfort."

Tea. Rosanna had a memory flash of a beaker of orange squash pressed into her hands. A memory of her drinking it because her mouth was so dry it hurt. A neighbour saying, "That's better, isn't it?" and it wasn't better at all.

"No, I don't suppose it would be," she said, following Ben into the drawing room.

Lofty and spacious, all blond wood, pale leather, everything tastefully subdued and just wrong. Nothing dark except a grand piano, occupying one corner. The wide windows would flood the room with sun in the day, and artful glows from strategically placed lamps would soften it by night but, under the bright unforgiving central light this evening, it seemed clinical and drained.

A man was standing at the marble fireplace, his back to them as he leaned on the mantelpiece, his face buried in his arms, his shoulders heaving. At the sound of their entry, he raised his head and stared at them in the mirror, before turning to face them, breathing heavily.

"Mr Simon Delaney?" asked Ben.

"Yes. Jesus, I don't understand it. Why? Why did she do it?"

"Let's sit down, shall we, Mr Delaney? I'm DC Morgan and this is DC Quillan. I know you must be in a state of shock, but if you're up to it, I would like to ask you some questions, just so that we can have a clear idea of what happened with your wife."

"What? Okay, yes of course." Delaney slumped down into an armchair. Head in hands, he heaved a sob.

Ben perched on a chair opposite him. "Your wife, Alison - I understand she was pregnant? Four months, I think the paramedic said."

"Nearly five!" The words began as a whisper and ended as a howl. "Nearly five. She's just had a scan. My daughter! How could she?" Delaney squeezed his eyes shut in a visible effort to control himself, his hands gripping together convulsively.

Rosanna, standing apart, watched him with detachment, leaving the compassion to Ben.

Despite the distraught dishevelment, Simon Delaney was gym-fit, taller than average, dark and handsome – probably knew it too. People that good-looking always did. Rosanna guessed that in normal circumstances he'd be immaculately groomed, never a well-styled hair out of place. But circumstances weren't normal. His hair had been raked through, and his linen shirt was crumpled, the front splattered with wet patches as if he'd either spilled drink or vomited and mopped himself down. Sweat stains were spreading under the armpits – no anti-perspirant was designed to cope with a wife's suicide.

Was his distress real or a performance for their benefit? Rosanna had witnessed a fake show of grief; she knew what that looked like. This seemed genuine enough. His wife had killed herself and he was left to struggle through a maelstrom of bewildered grief, rage, guilt, all the usual responses to bereavement. She knew how it worked.

"So, Simon. Is it all right to call you Simon? Good. I'm Ben. Now, as I understand it, you found your wife. Would you like to tell me about it? You came home from work? Where's that?"

"London. My main office is in London."

"And you were there all day? What time did you travel in, this morning?"

"I caught the seven-thirty train." Delaney mopped his damp forehead.

"From Oxford, would that be? Did you drive there, leave your car at the station?"

"Yes, why?"

"Just so we can confirm all the details. And you left your office when?"

"Er, the meeting finished just before five. I got the train back… no, I stopped for a drink first. Sorry. I forgot that."

"Don't worry, Simon, it's always difficult getting things straight in your head when something like this happens. You stopped for a drink. For ten minutes? Half an hour? An hour?"

"I – er – I don't know. Half an hour, maybe. I caught the six-fifty-something train back."

"And then you drove straight home from the station?"

"Yes. No!" He pulled himself up short with a squirm of guilt. "Yes, but I wasn't over the limit. I'd only had one. I had a couple of whiskies here, though, after…" He glanced at a half-empty bottle of Scotch on a cabinet.

"We're not worrying about that, just now. Just want to get the timing right. You arrived home then, about what? Eight-ish?"

"Yes, I suppose, about that. I don't know. I wasn't really thinking about it. I just drove home, that's all. And I found her lying there! I mean, how could she do it to me?"

Ben nodded understanding. "So you found her. How soon?"

"What?"

"You let yourself in – presumably you weren't instantly alarmed when you found that she wasn't there to greet you?"

"Oh. No. Well, I don't know. Maybe. Everything was so silent, which was odd. If she's not in the hall to greet me, I'd hear her around the house. I called, you know, 'Alison, are you there?' She didn't reply so I went up to see if she'd gone to bed, but she hadn't. So I went looking for her."

"The door of the back bedroom was shut, was it?"

Delaney's head jerked up a fraction. Trying to remember a detail? There was a momentary look of panic in his eyes, before they closed, and opened again full of tears. Rosanna's skin prickled.

"Yes."

"But you looked in there, anyway."

"Yes. Well, only after I'd looked everywhere else."

"You didn't just assume she'd gone out for the evening? Gone to see a friend maybe?"

A pause. He licked his lips. "Alison doesn't like going out in the evening alone – only if I'm with her. She's always waiting for me when I get home." He looked from Ben to Rosanna and back, adding hurriedly, "She hasn't been well. She gets nervous."

The prickling in Rosanna's skin began to claw. A confused picture. Little wifey dutifully waiting for hubby at home? Or a troubled woman scared to be without him? Either way he'd known she'd be there waiting, but it hadn't stopped him staying in London for a drink or two or three.

Ben nodded. "So you knew she must be in the house and you looked in the back bedroom."

"Yes. And everywhere else."

"Was that door locked?" asked Rosanna. "Had she locked herself in?"

Delaney was motionless for a moment, seemingly confused by a second interrogator. "No."

"So you didn't have to break the door down."

"No." He took a deep breath. "No, she didn't lock it."

"The windows are locked."

The sinews of his neck stiffened. "We always keep them locked."

"Do you know where the keys are?"

He stared at her, then exploded in irritation. "God, I don't fucking know. Does it matter?"

"Probably not," said Ben, throwing Rosanna a quizzical glance. "Never mind the window for now. The door wasn't locked and you went in."

"Yes! And there she was. It made no sense at first. Of course I immediately shook her, felt for a pulse, but it was obvious she was dead." It was a very pat response, rehearsed, but he trembled, despite his keenness to get the words out.

"It must have been very distressing for you. No wonder you needed a stiff drink. Did you immediately assume suicide when you saw her? Or did you suspect murder, for instance?"

"No, no! Of course it was suicide. All those bottles and…" Delaney struggled to get the words out. "…pills."

"When you made your 999 call, you asked for the police, not an ambulance."

"I didn't know who to call. She was dead. I could see that. I could feel it. Who are you supposed to call when someone dies? I don't know."

"No, of course not. So you were quite convinced, from the moment you realised she was dead, that it was self-inflicted?"

Delaney turned white. "Yes," he said in almost a whisper.

"Sorry if this is distressing for you. I'm afraid any case of unexpected death has to be investigated. So, I have to ask, did her suicide come as a total surprise? Did she do, say anything beforehand, to suggest she might be intending to do something like this?"

"No! Why would she? She was having my baby, for Christ's sake."

"She wasn't depressed? There was a lot of medication there. Did you know she had been prescribed Tofranil?"

"I…" He was fidgeting, hands clenching, one eyelid twitching uncontrollably. "I knew the doctor had prescribed something, but that was… She had been depressed, drinking too much – she'd had some professional setbacks and they left her a bit vulnerable, I suppose."

"What sort of setbacks would those be?"

"She used to be a music teacher. Dreamed of being a concert pianist, but it didn't come to anything. She was disappointed, really down about it, so she went to see her doctor. Quack gave her pills, but we'd agreed they'd stop with the pregnancy. No more pills, no more alcohol. We'd agreed. It was best for the…" He couldn't say the word *baby*.

"And yet there was plenty of alcohol in the house."

"Apparently," said Delaney, bitterly. Rage suddenly erupted from him. "She lied! She lied to me! We agreed no drink and she fucking lied!"

"You didn't know she kept a supply? Other than your Scotch?" Ben studied the bottle.

"No, and she wasn't allow… she never touched that. I certainly didn't know she'd stashed away bottles of gin! Do you think I'd have left them there if I'd known?"

"You'd have confiscated them."

Delaney almost blurted an answer but hesitated at the last moment. "We'd agreed she wouldn't drink. She knew it was for the best. And she didn't need the pills.

anything else. I thought it would be enough for her. It should have been enough for her."

Rosanna dug her nails into her palms. Judgements shouldn't be based on the words of someone deranged by sudden bereavement. She should be keeping an open mind. But she really wanted to smack this man.

Morgan merely nodded again. "And how was she when you left this morning?"

"She was asleep." Delaney was firm about this. His voice shifted to a different register. Back to the prepared script. "She was a bit uptight, last night. Sometimes she gets wound up. Pregnancy affects some women that way. They get overly emotional. Hormones running riot. Yes, she was emotional last night, a bit tearful—"

"About?"

"Nothing in particular. Just worried that the baby would be okay, that she'd be a good mother, able to cope, all that. So, as I said, she was uptight, didn't get off to sleep until gone one. So this morning I slipped out of bed without waking her."

"Did you contact her at all, during the day?"

"No."

"Didn't want to check that she was feeling less uptight?"

"No." Suddenly Delaney's head was in his hands again and he was blubbing wildly. "I should have done. I'll never forgive myself. Never!"

Ben was leaning forward with another question when the door opened and DS Gray came in. "Mr Delaney. Sorry for your loss. All done here, Morgan? Clearly an

21

open and shut case of suicide. No need to bother you further just now, but we'll have to check the scene thoroughly. Do you have friends you can go to?"

"I'll go to a hotel," said Delaney. "I'll just fetch a few things." He rose with a weary sigh and let Gray shepherd him towards the door.

"As I said, he likes speedy conclusions." Ben pocketed his notebook.

"It's not open and shut," said Rosanna.

"You reckon? You can't think it's anything other than suicide, surely?"

"Suicide yes, but not simple. What about mental cruelty?"

"Do we have any evidence of that? He's cruel because he won't let her drink while she's pregnant? Which suggests maybe she was an alcoholic, otherwise she wouldn't need telling."

"You think he's innocent as a lamb?"

"No, I don't. I think he was rearranging the truth to make himself feel better, the way people do. Keeping quiet about some things, like how much he drank before driving, or how much her being "emotional" last night was actually a blazing row, or how soon he panicked before he bothered to look for her. He's riddled with guilt. Guilty that he didn't phone her, didn't come straight home, didn't see it coming, didn't realise that she had booze and pills stashed away…"

"Stashed away in the spare bedroom where he'd never look. Never suspect. I think he locked her in there when he went to London. Never guessed she'd have the means to kill herself."

"Hey, hey! Locked her in? That's a big if. You've got to have some evidence before you start on that track."

"She's dressed but she has nothing with her. No mobile phone, that's over there." Rosanna pointed to a phone on the floor in the corner, along with a handbag, spilling its contents. She moved towards it.

"Wait." Ben held her back. "Leave it for forensics just in case. But it still doesn't mean she was locked in up there. That's just wild speculation."

"A back room out of sight, so she couldn't attract attention, couldn't be heard."

"So she could avoid nosy neighbours? You think his whole response has been an act? I'd say either he's genuinely upset at her death, or he's the best actor I've ever come across."

"He's shocked, yes. He wasn't expecting it. Doesn't mean he didn't bring it about. Look, he forbids her to drink but keeps his own Scotch in full view. If a caring husband wanted to help his wife give up alcohol, he'd give it up with her. And she likes to be at home to greet him? What is this, the fifties?"

"It is possible that she just liked playing the perfect housewife. Role play, you know? Some couples enjoy it. Or she really did have mental issues, agoraphobia, and she was scared to go out. It happens."

"Maybe, but let's see if I'm right." Rosanna strode out into the hall and back upstairs, Ben on her heels. Other doors led off the landing. Gray and Delaney were talking behind one. She opened another to a second pristine guest bedroom. Ben followed her in and she pointed to

23

a couple of keys in a china dish. "Windows and door. There's a dish like that in the back room, empty."

"Maybe." He tried another door at the back. It was obviously intended as a nursery, newly papered in pink, with a cot and packets still in cellophane wrappers, the room reeking of fresh paint. No key in the door but a couple on the window sill.

"Okay," said Ben.

"And this?" Rosanna looked into a bathroom, bolts on the door, a key in the window. On down a passage to a large gallery set up as a gym. Keys in the windows, front and back.

Ben rubbed his chin.

"No keys in the room where she died," said Rosanna. "I think he locked her in and went to London for the day. Not a chance of her breaking out. Those leaded windows are as good as prison bars."

"Oh, come on, Rosanna!"

"He didn't try to phone her once, during the day. Because he knew she couldn't answer. He'd left her without a phone. And—"

"Stop! At best, this is all wild speculation. You've got nothing remotely like proof of anything. You must realise it's more plausible that the keys are simply misplaced. In a drawer in the kitchen maybe."

"Supposing he has the keys on him now, would that be evidence enough?"

They caught a creak on the heavily carpeted stairs and hurried back to the landing to see Gray following Delaney across the hall to the front door. Delaney was carrying a holdall.

"Sir!" said Rosanna, but Gray was shooing Delaney out, a hand on his shoulder.

Ben scooted across to the master bedroom, looked round the door and held up a key. "But none in the room where she died. Okay, come on, you've persuaded me it's a possibility. Just a possibility."

They hurried downstairs. Too late. Delaney hadn't wasted time. He was already in his Porsche and Gray was slapping the boot to see him off.

He turned to face them, rubbing his hands. "He'll be staying at the Marriott. Okay for some, eh. Now, are we done here? Doc Richardson says she probably died between one and three this afternoon and no sign of anyone else present. He can't tell yet if the pills killed her or she drank herself senseless and drowned in her own vomit. Autopsy can settle that, so that's me done..."

"Sir." Ben interrupted before Gray could turn away. "DC Quillan noticed the keys to that bedroom seem to be missing. It's just a possibility that Delaney may have locked his wife in."

Gray growled annoyance. "Why the fuck would he have done that?"

"Coercive control," said Rosanna.

"Phwa!" He laughed mockingly. "Don't try to be clever, girlie."

"We ought to see if he has those keys on him," suggested Ben.

"Oh for God's sake, Morgan, I thought you had more sense. You seriously want me to take this to the DI? No way. You two finish things off here. I'm off. My stomach will give me hell if I don't get something to eat soon."

They watched him drive off. Ben sighed. "I'll go to the Marriott, follow it up anyway."

"No point," said Rosanna. "I asked Delaney if the room was locked. He'll have realised the keys would be awkward to explain. They'll be down a drain by now."

Ben nodded. "You're right. Well, I'll report your suspicions. Our suspicions. The possibility of coercive control has to be considered."

* * *

Rosanna stood staring out of the window of her flat. The tower block three streets away had been brightly lit when she'd come in, regimented windows each aglow like miniature screens, portals into hidden worlds. But one by one, the lights were going out as private lives became secret ones in the darkness of bedrooms.

"Okay, how about Black Mirror?" Luke was bent forward on the sofa, studying the TV screen intently. He really ought to get glasses.

"Fine," said Rosanna, watching silhouettes behind curtains come together, part again. You could never really know what was going on in other people's lives.

"White Bear, yeah?"

"If you like." She turned away from the window as Luke turned his attention from the TV screen to look at her.

"What's up. Work?"

"Sort of."

"Still thinking about that woman who topped herself?"

"Yes."

"And you reckon the husband really murdered her? Seriously?"

"Yes. No. She committed suicide. But…" She sighed, sliding onto the sofa next to him.

"You think he drove her to it."

"I don't know. I felt certain, but was that just because I wanted to think it?"

"Why would you want to?"

Rosanna shrugged. Luke was too recent for her to have shared her own history with him. Her very private obsessions that she carried around with her. She knew they coloured her thoughts, however objective she tried to be.

"So what was it about him made you suspect him?"

"I don't know, he had all the right reactions. He was angry. I know that's how people often are when suicides happen. I… people often are. Maybe I'm seeing too much, but he looked shifty, said the wrong things…. And then there's the keys. They were missing, the keys of the door and window where she was found."

Luke frowned up at the window she had recently vacated. "That window's got a lock. Do you know where the key is?"

"Not the faintest idea. Probably in the cutlery drawer. I've never bothered using it."

"Well then. You're letting it get to you. Let it go."

"Okay." She took the remote control from him and pressed play. "Let's forget it."

* * *

Ben caught Rosanna as she arrived for her late shift. "I don't know if you're psychic, but it looks like you might have been really onto something with that suicide in Soweridge yesterday. It's certainly kicked off today."

"How do you mean? What's happened?"

"Woman came in this morning, friend of the deceased, accusing Delaney of murdering his wife."

"Really!"

"Stansford interviewed her."

"Yes!"

"Mind you, the desk sarge thought the woman was hysterical, not making much sense, so don't get your hopes up too much. Just letting you know, they've brought Delaney in. He's with his solicitor now."

"Good."

Detective Inspector Stansford, hurrying down the stairs, paused at the bottom and beckoned Rosanna. "DC Quillan. You're in early. Settling in?"

"I hope so, ma'am."

"Good." The DI was a woman in her forties, stocky, always smartly dressed, reputed to have a sense of humour but not quick to show it. She glanced down at a file. "You attended the Delaney suicide with DS Gray. Morgan's report says you thought coercive control might have been a factor."

"Yes, ma'am."

"And DS Gray didn't agree."

"No, ma'am."

"Give you much grief, did he? Harry Gray? Say anything too inappropriate?"

"Nothing that hurt."

"Good. I'd hate to see him on a disciplinary charge with less than a month to go before he retires." The DI's tone was so dry, Rosanna wasn't sure if she was genuinely glad or the reverse. "You'll have heard that allegations have been made against Delaney. A woman, Danielle Brightman, claims to have been a friend of the deceased. Highly emotional. By which I don't mean drunk, I mean irrational. Not very stable grounds to build a case on. Under normal circumstances I would have treated her claims as outpourings of hysterical grief but combined with your doubts, I decided to invite the husband in. I'd like you to sit in on the interview. No interruptions. Sit, watch and listen, yes? You can give me your opinions afterwards."

"Yes, ma'am."

So Rosanna sat, watched and listened.

Delaney, waiting for them in the interview room, was clearly impatient, aggrieved that he'd been summoned. Which wasn't proof of anything; any grieving husband would be. And so would any guilty party who wanted to conceal his guilt behind a veil of indignation. He looked smart, polished, but his eyes were red-rimmed, though dry now. He sat quietly rapping his knuckles on the desk, his solicitor beside him, waiting for Stansford to begin.

"Good of you to come in, Mr Delaney. I'm sure you have enough on your plate as it is."

"Yes, I have a wife and child to bury. And I'm really struggling to deal with that, so what's this all about?"

"Our problem, Mr Delaney, is that a Mrs Danielle Brightman, who claims to be a close friend of your wife, has come to us and made certain allegations."

29

Delaney was clenching his hands again, but other than that, for two or three seconds, he was motionless, frozen. His jaw was set as if he had schooled himself to keep control whatever happened – but he couldn't stop the twitch in his eyelid. Then he licked his lips, a snake's tongue flicking out, and he said, with barely a tremor in his voice, "What allegations? I can't imagine it will be anything believable."

"We'll see. She claimed that your wife told her, the day before she died, that you were, quote, 'an evil monster' and she was intending to leave you."

"What?" Was it disgust or relief in his scowl? "Utter rubbish!"

"Mrs Brightman believes you murdered your wife rather than let her leave."

"Ha!" Definitely relief, Rosanna decided. "This is nonsense! How could I have murdered her? Even if I wanted to, which I didn't, I was in London all day."

"Yes, we did check with your colleagues."

"And they doubtless confirmed my client's alibi," added his solicitor.

"Alibi!" said Delaney. "It's not an alibi, it's what I was bloody well doing. So you know I can't be responsible."

"Yes. Not by literally forcing gin and pills down her throat, but there is such a thing as…" The DI smiled as she launched smoothly into the correct phrasing. "…coercive and controlling behaviour in an intimate or family relationship, causing serious alarm or distress which has a substantial adverse effect on the victim. Section 76 of the Serious Crime Act 2015. I'm sure you'd agree, wouldn't you, Mr Delaney, that suicide is a substantial adverse effect?"

"This is crap. This is complete and utter bullshit." He was loudly confident now. "I loved my wife. I took care of her. Our relationship was good. More than good. She was having my baby, my daughter. I've never raised a hand to her and she never talked of leaving me."

Stansford nodded, scrutinising a sheet of notes. "Financially, the marriage was very good for you, wasn't it?"

"How do you mean?"

"I mean your wife had just inherited the house in Soweridge and investments worth more than a million when you met."

"Yes. She came to me for advice. I'm a financial advisor. That's what I did. I advised her."

"You advised her to invest in you and your business. It expanded considerably, I understand, after your marriage."

"What are you implying? I advised her, yes, just as I advise all my clients, solely for their benefit. Yes, some of her money was invested in my business – that was her choice, because it was an investment in our joint future. But most of it is still invested elsewhere."

"Some of it in an offshore account in your name."

"Once we were married, yes, in my name. She wanted that. I am a financial manager so it made sense. Is that so unusual? That's what husbands and wives do."

"So the money in that off-shore account is now indisputably yours."

"I'm her husband, for Christ's sake, so yes. If I'd died first, it would have been hers. What are you trying to suggest? That I married her for her money and then killed her or drove her to suicide? Is that what that bitch has been saying?"

"That bitch being Danielle Brightman."

"She's claiming Alison called me a monster? She's lying. In case you didn't know, she's a pathological liar. I bet she didn't even speak to Alison."

"We checked your wife's phone and we confirmed that they did speak, at length, twice in fact, the day before your wife's death. First time for over an hour, when Mrs Brightman called your wife. Half an hour later, your wife called Mrs Brightman back and again the call lasted nearly an hour. We have also confirmed that yesterday, the day your wife died, Mrs Brightman called her a total of eleven times, from midnight onwards, before your wife's phone battery ran out. Some of those calls were probably made after your wife's time of death, but others were made when she was definitely still alive. Do you have any explanation of why your wife wouldn't answer her phone?"

Delaney was silent, blank. His solicitor coughed. "Are you asking my client to speculate on what might have happened while he was many miles away?"

"Speculation would do. A husband usually knows his wife better than anyone."

Delaney moistened his lips. "If they spoke the day before, maybe they'd had such an argument that Alison didn't want any more to do with her."

"It wouldn't be, for instance, that she simply had no access to her phone? Did you leave her, that morning, locked in the back bedroom?"

"What? What!" Delaney's eyes were bulging with indignation, instant and explosive. "No I certainly did not! Is this another insane accusation by that mad cow, Danny?"

"No, her allegations were not that specific. Just murder. Would you like to hazard a guess why she's so insistent on that point?"

"Because, I told you, she's a pathological liar!"

"But you must have an idea what her motives would be. How well do you know Mrs Brightman?"

Again, Delaney's eyes flitted sideways, not furtive but calculating. Rosanna thought *he's deciding if it's time to play his emergency joker.* He turned and leaned in to whisper to his solicitor.

The solicitor whispered back, then faced Stansford. "I'd like to confer with my client in private, if you don't mind."

"Not at all." Stansford rose with a pleasant smile. "Time for a coffee break, I think. Can I send some in for you gentlemen? Mr Delaney? Mr Wicks? No?" She rose. "Oh, just one thing. Do you know where the keys to that bedroom door and window are, Mr Delaney? We've been unable to locate them."

"No idea!" Delaney sprang up, held his arms wide. "Search me if you want. I do not know."

"Not to worry." The DI smiled again and ushered Rosanna out of the room.

Rosanna waited in the corridor for the DI to deliver a verdict on the interview so far.

"Mine's black, no sugar," said Stansford.

Their coffee was barely touched when they returned to the interview room.

"My client would like to make a statement," said the solicitor.

Delaney looked meek. Ashamed. Prepared. "I'm sorry. Yes, I do know Danny Brightman. She and Alison were childhood friends and they'd probably be friends still if… Look, I'm not proud of this, but Alison and I were going through a rough patch. She was drinking too much, and maybe I was impatient, not as sympathetic as I should have been. I bumped into Danny and we got talking. Danny's a flirt, you have to understand that. It's why her own marriage broke up; she couldn't keep her eyes off other men. So that's how it was. One thing led to another, and we finished up having sex.

"Like I said, I'm not proud of it. In fact, bloody ashamed. I was already kicking myself by the next morning. It was a stupid one-night stand and I wanted to forget it, but Danny wouldn't let it go. She kept phoning, wanting us to meet up again, trying to build it up into this great romance. Wanted me to leave Alison, which shows precisely how good a friend she was. I tried to be polite at first, but she wouldn't give up, kept phoning, ambushing me at the office, the gym, the station, and in the end, I told her to get lost or I'd report her for harassment. She went quiet for a bit then, but now I'm thinking…" He gazed into the middle distance and shook his head. "I'm thinking if she did phone Alison, it was to spin her some yarn about our great affair. Maybe she convinced her I was leaving her. Maybe that's what drove Alison to it.

"So." He slapped his hand on the table, shaking with righteous anger. "So if you think someone drove my wife to kill herself and my child, why don't you arrest that bitch, Danny Brightman?"

Stansford perused Delaney for a while before slowly nodding her head. "It certainly gives us a possible motive for your wife's actions."

"Yes. It does."

"Well, thank you for that, Mr Delaney. I don't want to detain you any further. If there are any more questions, I expect we'll be able to contact you?"

"I can go?" Delaney half rose.

"Of course, you were perfectly free to leave at any time. I'm very grateful that you were willing to come in and answer our questions."

He couldn't quite hide his relief as he grabbed his coat. Relief seasoned with triumph that he tried to pass off as resentment. "Let's go," he said to his solicitor and stalked out, muttering about heartless officiousness.

Stansford sat back, picked up a pen from the desk and poised it between fingers, measuring its length. "Well DC Quillan. What do you make of that?"

"He's a liar."

"Of course. But what is he lying about?"

"The affair for one thing. Brightman was a flirt and he couldn't resist but then he regretted it and she wouldn't let him go. That's pure male fantasy."

The DI smiled thinly. "I never believe anyone's account of an affair. It would, however, be an explanation for Brightman's avenging angel act. She made no mention of it when accusing him. I shall have to ask her if there has ever been anything between her and Delaney. If the answer's yes, that seriously undermines her claims and reinforces his. But would the discovery of an affair be enough to push Alison Delaney to suicide?"

"No, I don't think so. But locking her up, preventing her from leaving him, treating her like nothing more than the carrier of his baby – always his baby, not theirs – treating her like a doormat, tormenting her and belittling her—"

Stansford held up a finger for silence. She looked at Rosanna thoughtfully. "I know it's a possibility, but I also know why you are so ready to jump to that conclusion. I have read your records. I know where you're coming from."

Rosanna felt a chill anger sweep through her. "Where I'm coming from merely gives me an insight into the way that sort of control works."

"Yes, I expect it does." The DI pushed her chair back and folded her arms. "Whatever Delaney says, I am sure his marriage wasn't perfect. If it were, his wife would probably still be alive. Maybe he was possessive and controlling, or maybe he fussed over her too much, or he was neglectful, spending too much time away on business. Perhaps she was the possessive one. She was pregnant, remember. In killing herself, she also killed her child. Women have to be very disturbed to consider hurting their babies. Unfortunately, whatever the truth is, we have no way of establishing it. There were no witnesses. The neighbours say she was a lovely girl, they were a charming couple, he always seemed so considerate, etcetera. According to her GP she had been prescribed medication for depression and she did have a drink problem but she was delighted to be pregnant and eager to give up the pills and the booze. Apart from missing keys, which prove nothing in themselves, we don't have anything to act on. It was a suicide and that's all we'll be able to recommend to the coroner. So we leave it."

Rosanna shook her head, her lips pressed together.

DI Stansford winced sympathy. "Why did you join the force, Quillan? What were you looking for?"

"Justice, I suppose."

"Ah yes. The big one. What does justice mean to you? Retribution? Restitution?"

"Truth."

"Interesting. But then what is truth? Who said that?"

"Pontius Pilate."

Stansford laughed at the unhesitating response. "You know your Bible. A woman of faith?"

"No, a girl who was packed off to Sunday School every week for fourteen years."

"Well then, you'll have to accept that the answer, in the police force, isn't necessarily the one you want. The only truth we can afford to deal in is the truth that can be established beyond all reasonable doubt in a court of law."

"So we wash our hands of Alison Delaney?"

"A hard lesson for your first serious case, but I'm afraid so."

3. JUDE

Summervale. I'd always thought it a most inappropriate house name. On a hill, for a start, and the season it belonged to was surely winter. Or at least that was how I'd always seen it in the past.

I'd been here maybe a dozen times as a child… no, less than that, when I think about it. Summervale was Alison's residence, though it could hardly be described as a home after her mother died. She came to Madeleine and us for everything a family should be. Her father hadn't been unkind, just one of those focused businessmen who left domestic matters to the woman; his job was to provide. He wasn't emotionally equipped to deal with plaiting hair, sorting gym clothes and the onset of periods.

Summervale had seemed a forbiddingly brown house, enclosed in leathery shrubs that cast brown shadows, and full of unrelentingly brown vintage furniture, inherited from Granddad Greenold who'd built the house back in the thirties, all blackened timbers and London Brick in a land of golden limestone. It had never seemed right for Alison. She'd suited something more like Neuschwanstein castle. Maybe if her mother had survived, the place might have cheered up, but Mr Greenold and the succession of housekeepers he employed to look after Alison had never thought to move on from brown.

Things had moved on now though. Still too many copper beeches and evergreens but the looming shrubbery had been cleared back from the gravel drive. Sunlight could get at the house and brighten those oppressive mullioned windows. The detached double garage, with the loft that we'd attempted to turn into a Pitt Rivers Museum with shrunken Barbie heads, was less like a witch's cottage lost in deep forest. The door, flip-over now instead of the old heavy wooden ones, was raised and I could see a silver Porsche inside.

I smiled. First time I'd met Simon Delaney, I'd pictured him with a Porsche.

Next to it, a car shrouded in tarpaulin. My throat caught. It was hidden from me, like Alison. I had an urge to run across the gravel and pull the cover off to find her there. I could picture her so clearly; the worst driver in the world. She knew she was bad so she took extra care. It was a major achievement if she ever got as high as fourth gear. "One thing you can be sure of," I'd said. "You'll never kill yourself in this thing."

She'd laughed. "I hope not."

Not in her car. In her bedroom.

No point standing there, remembering and mourning. I owed it to her to focus on the living. I rang the bell, catching the echo of the resounding midnight clang that used to have Danny and me running back from the door, expecting Dracula to open it. In the case of one housekeeper, Mrs Snoddy, that hadn't been far from the truth. But nobody responded to it now. Unsurprising. A widower of barely a week was hardly going to come rushing to the door to greet an unexpected visitor. I hadn't phoned first. He was probably lurking somewhere in the back, praying for me to go away.

I suppose that's what I should have done, leave and come back when he'd had more time to get a grip. But I couldn't. There was too much I had to know and understand.

At last, I could hear slow footsteps. They stopped, started again. I saw a figure looming up through the stained glass. The door opened. Half opened. "Yes?"

He was the same Simon I'd last seen more than three years before, and yet subtly diminished. Crushed. Still incredibly handsome, well-groomed, but the confident authority that he'd exuded was now bruised and limping. There was a slight nervous tic in his left eyelid, something defensive in his stance. He had been put through the mill, by Alison's suicide, by the police, by Danny's hysteria. He must have thought I'd come to pile on the agony.

I was determined to ease the pain, for Alison's sake. "Simon." I held out my hands. "I'm Jude. Judith Granger. I came to your wedding and I was at one of Alison's recitals, but I don't think we've met since then, so you probably don't remember me."

"You were at the wedding?" He gaped at me for a moment, rearranging his muddled memories. "I don't… No wait. Yes. Jude. You were one of the friends, weren't you?" Enlightenment brought a surge of anger. "I don't know what she's said to you but if you're another crazy cow come to accuse me of murder—"

"No! Good God, not at all. I was so shocked when I heard about Alison's death and then Danny's allegations. That was appalling. It should never have happened. Danny's always been melodramatic. I'm so sorry if she's made things worse for you. That's what I came to tell you. To apologise for her, I suppose. As if losing Alison wasn't enough. It's beyond ghastly. You must be devastated."

"Yes. I am." He looked me over, the anger fading, though a hint of suspicion remained. "You'd best come in, then." He stood back to let me enter and I could see that the interior of the house had been transformed in recent years. I had only visited the place once since Alison's marriage, and that had been in the first year, when the place was still a shrine to her father. It had been transformed in the four years since then. Everything was now shining, modern and light.

But not quite tidy. Simon ushered me into the drawing room where a couple of empty beer bottles and a greasy pizza packet sat next to a closed laptop on the coffee table. He looked at them. "Sorry. Should have cleared away. I've not really been focused on housework since I got back from the police station."

"It's the last thing you want to be thinking about." I glanced around. Other than the mess on the coffee table, there wasn't much to complain about. A faint film of dust on Alison's piano, which was the only dark thing remaining.

I pictured Alison sitting here in this cocoon of light, dreamily playing Chopin on a quiet afternoon. It needed gossamer drapes stirring in the breeze, to create the otherworldly surroundings she deserved. Well, she was in another world now, a kinder one, please God.

But it was Simon marooned in this cruel world that I needed to concentrate on. "I can't imagine what you've gone through. How are you coping?"

"I'm managing. A woman comes in twice a week. It's okay. I'm getting by." He waved his hand at the pizza packet. "I was never much of a cook."

"Who'd want to think about cooking at a time like this? Alison – I really don't know what to say." I laid my hand sympathetically on his arm. "It's shocked me to the core, and I was just an old friend, but you were her husband, the love of her life, the last person I thought she'd want to hurt. I just can't believe she'd kill herself."

"And my child. She killed my daughter too."

"I know, your baby. That must be so difficult to forgive."

"It is." He was shaking. Staring at my hand still on his arm. "Look, um… sit down, yes? I should offer you a drink, or something."

"No, you don't need to do anything." I sat down, to encourage him to do the same. He dropped as if he'd been waiting for permission to collapse. I leaned forward from my chair to place my hands over his. "Please, Simon, I'm not here to be waited on. Quite the reverse. Let me help you. I tell you what." I pressed on his shoulder to keep him down. "I'll clear these things away and I'll make us some tea, do any washing up you need done. I want to do anything I can to help."

"Thank you," he said, meekly.

The kitchen wasn't bad. A few plates and mugs and a saucepan smeared with baked beans were piled up in the sink, empty Indian take-away cartons and various crumpled biscuit and crisp packets on the side, crumbs everywhere, a turmeric stain on the granite worktop and a cafetiere clogged with grouts, but I'd seen a lot worse. It only took a few minutes to load the dishwasher, sweep up and wipe down the surfaces. Easy even for me and I had never been particularly domesticated. That had been Alison, with her deep-rooted longing to look after people.

I filled the kettle and stood there, gazing around the room while it boiled. It was in this kitchen that I had first met Simon Delaney. Not as it was now, of course, all gleaming modernity and top of the range gadgets. What happened to the loose quarry tile under which we'd hidden Mr Greenold's study key? Did he ever find it? The larder was still there, where we'd shut Mrs Snoddy in, but not the Formica-topped table on which Alison had prepared tasty titbits to celebrate the arrival of her wonderful new man…

Danny is brooding over a plate of hors d'oeuvres. "Do you think she'll notice if I try one of those? Will it upset the arrangement?"

"Not if you take another one and I take two," I say, helping myself.

We hear, distantly, the roll of tyres on gravel and a gasp of panic from Alison in the hall. "He's here!"

Danny swallows quickly and moves to join her, but I tug her arm, wiping crumbs off my lips. "Not yet," I mouth. So we stand there, peering round the kitchen door as the doorbell tolls and Alison lurches forward, steadies herself, then quietly opens the front door.

Simon Delaney walks in, a bouquet in his arms, red roses, two dozen at least. "Alison. Sweetheart. You look gorgeous, as always."

Danny turns to look at me. I look at her, wide-eyed. He is an Adonis. We take our fill and then retreat into the kitchen, letting the door gently shut.

"Oh my God," whispers Danny. "Be still, my beating heart. Where did she find him? Can they be ordered from a catalogue?"

"Do they have catalogues in heaven?" I suggest.

We edge open the door to gaze again. Out in the hall, Simon has Alison in a passionate embrace and there's no stopping my feelings. Overwhelming jealousy. I shouldn't let it take hold but I can't help it.

"God's gift," breathes Danny, beside me.

We withdraw again, and I avoid her eyes. "Alison is all alone in the world now. It's up to us to take care of her."

"We should check him out," agrees Danny. "Make sure he's right for her, that's only fair." It's there in her, too, that self-same jealousy.

The kitchen door opens and Alison enters, her face radiant, as she leads in her Greek god. "Danny, Jude, my very best of best friends, this is Simon."

We smile our delight as he comes forward, beaming, to take our hands…

Were we cruel, Danny and I, to spend the rest of that visit monopolising him? Questioning, keeping him talking, leaving Alison to sit and gaze upon him with undiluted adoration. She was too kind, too generous to object and Simon had taken it in remarkably good part, more than happy to talk about his career and achievements. In fact, he'd barely needed prompting. He must have seen us as acting in loco parentis and he wanted us to know he wouldn't be a drag on Alison. It was so obvious that he was genuinely smitten. We'd had no choice but to accept defeat.

And now where were we all? Where had that suppression of jealousy landed us? Danny sick and deranged, Alison dead and Simon a crumbling wreck. Could I pick up the pieces of what was left?

The kettle clicked off. I found clean mugs and set out a tray. There was milk in the fridge, fresh enough, along with an acceptable packet of salami and some butter. A couple of chicken breasts looked suspicious and so did the blackening mushrooms and the wilted contents of the salad drawer. A week at least since the fridge had been stocked. I cleared it and wiped down the shelves, then I carried the tray through.

Simon had thrown himself back on a sofa, one arm flung over his eyes, what was visible of his face creased with emotion, crushed. I realised how little I knew of his inner strengths and weaknesses. Apart from that introductory meeting, I'd seen very little of him until the wedding. One or two encounters in Oxford, in which he was always the same charming self, barely registering me because he was only intent on Alison. I was mostly abroad. Danny saw more of them and sent me updates, but she had offered scant insight into Simon's character. We had understood implicitly that our feelings put us on dangerous ground, the less discussed the better.

Alison had wanted us both as bridesmaids, but Danny hadn't been up to it, and work commitments meant I couldn't be certain of making it to the wedding at all. But I had, and there he was, still looking so impossibly gorgeous in his morning suit, though humming with tension. He was one of those men, I could tell, who needed things to go exactly to plan and a wedding was guaranteed to overstretch such nerves. But he was still clearly besotted with his bride, and they had eyes only for each other, the perfect golden couple with nothing but good things awaiting them.

Odd to think that I had only seen him once in the five years since. It had been in a church in Oxford, where Alison had played a Clara Schumann's concerto. My eyes had flitted automatically to Simon, sitting at the end of a row, apparently mesmerised by her and the attentive audience, but this was Alison's triumph and I concentrated on her. She had been brilliant, as ever, made for such a moment. I did shake Simon's hand afterwards before going on to hug Alison, but we had barely spoken. For that night, her night, he was just a shadow on the side-lines.

And now, four years later, there was nothing but night for her, and he was lying there, looking as if the solid rock had cracked under his feet and was about to swallow him up. I couldn't allow him to go under like that. For Alison's sake, I wouldn't let him.

"Simon? Have some tea."

He opened his eyes with a brief flash of alarm and struggled up, looking pathetic.

"You look terrible. Don't you have any family to stay with you at this awful time?"

He shook his head, wiping his face. "No one."

"That's awful, having to bear this alone." He'd had parents at their wedding but whatever the dynamics of that family, he obviously felt himself alone now. He didn't have to be. I wouldn't let him be.

I poured the tea. He took the cup from me and set it down. "Thanks."

"You must take care of yourself, you know."

"I'm fine. Getting over it. Well, getting used to the idea – starting to believe it."

"Not easy, is it? It must have been unbelievably awful coming home to find her. Did you…" I paused. I should leave it alone but I needed his answer. "Did you have any inkling she might do something like that? I was told it was an overdose. Could it have been an accident?"

He was silent for a moment, fighting something within himself. At last he managed to reply in a reasonably calm voice. "No. It wasn't an accident. It was totally bloody deliberate." A quiver of anger surged through him. Then he shook himself. "No, I didn't suspect. I didn't even know she had pills and booze in the house. If I had known, I'd have got rid of them. She didn't need them anymore."

"She was on medication before? I'm sorry, I never realised. I've been out of the country so long. I had no idea she was having problems."

"She'd been a bit down, you know how it is, and doctors – well they just hand out pills like Smarties to any bored housewife."

"You think it was boredom, then? I know she'd given up teaching."

"There was no need for her to waste her talents on snotty-nosed juvenile delinquents. But no need for her to be bored, either."

"Well, of course not. She had her music."

"Yes… yes. That's right." He fidgeted and then shook his head violently. "God knows what it was all about,

47

because I don't. I thought she'd be happy if she had a child to focus on. And then she goes and kills them both." He had a hand over his eyes, his shoulders heaving.

I made no reply. What was there to be said? At last he dropped his hand and took a gulp, then cradled the cup, still shaking. So much for getting over it. He heaved a shuddering sigh, resorting to anger instead. "And then I'm carted off to the police station for questioning as if I'm some criminal, thanks to that bloody friend of yours."

I moved over to sit beside him and touched his hand. "I know. That was unforgiveable. I'm afraid Danny hasn't been well, and Alison's death has totally messed up her mind. She just wanted someone to blame, to make sense of it somehow. Because, truthfully, none of us can understand it, so the things Danny said—"

"What did she say?" The question exploded from him. "What did she say I'd done?"

I patted his arm. "She wanted everyone to believe you'd killed Alison and, to be honest, I wasn't willing to hear any more than that. Everyone knows it simply wasn't possible. I warned her, if she didn't stop it, she'd find herself facing a lawsuit for slander. She really is in a bad way, mentally and physically. But she's having treatment now and her mother's doing her best to look after her. I hope she manages to find some peace, I really do. I can hardly expect you to forgive her though."

He grunted. "God knows what she'll say next."

"She'll calm down. It's the way some people deal with shock and grief, lashing out wildly. Did the police give you a really hard time because of it?"

"What do you think? I'd just found my pregnant wife dead, I was turned out of my home while it was ransacked, and some crazed woman accused me of murder, so I'm interrogated at a police station as if everyone thinks it was my doing. How much harder can it be? Isn't it enough that Alison killed herself and my daughter? That's more than I can deal with." He slammed the cup down.

I put my arm around him. "Look, Simon, I know visitors must be the last thing you want just now. Sympathy must really grate. Is there anything else I can do around the house? Tell me, and I'll do it, then I'll go. I can come back another day, if you like. I'm sure you'll need someone to help you with the practicalities. The funeral, the inquest, whatever. You don't want to be doing it all on your own."

He nodded. "That would be… good of you."

"So can I do anything now? Tidy upstairs maybe?"

I felt him cringe at the thought. "It's still…the back room, where… I haven't touched it."

"Oh God no, no one would expect you to have to deal with that. Let me do it for you."

"You are kind."

I was ready to be kind. I left him staring at his empty teacup and went upstairs. Everything was quiet, tomblike. I opened his bedroom door, the bedroom he had shared with Alison for five years. The bed looked as if a rugby team had romped in it, but at least the linen smelled clean, freshly laundered. No need to change it. I made the bed neatly and adjusted the things on the dressing table. Hairbrush with long fair strands entangled in the bristles. I wound some onto my finger. A jewellery case, locked. A manicure set. In the en-suite bathroom, just one toothbrush and some masculine toiletries. A toilet bag had been stuffed with her things, its seams bulging. I ran a wet cloth over the basin, shower and bath, but they didn't really need it. The cleaning lady had kept it under control.

There was a separate dressing room, where black bin bags stood, bulging with Alison's clothes, ready for a charity shop. Simon wouldn't want to lie here surrounded by an ocean of memories. I could take them all off his hands.

I left the master bedroom in a reasonable state and checked other rooms off the landing – a guest suite at the front, spic and span, a gym, a bathroom, a nursery – that was a shock. Painful. A cot that would never be used. I had to fight down the emotions that flooded through me.

That left the second guest bedroom, at the back. I braced myself to face it, took a deep breath and opened the door.

The room where Alison died. I remembered it as her childhood bedroom, the only room in the house that had escaped the all-conquering brown. Turquoise and pink, unicorns, a poster of Robbie Williams and a ballerina musical box. *Oh Alison, what was there of you now?* It had become a guest room, devoid of emotional comfort, no better than an anonymous hotel room.

Not quite. Feeding in amidst the ivory and cream colour scheme, I recognised the misty grey-blue that had become her favourite colour when she'd migrated from turquoise and pink. She'd had half a dozen dresses that colour, back in the day when we three student musketeers had been all for one and one for all when it came to clothes. A wise choice. It looked insipid on Danny and me, but perfect on her. I picked up a cushion from the floor and stroked it. *Why, Alison? Show me why?*

Grey-blue and cream duvet cover, stained and contorted in her death throes. It still bore the imprint of her body. No wonder Simon couldn't face coming in here. Even the cleaning lady hadn't faced it. I sat on the edge of the bed and stared out of the window. Trees stood like shrouded funeral mourners at the end of the long immaculate lawns, beyond them, a glimpse of open field. A footpath skirted that field, but no one, apart from us as children, ever veered from it into the trees to peer into Summervale's garden. No houses overlooking this window. No one to see her die.

I felt a wave of nausea rising and fought it down. Best get on with it. I stripped the cover off the duvet, which was stained too. Maybe best to burn it. I pulled off sheet and pillowcases and gathered them up. They couldn't stay as they were. Was there anything else? Towels perhaps? I looked in the bathroom. Nothing. The mirror-fronted cabinet was wide open, its shelves empty. Anything relating to the cause of death would have been taken by the police.

I gently shut the cabinet. Smudges blurred the mirror. I breathed on it. Words appeared briefly. I breathed again, several times, more forcefully. This time the letters lasted enough for me to read. *Sorry, sorry, sorry, I can't leave you...* The rest was lost in a mess of fingerprints from the door being opened and closed. Alison's last despairing words.

What would Simon make of them? She wanted to leave him but she couldn't, so she chose death instead? Or she'd taken the pills and was now regretting it, wishing she hadn't chosen to leave him? Better he never saw it. I wiped the mirror clean with my sleeve, then I gathered up the bedding and tiptoed downstairs.

Simon was at the living room door, watching me descend.

"I'll take these and get them laundered," I said.

He nodded. "Thank you."

"Shall I come back?"

Another nod. "Please."

I left, my grief for Alison still burning inside me. But there was the inescapable truth. Alison and Simon had been a couple, he had been hers entirely. Unto death. And now Alison was dead, which meant that Simon was free.

4. SIMON

He saw the woman turn in through the gate and he froze. She could have been anyone, friend or foe, but it was all one. He couldn't face anyone yet, his nerves on fire. All he wanted was to shut out the world out until he could get a grip and breathe easily again, until the black snakes stopped writhing in his gut whenever he remembered what he'd done.

She rang the bell and he toyed with the idea of keeping quiet until she went away, but when she rang a second time, he forced himself to move. He needed to be in command again, the only way he could cope. He hated the feeling of being a leaf swept along on a current of circumstances that had slipped out of his control. So he made it to the door and opened it.

There was something about her that jogged his memory, but there were too many faces swimming in his head – clients, neighbours, police, doctors, reporters. He was having trouble pinning any of them down. But she was so striking, with that incredible red hair, those green eyes swimming with tears, that full mouth. Vivid colouring utterly different to Alison's pearl-like perfection. He had definitely met her before, but where? Then she said her name. Judith Granger.

Judith. Yes, of course, Alison's bloody friends. He felt himself shaking with rage at the memory of what that bitch Danny had done to him, terrified of what she might yet do. Was this Judith Granger just her lieutenant, come to lob another grenade at him?

Then it turned out she was anything but. It was tears and sympathy she was offering, not grenades. Someone on his side at last. God, how he needed that. He was still having nightmares about the interview at the police station, reliving the sheer bloody terror, waiting for the accusations to be fired at him. He'd survived it, kept his cool, come up with the only possible answers in the circumstances, and they'd sent him home, so he was in the clear. He must be, surely. He'd admitted to a stupid fling with Danny, just a brief one, none of his doing, really, and they'd accepted that it explained everything, or enough, anyway. But the memory still brought him out in a sweat.

Jude wasn't flinging accusations, merely trying to understand. After all, why would she accuse him of anything? They hardly knew each, there had never been anything between them, not like with Danny. Nothing like with Danny. She was just another sympathetic woman who wanted to mother him. He wasn't going to object. After five years of marriage to Alison, he'd grown accustomed to being looked after with the little things. Mrs Bilson, the cleaning lady, might be okay with a Dyson but she was hardly the same. If Jude wanted to fill the domestic void left by Alison, it was fine by him. When she offered to tidy up and make tea, he was grateful. But then, when she returned with the tray, he caught that look, through the long auburn fringe, the look he had learned to recognise in women. He was lucky that way. Even when they pretended they were just being business-like or making idle conversation, he could detect the flutter coming through. That was why he'd never had to beg for it. And he knew that he wouldn't have to beg for it now.

Except that it wasn't the done thing to make a pass at your wife's friend when your wife's only been dead seven days. Even if the woman was gagging for it. Besides, one flashback of Alison, lying there on that bed, had him shrivelling up inside. He still had to organise her funeral, people to face, never knowing what might be thrown at him next. He wanted a clean slate. He wanted to block Alison out of his mind, he wanted to expunge Danny entirely. If he could get through the next few days or weeks, he might just let Judith Granger do the job for him.

5. DC QUILLAN

Luke checked his latest text. "Matt says do we want to come over for the game?"

Rosanna was debating over her limited wardrobe. Not black, but something dark. The navy-blue jacket she hardly ever wore because it had looked smart in the shop but like a school blazer once she'd got it home. It would be right for today though. She unhooked it. "Sorry, can't. I'm going to a funeral."

"Oh. What, a relative or something? I didn't know anyone had died."

They're dying all the time, she thought. "No, not family. Not even friend really, but I feel sort of obliged."

"So, you want me to come with you?"

She smiled brightly. "No need. I'll be fine. You go to Matt's on your own."

He made a generous show of being willing to surrender TV, canned beer and pot noodles in order to accompany her, but she was resolute. Sweet boy. A bit immature, but they all seemed to take their time growing up. Or maybe she had grown up too fast. Anyway, she really didn't want him with her today.

The case of Alison Delaney had been buried as the team focused on a case of child rape. Rosanna had said justice was truth and this new case was one where truth was all that mattered, a vital commodity that just might help a child who was likely to be traumatised for life.

Rosanna had been as obsessed with it as everyone else but always, lurking in the back of her mind, was the image of Alison Delaney.

Alison's autopsy had confirmed that she had taken an overdose of a tricyclic antidepressant, washed down with enough gin to kill an elephant. There were only her fingerprints on the bottles and wrappers, apart from one packet, which her husband probably picked up when he found her. Only her fingerprints in the room, all over the windows, the door, the bathroom cabinet, washbasin, furniture. There were bruises on her legs, arms, temple, consistent with stumbling around in a drunken state. Scratches on her face and hands were self-inflicted, based on the skin cells under her fingernails. There was no trace of anyone else in the house. She had died alone, so suicide was self-evident and the body had been released without any further delay.

Which had left Simon Delaney free to arrange a funeral and as it turned out, he'd arranged it for Rosanna's day off. There was nothing to stop her attending. What she did in her free time was her business.

She drove, sorting her thoughts into objective order. Trying to be as dispassionate as DI Stansford. But the closer she came to the crematorium, the less objective her feelings became. She had stifled her suspicions on this one in the wake of the child abuse case, but now they swept back in full force until they became absolute certainty. Alison Delaney had been imprisoned in that room.

She could hear, once more, her mother's voice upstairs, faint and meek and hopeless. "Let me out, Craig, I promise I won't do it again."

57

Her father, smiling as he tossed the wardrobe key from hand to hand. "Drunken bitch. Right, you kids, get this place tidied up."

And her, Rosanna, trying to creep silently upstairs while her father sprawled in front of the football. His hand suddenly on her hair, yanking her back down. "Oh no you don't. She stays there till she's sober. I don't want to have to set eyes on her…"

Rosanna was gripping the wheel, her knuckles white, as she parked up. A woman locked up in punishment. A woman driven to suicide. She wasn't going to let this one go into the flames without one witness recognising her death as murder. Murder by bullying, degradation and slow dissolution of a wounded soul. Someone had to be there, watching her killer, even if he thought he'd got away with it. She wanted to stare into the soul of Simon Delaney and pray that he felt the stab of an accusing eye.

She could see how this would look at the station. DS Gray had retired at last, to general relief. Ben Morgan and others of his complexion didn't have to put up with any more jovial back-slapping comments about jungles and Bongo-bongo land. She and other women officers would no longer be greeted by cracks about the time of the month, but if the team could see her now, they'd probably all be labelling her emotional, highly strung or – since her own history seemed to have been bandied round the station – girl with a chip on her shoulder, needing to let her own trauma go.

She wouldn't let it go, though. Her brother had, but not her. That's why she wouldn't let the death of Alison Delaney go, either. She had chosen a career in the police because she wanted to see justice done, if not for her mother, then for any other woman in the same position.

Rosanna took her place in the chapel as the previous party was still milling around outside. Another woman followed her in, early-to-mid-sixties, medium height, weight on the light side, hair dyed but greying, smart dark clothes. She couldn't be a close relative because she slipped unobtrusively into a seat at the back, head bowed. Dribs and drabs followed, couples, businessmen and women, all in stylish sable. They looked and talked as if this were a social gathering for casual gossip. A few arty types, the women tearful, the men grave, gathered in an exclusive knot, their greetings hushed. One or two more mature people, in well-worn funeral gear, kept a respectful silence. Rosanna took precise note of each of them, not because it was necessary but because it was what she did, slotting them into the mental filing cabinet that was her means of blocking out unwelcome memories. Organ music was playing softly, but there was no one at the keyboard, so it must have been a recording.

A bustle outside; shadows filled the doorway; the congregation fell silent. The coffin came in, borne on sturdy professional shoulders. Behind it, walking solemnly, head bowed, came Simon Delaney – and a woman. Quite tall, very trim. Willowy. Chic elegance from head to toe, all in black of course, which threw into startling contrast her red hair under the broad-brimmed hat. Not ginger so much as cinnamon. Perfect but restrained make-up on a naturally pale face. Corel lipstick. Occupation: model? PR? PA?   She had

Delaney's arm and leaned her head towards him, throwing him little anxious glances, her free hand occasionally reaching across to pat his arm. So not his sister. Sisters didn't behave like that. Had he really moved on so quickly? So shamelessly? They did, though. That's exactly what they did.

She'd seen it all before, in her own home. In the home that everyone believed to be just one big bundle of laughs. Everyone knew Dad, Craig Quillan. He was the one who organised the darts tournaments, the whip-rounds, the trips to matches. A charmer, chatting up the girls with a wink, in a cheeky way, and one of the lads with the men, always ready with a chortle, a dirty joke, a slap on the back.

Only one fly in Craig Quillan's ointment: that wife of his, Mandy. Never sober, that woman. Pathetic. He deserved better. Plenty of sympathy for poor Craig when she killed herself, although, mind, he was well shot of her. Poor man having to put up with so much. All the fat wives competed to do the widower's washing, bring him casseroles, iron his shirts. All the unmarried ones, past romantic youth but still hopeful, were on his doorstep offering him a shoulder to cry on. Debbie Holsworthy had moved in less than a month after the funeral. She and Craig were married six weeks later.

"I'm your new mum," she said, making a great fuss of Ryan who came up with something sickly about hoping she made Dad happy. She made no fuss at all of Rosanna, because Rosanna was persona non grata by then in the Quillan household. Sulky spiteful child, telling lies, breaking her father's heart, as if he hadn't already been through enough, putting up with that woman all those years. Craig's heart wasn't really broken though. He didn't have one.

So she'd hardened her own. She heard them, Craig and Debbie, bitching about her one night.

"I can't stand her in the house any longer, Craig. She gets on my tits, she really does. And the lies she said about you… I'm scared she'll come into our room one night and cut our throats."

"I wouldn't let her lay a finger on you, sweetheart. Little cow, already stabbed me in the back."

"And she'll do it again. I mean it, Craig. Either she goes or I do."

"Just hold your horses, pet. How would it look if I chucked her out now? Too many questions, but just wait. The moment she turns sixteen, she's out on her ear."

Rosanna didn't give him the satisfaction. Early in the morning, on her sixteenth birthday, with her bags already packed the night before, she slipped out, while they were still in bed. She'd have gone before if she hadn't thought her father would play the caring dad card, with hell to pay afterwards. She went to stay with her friend Shelley Barlow, intending it as a temporary measure, but she made such an effort, helping round the Barlow house, taking a weekend job to pay for her keep, that when she mentioned looking for something permanent, Mrs Barlow told her to forget all about that and stay with them until she'd finished her A levels.

So she did. She never spoke to her father again, although once, in a supermarket, she ran into Debbie who swore at her – Debbie who was no longer looking quite the same glamour-puss. Debbie with the three bottles of vodka in her trolley. Rosanna met her brother Ryan once or twice, but he only looked pained and disappointed. He didn't want to talk about the family tragedy. No one did. Mandy Quillan was forgotten.

Like the dead woman in the coffin ahead of them now, already blotted out of Delaney's mind? There was the red-haired woman, another Debbie Holsworthy, wiping away Delaney's crocodile tears, and he could forget that he'd driven his wife to suicide. Rosanna knew he had. Gut feeling, yes, but there was evidence too. There were the missing keys. There was Danielle Brightman.

Or there should be Danielle Brightman, but she had been interviewed again and admitted that she and Delaney had been in a sexual relationship. Worse, she had unequivocally withdrawn her allegations. She must have been got at, threatened, or why had she done it? Nobody seemed bothered. Brightman was just a jealous woman having hysterics.

The canned music died. The committal was brief, uninterrupted except by a few sobs in the Bohemian set. The red-headed woman's shoulders quivered a little and Delaney turned towards her, whispering something in her ear. The curtain parted, the coffin rolled out of sight. Rosanna heard a gasping sniff from the older woman at the back, but that was all. The assembly rose, gathered coats and bags, and quietly made their way out onto the gravel where floral tributes were piled. Delaney and his companion stood side by side looking down at them, stooping occasionally to read messages.

Rosanna realised she wasn't the only one watching them. The older woman from the rear of the chapel was watching too, in silence, standing well back, her eyes fixed on Delaney's performance, with what was surely loathing. Or was Rosanna reading too much into it. The woman was just grieving, that was all. A couple of the arty men walked over to join her, one of them blubbing uncontrollably as the taller of the two supported him. They spoke in animated whispers with the woman, hugging her in turn. She kissed them both then bowed her head, turned and walked away. Rosanna caught a glimpse of her face, tear-streaked but with jaw set.

Delaney didn't appear to have noticed any of this. He was too busy shaking hands now with the other mourners.

"Very good of you to come…Yes, a great loss…She was my shining star…Thank you, you are very kind."

Rosanna walked away. *Somehow, some day*, she vowed, *I'm going to get you.*

6. JUDE

I thought Simon put in a remarkable performance at the funeral, dignity personified, holding himself together with iron determination. When I considered what he must have been feeling inside, I was amazed he didn't just collapse in a huddle on the floor, tearing his hair out. I'd helped with the arrangements, since it was the last thing I could do for Alison. Simon was struggling with all the stages of grief rolled into one. Shock, denial, guilt, anger. But he gathered himself together and faced it, because he had to.

I was there to support him, but in reality, it was my own grief for Alison that threatened to run out of control, and he was left comforting me.

When the last guest had gone from the restrained farewell gathering at the house, I gathered up my coat and held out my hands.

He squeezed them, pulling me closer. "You're not going, are you?"

"I really must."

"Have dinner with me. Tomorrow. Let me take you out. Just to thank you for everything you've done."

I bit my tongue to stop myself shouting "Yes!" too eagerly. I reined myself in. "All right. Yes. That would be nice. Not tomorrow, though. Friday."

"It's a… fine. I'll pick you up. Where do you live?"

"Oh, miles away! Seriously. Out by Gloucester."

"You're not driving all that way now. I won't hear of it."

"No, don't worry. I've arranged to stay with friends, heading back tomorrow. Friday, then. I'll get the train here after work. Then we can dine out."

"And after that? It's the weekend. No need to rush back to work the next day?"

"No need at all," I said, trying not to sound too eager.

* * *

He'd booked us a table at Chez Celeste, a relative newcomer on the local restaurant scene and very trendy. I don't know how he had managed to reserve a table at such short notice. It had been booked weeks in advance, the last time I'd been in the area.

"I pulled a few strings," he grinned, in explanation, sitting back to let a waiter set down our martinis. "I thought you deserved the best, as recompense for all your help." He loosened his blue silk tie. It suited his dark looks, as did the beautifully tailored heathery beige suit. I had dressed for an evening out, too. The good thing about little black numbers is that they can do for any occasion, funerals or dinner dates, but I was relieved that he was making an effort to cast off his sombre grief. So many men would have gone under in the wake of Alison's inexplicable suicide.

"I'm glad I could help," I said. "And now it's over." I raised my glass.

He raised his, with a smile.

I said, "To Alison. May she rest in peace."

65

He leaned back, the smile vanishing, and lowered his glass instead of clinking it against mine.

I reached out my free hand to touch his. "Can you really not forgive her just a little bit, even now?"

"Forgive?" He mouthed the word like an expletive.

"I know it's hard. I understand how impossible forgiveness can feel, with all that hurt boiling inside you. My husband—"

"Husband!" His glass came down hard on the table. "I didn't realise you were married."

"Oh, I'm not. I was, but he died."

"I'm sorry."

I waved aside his embarrassed sympathy. My marriage to poor Eddie had been a brief episode that hardly seemed real now. "It was six years ago. I'm over it."

"Really?"

"Yes. Honestly. We were young, ridiculously hot-headed. We'd only been going out a few weeks before we married, and then, two months later… an accident. It's like a brief shining bubble that floated away on the wind. Now it's burst and gone forever. I got over it. I moved on. I know it's far too early for you to think of moving on, but you will. In time. So please, try to forgive Alison just a little bit." I raised my glass again.

He raised his, with a slight grimace.

"Alison," I said.

His glass softly touched mine. "Alison." He managed it with an effort.

I smiled. "And now let her go. We'll talk of other things. I'm here to cheer you up. That's what Alison would have wanted." It was what I wanted, too.

He managed a smile, his eyes searching mine. "You're a good friend, you know. To both Alison and me."

"I'm glad you think so. Alison and I were incredibly close once."

The smile twisted. "Not all friends are so generous."

"Danny, you mean?"

"I hope you're not going to tell me I should forgive her too, are you? Now she's deigned to drop her allegations."

"Well…"

His fingers tightened on his glass and his eyes narrowed. "They were so absurd in the first place. How am I supposed to know what she'll come up with next?"

I sighed. "Things have been a bit awkward between us, I'm afraid, since I came home. She's always been extremely volatile, threatening suicide one moment, and immersed in her latest research project the next. And she's always been very possessive. We could see that with men. Once she had her claws in them…" I stopped. I was being grossly unfair to Danny. "I don't mean she literally clawed them, she just wouldn't let go. Same with women and Alison was her best friend, so she feels guilty that she didn't see it coming any more than you did. Her guilt made her lash out at you instead and she won't listen to reason. But at least she withdrew her allegation. That's something. I was a bit surprised, to be honest, that she didn't come to the funeral. Maybe she felt too ashamed to come."

"Just as well, because I'm not sure I would have behaved with appropriate decorum if she had." He was becoming loud.

"Shh." I stroked his hand, which was shaking again. "She's been quite ill, remember that. Not that it excuses—"

"Look, I really don't want to talk about her." He was breathing heavily.

Good, I thought. *Let's not talk about Danny. Let's keep her out of this. This is just you and me.*

Simon flicked his head to brush the subject away and knocked back his martini. "Tell me more about yourself. You've been a rock, but all we've done till now is talk about me. What about Judith Granger?" His smile was easier now. "I do remember you, you know. One of the Three Friends. The gorgeous one. You had Joe Miller panting all over you at the wedding. You'd flown in especially and Alison was over the moon to see you there. You lived abroad?"

"On and off. I have a talent for languages, so I got a job as a translator. A bloody good job too. It paid really well and it took me off round the world, with trade delegations. I think I flew home from Dubai for your wedding. Or was it Turkey? Anyway, that's all over now."

"No longer translating?"

I shrugged. "I fell victim to a merger. Personnel were pruned and I was one of the ones snipped. With a massive redundancy payoff, admittedly, but you can't just sit around living off two hundred K, so now I'm stuck with a tedious clerical job. Office manager."

"That can't be much fun after all the globe-trotting."

"Fun, no, but it earns a living. If I decide I can't bear it a moment longer, I can always fall back on the redundancy money."

He sat back, stroking his lip, surveying me thoughtfully. "You didn't get through it all, then."

"God, no, barely touched it before this present job came along."

"You've got it sensibly invested, I presume."

I wrinkled my nose. "Not really. Earning a pathetic pittance. I know I should do something better with it."

"Yes, you should! Go and see a financial advisor, get it earning a lot better than that."

"Yes, I know, I know."

He smiled, leaning forward and lowering his voice. "I can name one, if you're looking for some friendly advice."

"Oh Simon, please. I don't want you to think I only came to fish to free advice. Alison did tell me that was what you did."

"I certainly do." His smile broadened. "Investments, taxation, pensions, wealth management, my company does it all. Not pushing or anything, but you know, feel free to consult a friend."

"Seriously? If you've genuinely got room for another client, I'd love you to advise me. But only on a proper professional basis. I'll pay, of course. I insist."

"We'll see." His hand reached out to mine across the table. "It will give me an excuse to keep seeing you."

"Yes," I said slowly. "If you need an excuse."

I had expected our dinner date to be a tense, febrile dance of nerves as I strove to comfort an emotional

69

widower. But Simon was making a sterling effort so I did the same, and he was witty and entertaining. The wine flowed freely, possibly too freely, a Sancerre, followed by a St Emilion and then brandies apiece. We were steady enough as we finally rose to leave, but I persuaded him, with difficulty, not to think of driving us home.

"Actually, I drive better after a drink."

"Yes, but it won't do your business much good, will it, if you're stopped for a random breath test and lose your licence. Put the keys away and call a taxi."

In the cab, he put his arm around me and pulled me close, drunk enough to loosen any inhibitions. Back at Summervale, once he'd inserted the front door key in the lock with great concentration and let us in, there didn't seem to be any need for further restraint.

"Let's round the evening off," he said, walking, one hand on the wall for support, to the kitchen and opening a fridge in which six bottles of champagne were chilling.

I was giggling uncontrollably. "Maybe. Just a little."

The cork popped. We drank. His arm was round me again. We kissed. We drank more. We kissed more. There was no one around to disapprove now.

Wherever it might have led, Bacchus intervened. Simon finally fell on me, not in lust but in inebriation.

I sighed and put my arms around him, cradling him. "Time for bed, Simon."

His eyes half opened and his lips slipped briefly into a smile before he slumped into my arms.

"Come on." Somehow, marshalling what was left of his consciousness, I got him up the stairs and into his bedroom. I managed to flop him onto the bed and he was a rag doll. Getting his shoes off was easy. All I had to do now was wrestle the rest of his clothes off and get him under the duvet. He was going to have the mother of all hangovers in the morning.

* * *

I stood for a while in the back bedroom, staring out of the window at branches swaying in the dark, grey ghosts catching the first fingers of the coming dawn. Two casements, but neither of them would open. I wanted to fling them wide, something to do with letting the spirit free. Did Alison need to be set free, or had she done that for herself, the moment her heart stopped beating? I am not a religious person, but Alison needed more than the clink of martini glasses or the sanitised words of the funeral service. Words that politely made no mention of suicide, despair, desperation or whatever had driven her to it.

No key, but the locks weren't that difficult with a hairgrip and a bit of fiddling. More for show than to keep determined invaders at bay. The windows opened.

Out in the summer night an owl hooted. I could hear Alison's voice saying "Male tawney." She'd loved birds, not as an obsessive twitcher but just rejoicing in them. How many times had she stood here, at this back window, watching them in the trees at the end of the garden?

"Go," I whispered. "Fly with the owls. Be at peace, you and your child. All will be well." I wanted her to know that I was looking after Simon. She would want that, wouldn't she? I needed her blessing.

But the owl was silent now.

Weariness was beginning to overwhelm me. It wouldn't be proper, not yet, to curl up next to Simon on the marital bed. The guest bedroom at the front of the house was ready prepared with clean linen, but I didn't care to spoil it. The stripped bed in this room would do for me. I found an airing cupboard, pulled out a fleecy throw and wrapped myself, still dressed, on the bed where Alison had died.

* * *

The morning was enchanting, promising a perfect summer day. Too good to waste in bed. In the kitchen, I set out a tray with a pot of lethally strong coffee, and a tablet in a glass. I carried it upstairs on tiptoe and, as silently as possible, opened Simon's bedroom door. No need to be quite so quiet. He was still asleep, on his back in a pile of knotted bedding, snoring like a frightened bull. It was going to be an excruciating awakening.

I caressed the tendons on his neck, then laid my hand on his, stroking his fingers. When that didn't work, I tightened my grip.

"Simon?" Gently at first, then louder. "Simon!"

Blearily he opened his eyes, hurriedly squeezed them shut again, then, as I shook him, opened them once more and made a faint effort to sit up. He looked terrible and obviously felt it.

"Sorry," I said, letting him struggle to pull himself up on the pillows. "I didn't like to let you sleep on in case you were really ill. I've made you coffee, or there's an Alka Seltzer if you prefer."

He groaned. "Both." His voice was a barely audible rasp.

"Okay." I added water to the glass in his bathroom, watched it fizz and dissolve, then handed it to him. He drank it back in one gulp. I poured the coffee, gave him the cup in place of the glass, then I perched on the bed, holding up a bundle of keys.

"Yours. They were in your pocket. I've fetched your car for you."

Over the rim of the coffee cup, his eyes suddenly cleared and fixed on me. He lowered the cup. "You what?"

"I fetched your car. You didn't want it standing there at the restaurant for another day, did you?"

"You drove my car?" This was clearly a problem for him.

I explained hurriedly. "I knew you'd feel far too ill to fetch it yourself. You really knocked it back last night. It must still be in your system and you don't want to risk that breathalyser. I was only trying to look after you."

"All right." He took another swig of coffee. "Just don't… I'd prefer it if you didn't do it again."

I understood. Men and their cars. They could be very possessive. "I hope I wouldn't need to. Don't worry, I drove it very carefully, I promise."

He grunted. "How come you're not still drunk?"

"I am a little bit, but I didn't have nearly as much as you. A slight headache but no more. I'm fine, really. And you will be too. Why don't you have a shower? You'll feel better then."

The idea appealed. He put down the cup and threw back the covers. It was only then that he realised he was stark naked. He clearly had no memory of how he'd come to be undressed and in bed. He jerked the cover back up. "Last night… did we… were you…"

I sighed. "I'm afraid you were far too drunk."

He looked slightly disappointed.

"Don't worry," I promised. "There'll be other nights."

7. DR MADELEINE RACKMAN

I've been immersed in death for most of my life. For a doctor dedicated to healing the sick, that seems a negative way of looking at it, but it's true. Medicine, surgery, drugs will never defeat mortality. I lost my parents, I lost my husband four years ago, I lost a sister recently, and I've lost friends. I've worked shifts in A&E, and for twenty-five years in paediatrics I have been a witness to the worst of family anguish and loss. Without losing one's humanity, one learns to don a protective shell of professionalism to deal with it all.

But no professionalism in the world could protect me from the loss of my child. That was how I thought of all my girls, even though Danny was the only one biologically mine. I'd done my best to step into a mother's place with Alison. I'd loved her, fought for her, encouraged and supported her. I'd taken the part of honorary mother of the bride at her wedding, fixing her veil, stilling her nerves, watching from the front pew as my husband walked her up the aisle, and hushing Danny's diatribes against patriarchal gestures of possession. She had always been happy to confide in me as well as her two sworn sisters. The news of her death hit me like a hurricane, sucking the breath out of me. I'd wanted to howl in agony.

But I could not, because I had Danny's health to deal with. What with the cancer and Simon, she was in such a state that I wondered if I could do anything to save either her body or her sanity. It had only been made worse by her insistence on speaking to the police. There was such vengeful rage in her. I didn't want to think about what had gone on between her and Simon, it was so unspeakably wrong, but I was determined to encourage her to move on and put him out of her mind. Which meant dissuading her from attending Alison's funeral. It seemed unthinkable that Danny wouldn't be there, but in the circumstances, it was simply out of the question.

I went, though. Alison's mother in all but name and I didn't even receive official notification of when her funeral would be. If Simon even gave me a thought, it would have been as Danielle Brightman's mother, unwanted on the voyage.

I sat at the back of the chapel, prepared to keep my head down and my tongue still, but the sight of Jude on his arm nearly made me scream with disgusted outrage. Jude had sworn to help with Danny's care, and I was grateful for that, but did I have to see this? How could she do it? This was the man who had driven my darling into the arms of death, and she was pawing him, purring at him, treating him like the victim in all this.

Then it was over. So quickly, with no words of any meaning said. Alison was dismissed to the flames and I could barely breathe, I was trying so hard not to cry. People were rising to leave and I couldn't move. Simon and Jude passed me, neither looking my way, neither appearing to register my presence, but I felt a hand squeeze my shoulder. It was enough to break the spell. I staggered out after the last of them, but I couldn't bring myself to join the crowd gathering to examine the floral tributes, for all the world like wedding guests queuing up to admire the presents.

There was a young woman standing out of the crowd too, watching. My instinct was to approach her and encourage her, in case shyness was holding her back, but then I remembered that police officers might be present, witnessing and noting, and she could well be one of them, so I kept my distance.

Ade and Tim saw me and came over, looking considerably more grief-stricken than the widower. Ade was weeping his eyes out.

"Madeleine," said Tim, embracing me. 'No Danny?'

I shook my head. "It really wouldn't be appropriate for her to come. I persuaded her to stay at home."

"I should have done the same with Ade. He never could cope with funerals, least of all this one."

Ade just wailed and threw his arms around me. "Sorry. Sorry. Can't help myself."

"Don't apologise," I said. "Tears are what Alison's funeral deserves. A flood of tears. Better than this pathetic show, anyway."

"I know. It's an insult, isn't it?" Tim was shaking as he glanced back in disgust to where Jude was standing by Simon, stroking his sleeve. "What's happening there?"

"It's hard to stomach, isn't it?" I said. "Thank God Danny isn't here to see it."

"I wish I wasn't seeing it. How could she?'

"It's all too much for me, Tim. Is there more of this charade? Has Simon arranged something? A funeral tea?"

"If he has, I'm not interested." Tim almost spat the words, blinking back tears. "But some of us are meeting up at the Turf. Come and join us? Bring Danny. Let's remember Alison properly."

"No. Sorry, no." I let them embrace me again, but I couldn't cope with any more today. "Do, please, celebrate Alison in any way you can, but I'm not fit for company just now. You'll forgive me, won't you. Better if I just go home to Danny."

8. JUDE

"Jude. You're early." Tim Draycott, tall and rather saturnine, ushered me into the terraced house on the south side of Bristol that he shared with Danny's cousin, Adrian Merriman. It was a subdued greeting, compared with the usual jovial "Jude the eternally obscure!" or any number of variations on "Hey Jude!" It wasn't just the sobering effects of loss. I sensed the frost that had been evident when I'd phoned two days before. It grieved me but when you know what you want and you decide to go for it at any cost, you have to be prepared to pay.

"Hello, Tim."

None of the usual hearty kisses. He'd already turned and was leading me down the passage to the back room – or open-plan living space, thanks to a glass extension taking up most of the small garden. The front room was Tim's music studio.

"Ade. She's here."

Adrian Merriman didn't have it in him to be frosty with me. He lived up to his name, the light to Tim's dark, and he automatically broke into a broad grin at sight of me. "Hey Jude! How're you doing?"

"Oh, you know."

"Do we?" said Tim, waspish.

"I'm worried about Danny, just as you are, I imagine."

"Yes. No point in being worried about Alison anymore."

Ade looked pained. "He doesn't mean that. Yes, We're both worried about Danny, so I'll do anything you like."

I smiled. "I was hoping you'd be willing to come to Wales with me, that's all."

He was taken by surprise, as was Tim.

"Wales?"

"Why?"

"I've been talking with Madeleine," I explained. "You know what Danny went through first time round with the treatment. It was bad. It will probably be bad this time, too. Madeleine wants to take her away afterwards. Somewhere quiet, private, where she can recuperate in peace." I didn't add *somewhere far away from Simon Delaney*. It wasn't as if my sole concern was to separate them.

"She can come to Spain with us!"

"Maybe one day, but Madeleine thought West Wales. They rented a holiday cottage there once, so she thinks it will conjure up golden childhood memories. She's got the details of a few places." I held up a sheaf of papers. "She doesn't want to leave Danny at the moment, so I offered to drive there and take a look at them, find a suitable refuge for when it's all over. It's not much but it's something I can do. I was hoping you'd come with me, Ade."

"Well." He glanced brightly at Tim to see if he objected. Apparently not, though he said nothing. "If it's for Danny. I'll do anything for her, even venture over into bandit country."

"I've been assured it's all charmingly civilised."

"Well, okay!" Ade needed no more explanation.

"Why do you need him with you?" asked Tim.

"Because." I shrugged, slightly embarrassed. "I want a husband, okay?"

Tim snorted. "So I've heard." Ade gaped at me, his grin widening.

"Look, I'm trying to find a bolt hole for Danny. If I come across the perfect house, I don't want word to get around that it's going to be a convalescent retreat for a cancer patient. Can you imagine how Danny would react to village curiosity or well-meaning sympathy? So I thought, if we could pass ourselves off as yet another ordinary couple looking for a holiday place, no one would think twice. We can find a suitable property, sort out the purchase, get it all done quietly, and then Danny can move in without anyone noticing."

Ade waited.

"Okay," said Tim, cautiously.

"I'll pack a bag, said Ade, bounding for the stairs.

* * *

Mid-August and the school summer holidays were in full swing, so the traffic heading west over the bridge was horrendous. Ade was ebullient as we sped along the M4, slightly circumspect as we reached the end of the motorway and downright suspicious as we headed off along country roads beyond Carmarthen. Faced with placenames with an apparent lack of vowels, he actually whimpered.

"Do they even speak English?"

"You can always fall back on talking very loudly and using sign language, Ade."

"It's not natural."

"How are you going to manage in Spain? Your Spanish is hopeless."

"Yes, but Tim's is good. I'll just smile. Are you sure this is the way?" We were driving along a deep and increasingly forbidding valley. "Take the wrong turning and we'll be lost forever. Archaeologists will find our skeletons in a rusting car."

"This is what a satnav is for, Ade. The first one shouldn't be too far now. Turn left and near Cenarth."

"How many are we hoping to see?"

"Five, I think."

He grabbed the property print-outs from the back seat, and shuffled through them. "Not sure I'd fancy any of these, myself."

"Yes, but they're not for a city nightlife boy like you." I took the left turn. We were nearly there. "Listen, Ade, when we get there, just remember we're Mr and Mrs, John and Mary Smith, looking for a weekend cottage, okay?"

"Okay to the husband-and-wife bit, but not John and Mary Smith. That's so naff."

By the time we reached the first property on Madeleine's list, we'd settled on Jayne and Leo Camberley. All to do with his first pet dog and the road he'd grown up on. Make it easy to remember, I insisted.

The bungalow at Cenarth was nice enough, but too close to neighbours; a certain degree of privacy was desirable. We drove on, heading for number two, in the vicinity of Boncath.

"Speaking of loving couples," said Ade.

"Yes?"

"We've heard you're getting very tight with Alison's ex."

"Her widower, you mean? Simon. Can't you manage his name, or has Danny's bile been getting to you?"

"She does have it in for him, doesn't she?"

"She's hurting, Ade. We all are. Simon is too, though Danny won't accept that. He was Alison's husband. Remember them at the wedding? She adored him. She wouldn't want him left to fade away. If I can offer him some support, what's wrong with that?"

Ade's slow grin was back, spreading across his face. "Support, eh? A little bird's told me it's a bit more than that."

"Which is why Tim was so cool, I suppose."

"Well, you know how he worshipped Alison."

"We all worshipped Alison."

It was certainly true in Tim's case. He and Alison had been close friends since music college. Performing partners and we all thought they were an ideal match. He and Alison had thought it too, until she introduced Tim to Ade after one concert, and he discovered his true bent, as Ade liked to put it. But Tim had continued to idolise Alison in a purely platonic way.

"Tim's got it in for Simon too. Convinced he wasn't supporting her enough, and then, moving on... to you, I mean. It was pretty quick, wasn't it? Especially after what Danny said."

I concentrated on the road for a minute. "What did Danny say? How much did she tell you?"

"Just that she's convinced Simon killed Alison. Isn't that enough?"

"Did she tell you that she and Simon had had a close encounter of their own?"

"While he was married to Alison?"

"Yes."

"Blimey! That puts a different complexion on things. But he's not seeing her now."

"I hope not! Look, Ade, I know about it, but let's not broadcast it round the houses, okay. It's a bit awkward for all of us."

"Does that mean it's really serious, you and him?"

"It might be," I said carefully. "Let's say it is."

"Blimey," he repeated.

* * *

The cottage at Boncath wasn't suitable at all. The third, not far from Cilgerran, was a possible, the pros outnumbering the cons. I let it be understood that Mr and Mrs Camberley were definitely interested but we'd need to discuss it, and we headed west, to the fourth cottage, called the Boat Shed, beyond Cardigan. The satnav brought us along the valley on a narrow road, to a gateway with a For Sale sign. But the name on the wall of the cute pink-washed house beyond was Curlew Cottage. I stopped to check the paperwork again.

"A lane. I've got it."

"I told you it was bandit country," said Ade, as I turned us down a track winding into the bushes beside Curlew Cottage.

"Nonsense. Pirates, maybe." We'd emerged from the bushes onto a sweep of pasture that sloped down to a tidal estuary and the Boat Shed lay before us. The details boasted a sea view, but since the tide was out, it was more of a mud view. A thin glimmer of river was visible, threading through a glistening expanse, raucous with feeding birds. The name made it clear what the property had been in a former life. Another floor and extension had been added and French doors and wide windows inserted where large barn doors had been. The upper half of a crumbling slipway had been demolished, replaced by a raised patio with a stack of plastic chairs. There was still a boat, a small dinghy, moored to a wooden jetty that ran out beside one of the streams cutting a dark creek across the mud. Thorn bushes below the patio, mingled with a few flowering shrubs, suggested that the house was safely above high-water level, reassuring to know.

The estate agent arrived shortly after us and showed us in. The Boat Shed had been rented out as a holiday cottage and he assumed we would want to keep it as such. He didn't put much effort into selling it to us. No need. It was rather neglected and in need of a thorough refurbishment, but any property in that situation would probably fly.

"How far is the last one?" Ade asked, as I dragged him upstairs. "I never realised there was so much of Wales. Tell me it's not another fifty miles."

"No need," I said, glancing out of one bedroom window, which offered an unobstructed view over the mudflats to the wooded shore beyond. The other bedroom looked out straight up the lane leading to Curlew Cottage. "This is the one. Come on, darling. Let's tell the agent we'll have it. I think it's perfect, don't you?"

Ade put on a good show of being an excited husband. Too good a show. What had been intended as a discreet bit of subterfuge was turning into a theatrical drama as Ade launched into a detailed account of our courtship, our wedding and our expectations of tiny feet. I winced in the background. The agent was almost embarrassed, but pleased to have wrapped up a sale within two days of the house going on the market.

We stayed a little longer, to introduce ourselves to the neighbours. Mr and Mrs Godfrey, quarter of a mile away up at Curlew Cottage, were delighted to have a couple of newlyweds moving in as neighbours.

"It's sad that the Boat Shed stands empty for half the year," said Mrs Godfrey. "And no one's had it this year at all, because of Mr Lawson dying, although he never had any trouble letting it to summer visitors."

"Despite the name," I said. "It does sound rather industrial. We might change it."

"Whatever you call it, it will be lovely having a young couple taking it on. Will you be letting it too, or do you intend to live there permanently?"

"Probably just occasionally," I said, as Ade declared "Oh yes, and raise a family."

"Can you tone it down a bit?" I whispered, as I guided him back to the car. "At least get our story straight. We want to come across as a boringly normal couple, friendly but keeping our business private, okay?"

He promised to keep quiet from then on, but when we stopped to check out the facilities at the nearest village, the riverside pub where we stopped for dinner proved too much of a temptation. I should have known better. Ade never could take his drink. One round and he was pouring out all our marital plans to anyone who would listen, whether they spoke Welsh, English or the occasional German. I steered him away when he started naming our proposed progeny.

"That's enough, dear. We have to keep some secrets, don't we? Time to go."

"Oh God, We're not driving back tonight, are we?"

"You can sleep the entire way if you like. I'm fine for driving. Come on."

Several glasses were raised to cheer us on our way.

"That was fun," said Ade, settling into the passenger seat and preparing to doze.

"Which bit? Your fantasy of being the father of seven children?"

"Yeah, that." He yawned. "Four boys and three girls."

"I'll tell you one thing. No child of mine will ever be called Tarquin."

"Why not? I like it."

"Adrian Merriman, are you actually getting broody?"

He managed a somnolent chuckle. "Wouldn't mind there being a mini-me out there somewhere. Always fancied being a dad. Without the nappies and stuff. Just in an abstract sort of way."

"Very abstract." I finished a text to Madeleine, letting her know I'd found the perfect place, then I started the engine.

Ade shifted to get more comfortable. "You wouldn't marry Simon, would you? Tim would throw a fit."

I was debating how to answer but his snoring saved me the trouble.

He slept most of the way, apart from making use of an urgent pit stop at Cardiff West. I nudged him awake again when I finally pulled up by his home. A light was on.

"Come on. In."

"Uh? Are we there?"

"Yes. Move."

Tim opened the door for us.

I'd made a decision on the journey. I'd decided it was time to be totally honest and get everything out in the open. "I'm glad you're still up," I said.

"Had to make sure you didn't abduct him too, didn't I?"

I followed Tim through to the Space, where he had coffee brewing, before I responded.

"Okay, start again. I'm glad you're still up, Tim, because I want to talk to both of you. I've been thinking about things Ade has said today, and I know that you think I'm a callous cow, just intent on snatching my best friend's widower, which I don't deserve. Whatever I felt about Simon before Alison's death, he was her beloved and I would never have done anything to mess that up for her. But she's dead and that changes everything. So listen. Yes, I am seeing Simon Delaney. I am seeing a great deal of him. I don't know how it will play out, but if he asks me to marry him, I shall say yes. Don't look like that. I need you both to accept it, because you are not going to make me change my mind."

A painful and sometimes heated discussion went far into the night.

9. DC QUILLAN

The woman, Kylie Thompson, hurried forward and grabbed Rosanna's arm as she headed for the entrance of the police station.

"Have you seen this? Have you read it?" She was thrusting a letter in Rosanna's face. "What the fuck?"

"I am so sorry, Mrs Thompson." Rosanna took the letter, although she guessed the contents as soon as she saw the CPS logo at the top. She scanned the anodyne phrasing with revulsion. A woman was being told her twelve-year-old daughter's rapist was not going to be prosecuted and all they could say was *I hope you will not be too disappointed.* A mother was hovering on the brink of a nervous breakdown, a child, already traumatised by the belief that she had been responsible, had been pushed and prodded into details that had left her howling with misery, and *I hope you will not be too disappointed.*

"I don't get it. Why?" Mrs Thompson wouldn't let go of her arm. "She told them what happened. Why are they letting him get away with it? How can they fucking do that?"

What was she to say? That the CPS had measured the evidence against a table of percentages and had decided that the certainty of getting a conviction wasn't sufficiently high to waste court time and money on justice for her daughter? "I really am sorry, Mrs Thompson. We did our best."

"So why wasn't that good enough? Are they saying my girl's a liar?"

"No! I know she was telling the truth, and I knew how painful it was for her to tell it. And for you. Believe me, if I could have done anything more…"

Ben Morgan was hurrying towards them, ready to intervene, but he slowed as he realised who was involved. "Kylie, we are all very disappointed that your daughter's case isn't being taken forward."

"She's scared to leave the house now, you know that?"

"I can imagine. But there's really no need for her to worry. Go home to Grace." Ben was good at sounding earnest and reassuring, probably because it was genuine. "I'll make sure your family liaison officer calls round and talks to both of you."

They watched Kylie Thompson walk away, shoulders shaking. "She's angry," said Ben.

"I'm angry! Why did we bother?"

"I ask myself that sometimes." He turned with her towards the station. "Another case is being tidied up, too: the DI has asked me to attend the inquest on Alison Delaney. You remember her?"

"Of course I do."

"It's going to be an open and shut verdict of suicide, you know that?"

"With no mention of coercive control?"

"No evidence."

"What about the missing keys?"

"Circumstantial. Hypothetical. The DI doesn't want it brought up. Don't look at me like that, Ros."

Rosanna sat down at her desk, switched her screen on and stared at it, fuming with inner hatred. Then she decided that hating a computer screen was no solution to anything. She cornered DI Stansford.

"I understand—"

"The Delaney inquest? Morgan says you're still fretting about the case."

"I just think—"

"That we should be raising the issue of missing keys. I'm sorry, Quillan. I know you feel strongly about this one, but a missing bedroom key isn't enough to raise doubts at an inquest and lead to a futile police investigation that I guarantee would get us nowhere near a courtroom. There is simply no corroborating evidence that Delaney exerted undue mental or physical pressure on his wife. I have to consider the best use of police time. We've already had one disappointment this week with the Thompson case collapsing and, believe me, you're not the only one upset about that outcome."

Rosanna said nothing.

Stansford half turned to go, then stopped. "Morgan will be attending the inquest. You haven't been to one yet, have you?"

"Not as a police officer, ma'am."

"Ah, yes, of course. Your mother. Well, you can go with Morgan, see it through, if that will help."

"Thank you, ma'am."

"Just to observe, you understand that? No interruptions."

"No, ma'am.

* * *

Had she given the impression she'd attended an inquest before? It wasn't true. She would have gone when her mother died, but everyone said she was too young. Only fourteen. They said she'd only be distressed. What they meant was, they didn't want her coming out with her wicked fibs, so she was left in the care of Aunty Annie Prothero who lectured her on how lucky she was to have such a kind man for a father and she ought to learn to pay him proper respect.

Such a kind man, Craig Quillan. Kind to take on that little mouse, Mandy White, for a start. Wouldn't say boo to a goose, that woman. Most men wanted a girl with a bit more spirit, but then, there were benefits to having a wife who wasn't always nagging, or making a fuss if her man went to the pub. Should had appreciated how cushy she had it, because Craig Quillan worked hard and always brought home the dosh. No need for her to go scrabbling for jobs at the local shops, like other wives. All she had to do was sit at home, keep the house tidy, put food on the table, mind the kids. They were all right, the kids, Ryan and Rosanna. Quiet, but well-behaved, not like some. So what did Mandy Quillan have to complain about? Okay, she was a bit down occasionally. All women were. Pills usually sorted them out. But no, she had to drink, too. Tried to hide it, slipping off on the bus to different parts of town and coming home with clinking carriers. And see her struggling to walk down the street in a straight line! No

93

wonder the neighbours heard crashes and bangs now and then, coming from their terraced house. Daft woman probably fell downstairs, she was so pissed. Explains why she finished up under the wheel of the No.16 bus. Poor Craig Quillan but, let's be honest, he was better off rid of her.

A different picture inside the house though, witnessed by Ryan and Rosanna, as they watched him systematically destroy their mother. Yes, there was physical violence, a backhander across the face, a savage push between the shoulder blades while she was carrying boiling water, but mostly it was verbal. Non-stop, never ending. Seldom shouting, but softly spoken jibes and sneers and insults in her face. Interrupting with a new subject if she tried to say something. Sometimes it wasn't even verbal, just looks of utter contempt, the curled lip, the studied disdain, turning his back on her as if she weren't there. All he did was mock her, for her stupidity, for her inadequacy and, once he'd driven her to it, for her pathetic drunkenness.

The children knew better than to stand up for her. Who'd want to be on the receiving end of the same treatment? Ryan dealt with it by pretending to see nothing. Rosanna dealt with it by saying nothing, but she saw everything. She said nothing, even on that last day, when her father leaned down to speak to Mum, face so close their noses almost touched, though she tried to flinch away.

"Drunken cow. Fucking millstone round my neck from day one, that's all you've been. Do you know how pathetic you are? I don't know why you waste your energy breathing. Why don't you just get out of our lives? Go and throw yourself under a bus, why don't you?"

So she did.

Rosanna didn't see it, but she heard it. Walking to school, she heard, behind her, a hundred yards down her road, the hooting, the squeal of brakes, the screams from bystanders, and she knew, even before she turned to run back, what had happened. They tried to hide what the bus had done to her mother, but she saw it all before she was whisked away to the house of a neighbour who cried over her and worried that Rosanna wasn't crying too. Must be shock, they decided. She's not saying anything.

Nor did she until a couple of policewomen came to speak to the son and daughter. Was Mrs Quillan so drunk she fell into the road, as neighbours suspected, or did she, as the driver claimed, stand staring at the approaching bus before deliberately stepping in front of it?

They spoke to Ryan first, three years older, upset, bewildered, everything he was supposed to be. "I can't understand it. It can't have been deliberate, can it? I mean, she does get a bit tipsy now and then. If she was feeling that bad, why didn't she talk to us?" He genuinely meant it, Rosanna thought. He had opted not to see or hear, so he hadn't. But she had. While one police officer comforted Ryan, the other turned to Rosanna, not expecting much.

"Do you think you could talk about your mum?" As if she were a four-year-old.

"Yes," said Rosanna.

"It was a very sad accident, wasn't it?"

"No, it wasn't an accident. She jumped under a bus because Dad told her to."

Eyebrows rose. Ryan looked horrified. "Oh no, no, he didn't mean it. It was just because she'd got a bit drunk. He didn't mean it. He loves her."

"No he doesn't," said Rosanna. "He's horrible to her, all the time. He's a bully and he's cruel."

"No, that's not true!"

It was true though, and maybe the police realised it, but nothing was done. There was no hand on Mandy's back, pushing her. Suicide, whilst under the influence of alcohol. End of story. Rosanna wasn't to talk about it anymore. Not if she knew what was good for her.

"You're not going to enjoy this." Ben ushered Rosanna into the court before him.

"Really? I thought it was going to be a bundle of laughs."

"You reckon you can keep quiet about keys and things?"

"I plan to."

"What do you plan to do instead? Stare at Delaney and shame him into confession? Nice if it did work like that."

"But it doesn't. I know that."

Of course it wouldn't. And it didn't. The inquest went exactly as everyone had predicted. The police were settled on suicide. The GP confirmed a history of stress and panic attacks for which some mild antidepressants had been subscribed, but not the Tofranil found at the scene, which had probably been obtained illicitly over the internet. A neighbour commented on her heavy drinking, the husband expressed surprise and shock at her action but spoke of the stress she'd shown through the pregnancy. He looked solemn, but no longer crippled by grief. He couldn't have carried that off, as everyone could see he was already over it. The red-haired woman was by his side, her head leaning close to his throughout, her hand on his arm. Rosanna caught meaningful glances round the courtroom at the sight of them, but they seemed content with their mutual support and shrugged off the raised eyebrows.

Once the inevitable verdict was given, the couple rose and turned to leave the court, deaf to the whispering. As they passed Rosanna, she caught the flash of gold, the wedding ring on the woman's finger, as it stroked Delaney's sleeve. She was about to point it out to Ben, but her attention was caught by the sight of two women at the back of the court. Rosanna immediately recognised the older one as the solitary women at Alison's funeral. At the back again and watching. The other woman with her, dressed entirely in black, was younger, with dark hair trimmed short, dark eyes in dark shadows, her face thin. The Dark Lady, Rosanna thought.

Both women had their eyes fixed on the newly married couple, but the Dark Lady's gaze was fixed specifically on the bride. A look of disgust and fury. The red-head stopped and met her gaze, though Rosanna couldn't see her expression.

She heard the words, though. The Dark Lady stepped forward, despite the restraining grip of the older woman, and said "How could you do this to me, Jude? Do you have any idea what you've done?"

The reply was quavering, straining to keep calm. "You've got to stop this, Danny. It's not doing anyone any good. Let it go. Let him go."

"Never!" The Dark Lady's voice rose as her companion dragged her back. "I'll never let him go!"

With a slight shake of her head, the red-head walked on, on Delaney's arm. Throughout the exchange he had stood silent, a hint of pained distress visible on his profile, studiously not looking at their attacker.

"Is that Danielle Brightman?" asked Rosanna, as the Dark Lady was hustled from the court.

"Yep."

"She accused him of killing his wife. Why wasn't she called?"

"You know she withdrew it. Admitted she'd been involved with him. A case of hell having no fury, because he decided to stay with his wife? Probably feeling doubly scorned now, if he's gone and married the red-head instead. She must have thought she'd be in with a chance with the first wife dead."

"That sounds like bullshit to me."

"What do you make of it, then?"

"I…" The truth was, Rosanna couldn't think of any other interpretation. It was just so sordid. She wanted it to be something more sinister. She shrugged. "Did you know he'd remarried?"

"He told Jen when she spoke to him about the inquest. It was only last week apparently."

"You don't think that's suspicious? Or at the very least, bad taste?"

"Oh, yes, bad taste all right, but there's no law against that. And I can't see many men blaming him. The second Mrs Delaney is certainly a stunner."

"Oh well, enough said. Just like that, Alison Delaney is forgotten."

"You haven't forgotten her though."

"No. Nor will I."

Ben smiled grimly. "I know, Rosanna, and that's why I think you're going to find this job bloody hard."

10. JUDE

It was my idea. I know a lot of people were going to disapprove, but I felt I had to make a statement. It was common knowledge that Simon had been questioned when Alison died, and although he had been cleared of all suspicion in the eyes of the law, mud would stick, rumours would never quite die down. Our marriage, I hoped, would settle the matter. We had to move on.

After all, I had already practically moved in, and it was the natural next step. The only thing that had held him back from proposing was the relatively short time since Alison's death.

"Not five months yet, Jude."

"That's two months longer than I'd been dating Eddie when we married. Does it matter?"

"But with Alison… You know what people will say."

"I know that when we walk into the inquest together as a married couple, they'll be saying that one of Alison's closest friends trusts you implicitly."

"More likely, they'll say that I'm a devious heartless bastard."

"Are we going to care what they say?" I slipped my arms around him. "I want to show the world I believe in you."

Slowly, the worry frown faded and he smiled, impishly. "You're right. I don't care. Let's do it."

So we did. A big church affair really would have been tasteless, so, a week before the inquest, we drove to the register office, picked up a couple of witnesses on the street, and did the deed. I didn't need flowers and white lace, I told him. I just wanted a wedding ring. He was more than happy to buy that.

"Do you really want to be driving off every day at the crack of dawn to that stupid job of yours?" he said, as we drove back to Soweridge. "I'm doing perfectly well enough to support a wife."

"That sounds disgracefully old fashioned. Wives generally do work these days. I don't mind."

"Okay, if it was a job you loved… but you don't like it, do you? You told me that. Office management, dull, dull, dull, isn't that what you said? So why bother slogging away at it when you could be free?"

"I admit it's not exactly my dream career. But if I did give up, I'd expect to pull my weight here instead."

"You're got your redundancy pay and I reckon that's all the weight you need to pull. Leave it to me. I can manage things. That's what I do, remember."

"Yes, but still, I want to do something. I could work for you, instead."

He laughed.

"No, I mean it. I've had all the experience of office work you'd need. And you wouldn't even have to pay me."

"I've got a pretty good team in the city, darling. Not sure how the dynamics would play out if I suddenly brought my wife in out of nowhere."

"All right, I can see that. But you do have an office here too." One end of the house was a business suite, where Simon operated from home. The real work was done in a back room that I remembered as smelling of hot starch, because the housekeepers had ironed there. Now it smelled of enterprise, a very efficient workstation with computers, printers, telephones, box files, locked cabinets and a safe. A command centre. Adjoining it, overlooking the gravel drive at the front, was Mr Greenold's forbidden study, now a reassuringly opulent reception room for clients. "I could act as your secretary here."

He smiled, shaking his head.

"Why not? After all, I'm your wife now. I've invested myself in you and I want everyone to know your name."

"And I'll be proud and happy to have you standing beside me. My wife." He raised my hand and kissed the gleaming new ring on my finger.

I flashed the ring proudly at the inquest.

It was a sad occasion rather than harrowing. Everyone knew what had happened, even if the world would never understand what had driven Alison to it. It was a time to close the book… or it should have been.

I wasn't as calm as I seemed, worried how Danny might react, although it had been a relief to hear that she wasn't going to be called as an official witness. The police must have concluded there was sexual rivalry at the root of her accusations. I was painfully aware that friendship and sex can be competing forces impossible to reconcile.

I knew that Danny had been involved with Simon, fixated on him, before Alison died, and my marriage was bound to be awkward for her. But I had made my choice and I was going to support Simon through this last ritual, so I held his hand and prepared for the worst if she decided to let rip. She was there at the back, in the shadows, and all through the proceedings I could tell Simon was aware of her, expecting loud screams of accusation at any moment.

As the coroner reached his conclusions, we seemed to have passed the danger point. We rose to leave at last, with the coroner's condolences, and it was only then that Danny made her presence felt. Madeleine was with her, of course. I tried to shield Simon as we passed, and sure enough Danny broke free from Madeleine's grip and was in my face, blocking my way. I felt Simon's arm tense as I squeezed his hand.

"How could you do this to me, Jude? Do you have any idea what you've done?" She was almost spitting at me, but her eyes were drilling into Simon.

He was rigid by my side but determined not to respond, his eyes fixed ahead. I could feel his palm sweating.

I needed to get him out this distressing situation without violence breaking out. I took a deep breath, my voice unsteady. "You've got to stop this, Danny. It's not doing anyone any good. Let it go. Let him go."

"Never!" Danny was anything but calm. "I'll never let him go!"

"Dearest, don't do this." Madeleine had her arms around Danny and was pulling her back. "Come away now, please. It won't help."

I didn't wait to see if Danny would heed her mother's advice. I marched on resolutely, taking Simon with me. Only when we were outside did I let myself tremble.

"I'm so sorry, darling," I said as I let Simon guide me, stony-faced, towards the carpark. "I don't know why she's taken against you so violently, when she must know how much you loved Alison, how much Alison loved you."

"Ignore her," he said, through gritted teeth, and it was clear how upset he'd been by it. His pulse was racing. That tic was back in his eyelid.

"I hate it that she talks about not letting you go. Is she going to haunt you forever out of some delusion—"

"Let it go!"

"I can't. This can't go on. I'm going to have to go and see her, have it out with her, find out why she's doing this."

"No!" We'd reached his car and he swung the door open for me with violent force. "Don't go anywhere near her, you hear!" He must have realised how aggressive he sounded, because his tone immediately softened. "Please."

"But I have to know what's going on in her head. I know she hasn't been well, but this obsessive reaction is too much. It's poisoning everything. I've got to put things straight."

"No!" He settled himself in the driving seat, inserted the key and sat there staring at it. "Don't speak to her.

104

Look." He turned the key, letting the engine purr into life, then he turned it off again and gripped the steering wheel. "All right. You want to know what it's all about, and I'll tell you. We had an affair, okay?"

"You and Danny?"

"Yes. I didn't tell you before because I knew you'd be disgusted. You must be."

Disgusted wasn't quite the right word, since I already knew about his involvement with Danny. I had been determined not to mention it unless he did, because I could sense how guilty he felt about it. He'd want to bury it forever, pretend it had never happened. But after that showdown at the inquest, it really needed to be lanced, to let the venom out. I looked down at my hands. "Was this while you were married to Alison?"

"Yes. You see, I knew you'd be disgusted. I'm disgusted with myself. Alison and I were going through a rocky patch – you know how it was when the recording malarkey fell through. Well, maybe you don't. You weren't around. But Alison was depressed, distant, wouldn't let me comfort her. And… oh, never mind how it happened. It shouldn't have happened, but it did. Inexcusable. That's why I broke it off. Or tried to. But Danny wouldn't let it go. She even took it into her head that I was going to leave Alison for her. Can you believe that?"

I swallowed hard, unable to find words. An image came back to me, the three of us…

We are sprawled on the grass in University Parks, all dolled up in running gear. At least Alison is dolled up. She's wearing pink trainers, turquoise shorts, a T-shirt with a sparkly kitten on it and her golden hair is tied back with a pink bow. We'd debated long and hard about her choice of clothing. I thought it made her look too cute, My Little Pony. Danny said no, it made her stand out and that was what mattered. She is certainly a contrast to us in our dull P.E. kits, though it's not as if we're really keen to run. I prefer sprinting to long distance. Danny avoids any sort of exercise if she can manage it. Alison quite likes netball, but she wouldn't dream of weekend athletics if it weren't imperative.

It is imperative because it's the only way to catch the attention of Michael Someone. Alison thinks it's Michael Sandbridge and she looks hurt if I call him Michael Sandwich or Sandbag. All we know is that he's a student and he runs here every Saturday and Alison has the hots for him. I think Danny does too. When Alison pointed him out, Danny said "Swoon! And they both say "Swoon!" now, whenever he's mentioned, which is most of the time at the moment. He is quite hot, I suppose. At least he sweats a lot. We're not sure which college he belongs to or where he lives. We're not sure of anything except that he runs, so we're going to run too and he can't fail to notice Alison. He wouldn't notice us normally because we're fourteen and invisible to young Gods of Oxford, but if we're virtually tripping over each other on the path, he'll have to pay attention.

"He's coming!" squeals Alison and we spring to our feet, bouncing around as if we've been running all morning.

"Okay," I say. "Let's get ahead of him." I lead the way onto the path with Alison and Danny at my heels.

We spread out, me in front because I'm fastest and Alison last because that's the whole idea. Anyway, she runs like a duck, legs and elbows all over the place.

Michael Sandwich is coming up behind us, long legs and long strides and glistening sweat on his brow. He catches up with Alison, he's beside her, head turning to grin at her and she smiles back, blushing with hope.

But he just laughs, passing her with easy lopes. I've already rounded a bend so it's easy for me to look back and see what's happening. I see Alison's quivering lip, the welling tears of tragedy and my pace slows. Danny is still running stoically, her dark hair flopping into her eyes. She doesn't realise what's happened, not until the Sandwich falls in beside her, slowing to keep pace with her. He's grinning still, asking her something. Danny looks confused. This wasn't part of the plan.

He speaks again. I've come to a halt and they're almost on me. Danny's confusion turns to indignation.

"No! I don't want to. I'm with my friends." She jerks away from him and jogs back to Alison's side, hugging her round the waist.

The Sandwich shrugs, turns and finds himself almost nose to nose with me. He jumps, then dodges round me, muttering something. Alison bursts into tears as he disappears into trees.

"Cheek!" says Danny. "He was supposed to talk to you, not me."

"I wouldn't have minded," says Alison, weeping but generous.

"Never!" says Danny…

Never say never. We had been so young and innocent. Why couldn't we all have gone on believing that nothing could ever come between us? All it had taken, in the end, was one man. One man who had sparked an overwhelming desire in each of us – and now I had him. I wasn't going to let him go.

Simon switched the engine on again. "God knows what's behind all this now. Love turned to hate, I suppose. Or maybe shame, once Alison… Or sick anger because I didn't rush to Danny's side the moment Alison…" He sniffed and got into first gear decisively. "She phoned me, you know, as soon as she heard. I told her I never wanted to see her again and I cut her off. So. Now you know everything. What do you want me to do?"

I laid my hand on his. "Let's go home."

"Our home?"

"Yes. Our home."

He released the clutch, letting out a sigh of relief.

"I'm glad you told me," I said. "If I am disgusted, maybe I'm more disgusted with Danny than you. I can't believe that she'd betray Alison like that. Not just by sleeping with you, but by expecting you to abandon Alison. It must have been the illness getting to her."

"Maybe." He turned out onto the road. "But can we not talk about her anymore? We have our new life to lead."

"Yes we do!" I had to say it though. "If Danny was so desperate for you, she'll really have it in for me now."

"Don't worry," said Simon. "I won't let her do anything to you."

11. SIMON

It crept up on him almost before he was aware. He'd quite enjoyed the clandestine thrill of being Jude's lover, but then suddenly there he was, signing the register, side by side with a new wife and what had been clandestine became open and somehow disgraceful.

It wasn't the fact of being married again that worried him. He'd intended it almost from the first time they'd slept together. She was perfect. Alison had been perfect but Jude was different. He wanted her. What he didn't want was the reception that followed, the looks, the pursed lips, the mutterings as soon as his back was turned. It was stupid, he knew, but it was annoying, when all he'd ever wanted was respect.

"Let's show the world," Jude had said, and he loved her for that, for her sublime faith in him, ready to face down any criticism. He just didn't want the criticism. He didn't want Mrs Hargreaves, across the road, looking at him with sad disappointment.

Even the boys and girls at the London office stared at him speechless for half a minute when he told them, but it didn't take longer than that for them to rally and shower him with congratulations. They never missed an opportunity to bring out the champagne.

Jude resolutely ignored all barbed comments and looks, and her strength bolstered him. He needed her. Somehow, he was going to have to get through Alison's inquest, and he felt sick every time he thought about it, imagining what evidence might come out. Supposing they discovered…

But there was nothing that he hadn't already heard, none of the hostile questioning that he'd feared, just courteous and sympathetic requests for his account. There were unanswered questions, like where Alison had obtained the unprescribed pills she'd taken, but it seemed that everyone was doing it these days, via the web, or enough people for it to seem commonplace. He'd made sure to wipe his phone and laptop of any trace of dealings and no one accused him.

Best of all, Danny Brightman wasn't called. He'd lain awake night after night beside Jude, sweating over what Danny might say, telling himself that they'd surely see she was hysterical. But in the end, she wasn't even asked to speak. His legs were trembling with relief when they rose to leave. He offered Jude his arm, but it was questionable who was supporting whom.

And then it all seemed to fall apart. Danny was in front of them, spitting like the cat she was. He fought to keep his cool, choking on his own terror as he waited for her to start screaming accusations in front of the whole bloody courtroom. But it was Jude she went for. Of course their marriage must have been acid in her wounds. He marvelled at the way Jude coped, quiet but firm, refusing to snarl back, while he did nothing, useless until they were out of there. Then his breath returned, he seized Jude's arm and marched her to the waiting car. He had to get away from there. It was a question of protecting Jude, wasn't it?

But there was no escape. Danny was left behind but Jude started up, setting him on edge. She wouldn't let it drop, wanting to know why, why, why. He wanted to scream Shut Up, but he couldn't, not there, not then.

So he came out with it, his confession of an affair with Danny. What else could he do? He expected hysterics, or fury, a slamming of door. That was what any other woman would have done, but not Jude. She was almost too understanding. It was Danny she blamed, rather than him. It was all he could have hoped for. Surely it was over now.

Except that it wasn't. It would never be. He wanted more than anything to have Danny out of his life and everything simple and honest again, but her hold on him was too strong. Too much had happened between them. She was never going to let it rest, so neither could he. He knew, that night, as he made love to Jude, that Danny would always be in his head. He couldn't put it off any longer. He would have to go to her.

12. DC QUILLAN

Rosanna Quillan had a spate of housebreakings to attend to. Which meant logging the details in case a pattern emerged that would require some actual detection. Her chosen career was proving to be a depressing victory of despair over hope. God knows what trauma had been endured by those who'd been burgled. How many wouldn't be able to sleep, terrified by every creak in the house? For the victims, each burglary was a major damaging event. Here, at her desk, they were nothing more than a string of statistics involving insignificant assets. Manpower was limited so nothing would be done.

Just as nothing had been done about the death of Alison Delaney. Files closed, another case to be stamped and forgotten, as dead as Alison herself, and Simon Delaney was free to brush her away.

It shouldn't happen that way. What was the point of law if it did? It wouldn't be allowed if Rosanna had any say in it.

When she was fourteen, she had established herself as a stubborn and contrary creature, saying things that people didn't want to hear. Why should she change now? Ben was still keeping an eye on the Thompson case, letting the matter simmer rather than go cold, so she would do the same with Alison Delaney.

She delved into Delaney's history. He did have a criminal record. Nothing involving a prison sentence, unfortunately but still, five speeding tickets over eight years proved something about him, didn't it? That he was an arrogant bastard who didn't think normal rules should apply to him.

Did it mean that? She'd had one endorsement for speeding herself. She'd been driving with a car full of rowdy colleagues who'd distracted her. And there was Peter, an anal-retentive boyfriend, infuriatingly observant of all rules. He'd confessed that he'd deliberately exceeded the limit through a forty-mph zone when he'd been summoned to his dying father in hospital. The infringement had been worrying him ever since, even though he hadn't been caught.

She was willing to bet infringements didn't worry Simon Delaney in the slightest. He probably thought of speeding endorsements as a proof of virility.

Occasionally Rosanna would force herself to face the question she'd have resented anyone else asking. Was she just obsessed with Delaney because she wanted to nail him for the sins of her father, the shadow that she carried with her, night and day? Because she had simply taken a dislike to him from the moment of meeting him? She ought to accept that he might just be an innocent guy wounded by his wife's suicide.

Except, every time she hesitated or began to doubt herself, those missing keys jingled loudly in her brain and she knew Simon Delaney wasn't innocent. He was an abusive husband responsible for one wife's death and now he had another at his mercy.

So she kept digging.

Delaney was a financial advisor and wealth manager, and his company, Delaney Asset Management, had a plush office in London, where he entertained rich clients who wanted to be even richer without having to lift a finger. Probably swindling them left, right and centre... Except that Rosanna could see no evidence of financial misconduct.

Be objective. Look at him all round. What worked in his favour?

His looks, obviously. Change the expensive suit to something more casual, rumple the dark hair a little and he could be a film star. After all, he was certainly an actor, perpetually performing, confident advisor, loving husband, grief-stricken widower, repentant adulterer. Everyone else seemed to be convinced. Everyone except Rosanna.

She rifled through the records of the suicide and opened up the interviews with other residents of Tork Lane. What had they had to say about Simon Delaney? Nothing negative, except that he drove a bit too fast for such a quiet country lane. They were all in agreement that he was a nice young man. Alison had grown up among them, a lovely girl, looking after her father and so talented. They always emphasised that; so talented. She had seemed very happy with her new husband although, as a couple, they hadn't socialised much. There were rumours that she drank too much. Some accounts were less coy and stated it as a blunt fact.

Mrs Kathleen Hargreaves in one of the houses opposite, was one of the coy ones, an elderly widow finding occupation by keeping a close eye on the comings and goings in the lane. Mrs Delaney had sometimes seemed to be a little the worse for drink. Mrs Hargreaves had seen her staggering around in the garden some days, and she often just collapsed on the sofa in the house, looking dead to the world and doing nothing for hours on end. Not that Mrs Hargreaves made a point of peering into other people's houses, but from her window she couldn't help seeing. Mr Delaney would come in and struggle to get his wife to her feet. She'd be all over the place. No longer played the piano, which showed how bad it had got. Her husband had to stop her driving more than once. Took the keys from her. In fact, Mrs Delaney hadn't driven for months, although her car was still in their garage, but she had occasionally called a taxi when Mr Delaney was out. He often worked very long hours, gone before seven in the morning, home after seven at night. Sometimes as late as ten. Sometimes he didn't come home at all, but Mrs Delaney was always there, at home. Except the times when she called a taxi. When he was home, Mr Delaney would drive her when she needed to go out. To the doctor's or such. He took great care of her. She'd been a lot better though, in the last few months, with the baby on its way. She was so pleased about that, which makes it even more tragic.

Mrs Hargreaves had seen a light in their bedroom very early on the morning that Mrs Delaney died, but she hadn't seen the wife. It was a bit odd because the bedroom curtains stayed shut and Mrs Delaney always pulled them back first thing. Usually still in her nightdress, but not that day. Mr Delaney had left the house half an hour later. Very smart as usual. His wife hadn't been at the door to see him off as she normally did. Mrs Hargreaves didn't see any sign of anyone else at Summervale during the day, apart from the postman and a lady collecting for charity in the afternoon. The lady didn't enter the house, she just knocked a couple of times, then tried around the back, before going away again. She was middle-aged, short greying hair and a nice coat. No, Mrs Hargreaves didn't recognise her but she looked as if she might be a charity collector. There was no one else. It wasn't the day for Mrs Bilson, the Delaney's cleaning lady or Derek, the man who did their lawns. The whole place was quiet, no lights, until Mr Delaney came home about eight o'clock. She didn't notice anything really untoward except, a minute or two after he'd gone in, the light in the living room came on and she saw Mr Delaney open a cabinet and pour himself a drink. Then he threw the glass against the wall, which seemed a bit odd at the time, but then if he'd just found his wife, that would explain it. Mrs Hargreaves didn't know that then, of course. There was nothing else, really, until she heard sirens and an ambulance, and a police car, and she had no idea what was going on because she hadn't suspected a thing, and it was a great shock when they told her Mrs Delaney had killed herself.

Rosanna sat staring at Mrs Hargreaves' statement. Then she read it again. How much more did they want? She called Ben over. "You read this, did you?"

"What's that?" He peered at it. "Don't tell me, the Delaney case. This is the old biddy who lives opposite, yes?"

"Yes. Can't you see what she's saying? No sign of Alison Delaney at all, that day. A woman calls and no one answers?"

"In the afternoon, wasn't it? Alison was probably already dead, or comatose."

"And the curtains still shut?"

"Didn't the husband say he'd left her sleeping because she'd had a bad night?"

"I bet she did. Those curtains were never opened because Alison Delaney had been locked in that back room all day and probably since the previous evening."

Ben said nothing.

"And see, one or two minutes after he gets home, he's drinking and hurling glasses around. Just one or two minutes and he's already discovered she's dead. He didn't waste time searching the entire house and garden trying to figure out where his wife had got to. He'd gone straight to the room where he'd left her."

"Look." Ben rested his knuckles on her desk. "We're still back where we were. We have no proof. It could just as easily be an entirely different scenario. He leaves the curtains drawn because she's still sleeping. She doesn't pull them back when she wakes because she's already in a dark place in every sense. She's not going to answer the door to anyone. She's already intent on suicide."

"But she got dressed?"

"Like I said, she was in a dark place. Who knows how her mind was working? He comes home... Mrs Hargreaves says he was knocking back the Scotch a couple of minutes later, but was she keeping a written record of times? A few minutes for her could have been half an hour in reality. I'm not dismissing your suspicions, Rosanna. I find them quite compelling, but unless we can bring some actual evidence to court, it's going to get us nowhere. If Delaney was responsible, let's hope it weighs on his conscience, but that's the best we're going to get. She did kill herself, and everyone who's looked at the facts, including the coroner, agrees on that. She did have a history of mental illness. Maybe Delaney failed to give her the support she needed. Maybe he was a lousy husband, a bully, but there's nothing we can do about that."

"And we just leave him to move on to wife number two?"

"Yup. No law against it."

He was right, of course. There was nothing more the law could do. Simon Delaney had got away with it. And if he could do it once…

What about the second Mrs Delaney? Next potential victim or accomplice? How innocent was she? She and Danielle Brightman obviously knew each other. Delaney had admitted to having an affair with Danielle. Had he been involved with this one too before his wife died? Rosanna wanted to know.

Judith Theresa Granger, widow, according to the marriage certificate. Father: Ronald Cartwright, civil servant, deceased. Address at the time of marriage: Summervale, Tork Lane, Soweridge. How soon after Alison's death had she moved in with him? Where had she lived before? No records on the police computer. Way too classy to soil herself with crime.

"The new Mrs Delaney?" DI Stansford caught her unawares. "You're not still rooting around in that case, are you? It's closed. Put it behind you. We're not paid to be avenging angels for every failed marriage. You have a pile of break-ins to deal with, and I've got two more for you. Now, leave your personal obsessions at home and get on with the work in hand."

Rosanna had no choice. The DI was watching her now, so she ploughed on with cataloguing forced locks and smashed windows. Leave her personal obsessions at home? Yes, she still had a home, and in that home, she had a laptop and the internet.

* * *

Judith Theresa Granger, formerly Cartwright. Roughly the same age as Alison and Danielle? Some years older, it turned out. Rosanna found a birth, Judith T Cartwright, mother's maiden name Davison, registered in Doncaster in 1983. But since then, nothing. How could there be nothing in the age of the internet? Judith Theresa Delaney, formerly Granger, née Cartwright was a woman without any on-line presence whatsoever, which was almost as good as not existing, these days. None of the Judith Cartwrights, Grangers and Delaneys on Facebook and Twitter matched the new wife. No LinkedIn or Whatsapp or Instagram accounts. What about her first marriage? She could just check…

"For Christ's sake, Ro, it's three in the morning." Luke sat up, wrestling with the duvet. "What the hell are you doing on the bloody computer?"

119

"Just searching." She tapped away, her eyes fixed on the laptop screen.

Luke rubbed his eyes with the heel of his hand. "For what? Insomnia cures?"

"Judith Granger."

"Who?"

"She's married to Simon Delaney, the wife killer."

"Oh great! This is work?"

"Yes. Sort of. Three women, three friends, all scrabbling to get their hands on him."

"Lucky guy!"

"But he's already killed one of them. I know he has."

"Can't it wait?"

"I just need to see…"

Luke heaved a dramatic sigh and threw himself back down, pulling a pillow over his head, muttering. She caught "Never date a fucking policewoman."

Rosanna hesitated. She and Luke had been together for nearly a year now. That was a record for her. If she carried on with this obsession, he'd probably go the way of the others who'd thought they deserved one hundred percent of her attention. All that neediness in men was only a hair's breadth from the egoism that made her father think his women should be his doormat. Luke was nothing like her father, really. He could be fun, have her laughing in ways she'd never laughed before. Maybe she should drop this thing and move on, as everyone said.

Or maybe she should work it through, let Luke drop her, leave her to finish the job and get the obsession out of her system before she cut herself loose to concentrate on relationships. Besides, was being fun really enough?

When she'd mentioned three women fighting over Delaney, Luke had said, "Lucky man." What sort of a response was that? Yes, Delaney was lucky, like her father was lucky. That's what lucky men were – killers with impunity. Only this time, this one wasn't going to get away with it.

13. JUDE

I was pregnant. It happened very quickly – far quicker than I was expecting – and it was something I needed a little time to come to terms with. I'd never fantasised about having a child, but then I'd never fantasised about getting married, either. Alison had been the one for that. The mothering one, nursing dolls or kittens. I have a vivid image of her bandaging a bird's wing, which I could almost swear was a memory but it may just have been a Victorian painting that made me think of Alison.

She wanted to look after people. That's why she gave up her career in order to care for her father. She had only ever been a dutifully attended irritant in his life until he needed her, but she didn't mind. The slightest show of affection from anyone was enough to make her their willing slave, to do anything and everything for them. I suspect it was a sort of survivor's guilt. She had lost a mother and two brothers by the age of ten. She felt the need to justify her own survival and to recreate all the potential love and caring of the family she had lost. A child would have made her life worthwhile.

I remembered her phone call. *"Jude! I'm pregnant! I'm going to have a baby! Jude, oh Jude."* Christ, when was that? Nine months ago? She should have been sitting in Summer-vale with her baby pressed to her breast by now. The fulfilment of her existence. I shook, thinking of it.

Here was I, instead, pregnant in her place. Jude, the one who'd never been bothered about having children. I wasn't negative about my pregnancy. Far from it, once I knew for sure, I desperately wanted that child. It didn't make it any less disturbing, though, the thought of another being inside me, living off me, feeding on my blood. The image bewitched rather than horrified me, but my emotional and physical responses caught me off guard. Hormones are such an irksome slave-driver. I wasn't plagued by morning sickness, but there were moments of nausea. I kept flagging. Having been super-fit and totally in command of my body until now, it was an unsettling experience.

I kept it to myself for a week, then I visited my GP. I'd only just switched practices, so this was my first sight of my new doctor, Eldridge. I was given a thorough check-up and she assured me that everything seemed fine.

"It all happened rather sooner than I was expecting," I explained. "We've only been married a month."

"Mm." Dr Eldridge busied herself entering details on the computer. "Your husband is Simon Delaney, yes?"

"You know him? Of course you do, he's with this practice too, I was forgetting. And you must have known his first wife, Alison, I expect."

"Yes." She was succinct. I could sense disapproval of the situation, and not for the first time. The neighbours hadn't been overly welcoming. There had been a lot of tightened nostrils and studied politeness. The very nosy old lady who lived on the other side of Tork Lane had a way of turning her head slightly, when we faced each other at our gates, so that she could look at me sidelong, assessing me. But she certainly did look at me. More than once I'd stood at our bedroom window to find her watching me from one of hers.

I suppose we were bound to be the neighbourhood scandal, feeding comfortable outrage. I was the interloper, the woman replacing their own sweet Alison. But I was here now and they would have to accept it.

Our nosy neighbour, Kathleen Hargreaves, was beginning to accept, grudgingly, that I was not a scarlet Jezebel. I kept nodding hello to give her time. Maybe the doctor would become friendlier too.

"Alison's death must be an awkward subject for you, if you prescribed her medication," I said. "Wouldn't that have been dangerous for a pregnant woman?"

"I'd stopped her prescription long before she became pregnant," said the doctor, crisply. "And I'm sure you'll appreciate I can't discuss other patients with you. But I believe it's on public record that the drug she took when she died, Tofranil, was not prescribed, by me, nor would I ever have prescribed it for her."

"Oh yes, of course. Sorry. She got it on the internet, didn't she? I'm just wondering really if I need to take care with medication now."

"Yes, you should certainly take care with any drugs, and if you are in doubt, consult me or your pharmacist, but you're not on anything at the moment, are you?"

"The odd paracetamol for headaches, that's all."

"Well then, as you are perfectly fit otherwise, there should be no problem with the occasional couple when you need it. If things change, I'll let you know. Now, I've fixed up an appointment for you with a midwife. You're about five weeks, and that's very early days, so just get on with life for now. You're working?"

"I handed in my notice at my old job when we got married. Finished officially last week. Now I'm helping my husband, just light office work."

"So no stress, I presume. You don't smoke, but give up the alcohol, stick to a healthy diet and you'll be fine."

She smiled as she opened the door for me. A professional smile that told me she still didn't like me. I was reconciled to that. I refused to be deterred. I had Simon and that was all that mattered.

I had a celebratory dinner waiting for him when he got home that evening. Although he occasionally worked from home, seeing local clients in the oak-lined reception office, he mostly worked in the city. He rented an apartment there and he'd warned me that he often had to stay over, but that hadn't happened yet since our marriage, so I knew he'd be home by seven-thirty and I had the table laid, candles lit.

"Good day?"

"Yes, as it happens." He gave a modest smile but I could sense the satisfaction swelling in him.

"I've had a good day too."

"Yes? What have you been up to? Fun and games or work? You've already got the office spick and span."

"I did take a couple of phone calls. Assured Mr Willis that the paperwork was in the post – which it is because I posted it. And there's a message from a Neville Burns. It's on your desk. But apart from that, I've been to the doctor's."

"Yes?"

"And I'm pregnant."

Simon's jaw dropped for one second, then clamped shut. "You are?"

"I am."

"Good God. You're sure?"

"Yes, positive. Do you mind?"

"No. No, of course not. I'm delighted." He didn't look it. For a moment he looked horrified. Or maybe just scared. Of course, he'd been here before. He recovered and managed a broad smile. "You're having my child. Of course I don't mind! It's wonderful. Now, you've got to take care of yourself, you hear?"

"I will, I promise."

"You're to eat properly, no more wine, no excessive exercise."

I laughed. "I know. You'll take care of me."

"Yes I shall." He was positively fierce. "This time."

"Oh Simon! I'm so sorry. Alison, your baby, I wasn't thinking."

He said nothing, his fist gripping the back of a chair, squeezing the life out of it.

"It will be different this time." I put my arms around him. "I'm not like Alison. I don't have depression. I'm not remotely suicidal. I'm not on any medication, like she was."

"She shouldn't have been," he said through gritted teeth. "I stood over her, made her throw it all away. We agreed, she didn't need it."

"I wonder if it was that Dr Aldridge who gave it to her. She claimed she didn't, but she seemed very off with me."

"How dare she? I'm not having that. We'll change. Go private. I don't know why I hadn't done it before."

"Hush. Don't get angry. I've made us a beautiful dinner. Let's just sit and celebrate our good news, shall we?"

"Yes." He kissed my neck, his hand on my stomach as if he expected to feel something already stirring. "We are going to celebrate. With orange juice."

* * *

"Now, you drink this." Simon handed me a cup of tea and smoothed my forehead solicitously. "Just rest and I'll bring you some breakfast in bed."

"Don't be daft. I'm not going to let a slight headache stop me working just because I'm pregnant," I downed a couple of paracetamols he'd proffered with the tea. "I'll be fine."

"But you must take it easy."

"This has nothing to do with being pregnant. I shall have a shower, and by the time your Mr Grimstock arrives at eleven, I shall be there to smile and serve tea while you look earnest in your pinstripes."

"I don't know what you mean." He frowned. I was laughing and I realised he must think I was mocking him. We had married before he'd really had a chance to understand me.

I sobered. "I do understand, Simon. You know your customers; you know what they want and that's what you give them. It's how you're able to serve them so well. Good business, that's all. That's why you're such a brilliant success."

"Well, maybe." He was still cagey about admitting that he had any tricks of the trade, but of course he did. They were all about image. I hadn't visited his city office yet, but I'd seen pictures of it on his website. Ultra-cool, ultra-minimalist, ultra-smart. It was where he dealt with the young and eager, the go-getters, the world-shakers, impressed by modernity and stylish confidence. The reception office at home, by contrast, was a perfect reincarnation of the sepia house I'd visited as a girl, a vast mahogany desk and buttoned chesterfields, glass-fronted bookcase filled with finely tooled leather-bound volumes in dark brown, interspersed with a touch of dull crimson and olive green. The décor had been chosen quite deliberately to reassure his elderly clients that Simon was safe, solid. He even had different suits and ties for the different offices. The ones for the city deducted five years from his age. The ones he wore at home added at least ten.

"You really need a hat," I said. "A bowler, with umbrella. The final touch to the image. I shall buy you one."

"You will not. And if you do, I won't wear it. Utter nonsense."

"No it isn't. It's about projecting the right image to the right customers. I am guessing that at your London office, you have a glamorous young PA serving your clients Blue Mountain and almond croissants. What your office here needs is a charming wife, offering Darjeeling in fine bone china with a plate of Viennese fingers."

He grinned, and then was serious again. "You don't have to do that sort of thing."

"But I enjoy it. It's not a problem. I am fit and well and I can pour tea like a geisha. Your clients won't be alarmed by a visible bump for a few months yet, and I want to help, as long as I can."

"You're already helping, by carrying my child."

"I can do much more than that if you'll let me." He opened his mouth to object, but I didn't give him time. "Don't worry, I'm not planning to sit in on your advice sessions, hovering quietly with a shorthand book and serious spectacles." I got a hint of a smile from him. "But behind the scenes…"

"You've already working miracles."

"Typing a few letters? Sorting a few files? Fielding a few phone calls? That's hardly miraculous. I can do that in my sleep."

"Yes, and I appreciate it, but I didn't ask you to marry me so that you'd be stuck with the same tedious office routines you were desperate to escape."

"It isn't the same at all. It's for us. You and me, Simon, working together, for our future. There's nothing tedious about anything I do for you."

"You know I just want to look after you, Jude. You and the baby."

"And you do, you will. So let me look after you too. And buy you that hat."

So I played my small part in his business, or some of it. The rest remained his private domain. I wasn't told the combination to his safe or his passwords for confidential files, but I could keep things neat and orderly, and dish out the Viennese fingers to whiskery old gents.

I did buy him a hat though. Not a bowler – that would have been taking the joke too far, but a rather stylish fedora that would have suited him perfectly, if he'd agreed to wear it. He adamantly refused, though I made a point of stowing it in his car every day, just to give onlookers a hint that there was an Indiana Jones waiting to leap out.

As I was allowed into the periphery of Simon's affairs, I began to fit into village life, too. Kathleen Hargreaves, across the way, was too nosy, or perhaps too lonely, to keep me at wary arm's length for long. She started smiling at me, so I took to admiring her garden, still chocolate-box pretty with blazing red berries and the last roses and chrysanthemums of autumn. She invited me in for afternoon tea, where I discovered that doilies were still in vogue and that her front window offered a full-frontal view of our house.

"Are you all right, my dear?" she asked. "You look worried."

I was actually thinking that it would be a good idea to keep some curtains closed, but I couldn't tell her that. "Just checking that Simon hasn't come home yet. He likes me to be there for him."

"Ah yes. But he doesn't come home till much later, does he?"

"Not usually, no." She'd know, of course. She probably kept a log of every movement.

The next day I was beckoned over and introduced to her friend, Barbara Isaacs, from the other side of the village, who collected her regularly for shopping trips in Oxford.

"Why don't you come with us?" suggested Kathleen, sealing our friendship with this favour.

There was a lot to be said for a day in Oxford. Village life had its charms, but I could see it becoming a little stifling. On the other hand, I didn't fancy an entire day checking out M&S thermals with Kathleen and Barbara, and it would have been rude to abandon them, so I declined. "That would lovely, but Simon doesn't like me going out when he's not here."

"Pfft." Barbara Isaacs snorted like a bull, which she actually quite resembled. "Show a bit of independence. What are you going to be doing with yourself while he's away? Bored out of your skull. Much better coming with us."

"Now don't bully her, Barbara," said Kathleen. "She's, you know…" She added in a whisper behind her hand, "having a baby."

"Well. What difference does that make? Life doesn't stop because you're pregnant. Take it in your stride. Other women do."

Kathleen tried to make amends for Barbara's forthright manner. "I expect Mr Delaney is delighted."

I sighed, resigned to being the focus of more gossip. "I'm sure he will be, when it's born."

"Hm. Delaney." Barbara's eyes narrowed. "In finance, isn't he? Investments and such? You must pick up a few useful tips from him. What's in the wind at the moment?"

"I'm afraid I couldn't tell you. Simon doesn't like me having anything to do with his business. I know nothing about it."

"Well, he has got you well trained. And I suppose you're just going to sit at home making his supper for him? Not good for you, or the baby. Now." Barbara was willing to forego my trip to Oxford in exchange for another scheme. "You need to get involved in village life. You must join the book club. We meet every other Monday, Jenny Parker's place on the High Street. Couldn't get the other one to come. Alison Greenold, Delaney I mean."

"Barbara! Hush!" said Kathleen, quite distressed.

"Oh nonsense. She knows there was a first Mrs Delaney, doesn't she?"

"I do," I said. "She was a friend. Didn't she give piano lessons on a Monday?"

"So she said. But you don't have that excuse, so I insist. Can't persuade Kathleen to come, but we must keep our numbers up."

"I'm not much of a reader," said Kathleen apologetically.

"Nonsense. You've always got a book on the go."

"Yes, but just light-hearted romances, you know. Not your serious books."

"Stuff and nonsense. Now Judith, I insist you set an example. Show Kathleen here we're not too high brow. Next Monday; I'll introduce you. We're reading *Milkman*."

* * *

"I have to read *Milkman*," I told Simon, holding up the book as he brought me my coffee after dinner.

"Why?"

"Because I have been press ganged into the local book club and that's what they're reading. If I don't do my homework, Barbara Isaacs will probably have me flogged."

"That battle-axe. I'd keep well away from her."

"Coward."

He laughed. "Well, you've met her. You don't really want to join the ladies' circle, do you?"

"Why not? I like books. I'm told there's a couple of men in it too, so not just ladies. And it will be good to get involved. Up to a point. I think Barbara really wants me there so she can worm investment tips from me."

"Like hell. If she wants advice, send her to me and she can pay for it."

"That's what I thought. So I told her your business is a complete mystery to me. You don't allow me past the office door."

"That's right. I keep you chained to the sink where you belong."

"Yes, sir. There's a yoga class I might join, too. Just to keep supple."

"Won't harm the baby?"

"I'll make sure it doesn't."

"That's all right then."

So with Simon's permission I was duly initiated into the joys of Soweridge society. I was right about Barbara Isaac's aim in having me in the book club. She grilled

133

me unsuccessfully for investment tips at every meeting. The other members were much more restrained, friendly, full of advice on pregnancy and where to buy fish and politely curious about me. Behind it all, I realised that there was an itching desire to know all about the mystery of Alison. Her suicide was the most shocking thing that had happened in Soweridge for years. Not as shocking as it was to me. I refused to speak about it at all.

14. DC QUILLAN

The case of Alison Delaney was closed, but the files still existed, including the record of Mrs Danielle Brightman's visit to the police station, and her later retraction of her allegations. *I was mistaken. I was upset and angry and not thinking straight. I did have sex with Simon Delaney. I hope that was not what drove Alison to it. I did speak to her on the phone the day before, but it was just for a chat.*

To Rosanna, the retraction didn't ring remotely true. The woman had had two long conversations with Alison the day before she died and had tried repeatedly to phone her on the day itself. Just for a chat? Why had Danielle Brightman claimed so much and then denied it all? Why had she said nothing at the inquest, except to the new Mrs Delaney?

Rosanna wanted to know. If she couldn't follow it up at work, she could do so in her own time. On her next free day, she drove to Oxford and found her way to St David's Road, the address on Mrs Brightman's file.

She looked along the barricade of trees, walls and iron railings that gave the substantial houses an illusion of isolated privacy. In her northern town, there had been just one street, Manchester Road, with houses to match these, among a web of Victorian terraces and post-war council housing. Here in Oxford though, St David's Road was one of many such, off the Banbury Road, the houses all individual and yet alike, brick and golden stone and sharp gables. Many seemed to be guest houses or had been converted into flats, their front lawns replaced by tarmac to provide parking for the numerous residents.

Number 42 had parking space through its gates for a couple of cars but it had kept much of its garden, shielded by a huge copper beech. Like its neighbours on either side, it had been divided into apartments. Vertical blinds in the basement windows were opened enough to reveal a stainless-steel sculpture and a bowl of pebbles. Indian print fluttered around a bamboo mobile hanging in one of the narrow garret windows high above. The windows of the ground and first floor, 42A, were guarded by plain linen curtains and a few pot plants. Earnest, sensible, not remotely frivolous, thought Rosanna. The more she focussed on detail, analysing it dispassionately, the more she could dampen the restless anger within.

She took a deep breath, climbed the three steps under a gabled porch to the arched front door and rang the bell. She could hear its muffled chimes echoing down passageways. A big house, even when confined to just the two floors.

A tabby cat strolled round the corner of the house as she waited and came to sit at her feet, tail curled neatly round, eyes fixed on the door, ignoring her. As the door opened, it promptly slithered inside, greeted by "No, Thea, not in the living room!"

A woman looked out, the same one Rosanna had seen at Alison Delaney's funeral, and at the inquest, restraining Danielle Brightman, so it was no surprise to find her here. There had been deep suspicion in her eyes as she opened the door but, seeing Rosanna, she shot one quick glance out to the street, then asked politely, "Yes?"

"Detective Constable Quillan." Rosanna flashed her warrant card. "I was hoping to have a word with Mrs Danielle Brightman, if she's in."

"No. I'm afraid my daughter's not at home today. What is this about, may I ask?"

"I'd rather discuss that with your daughter, Mrs...?"

"Rackman. Though strictly speaking, Dr Rackman, not Mrs." It was Oxford, after all. The doctor stood scrutinising Rosanna for a moment, thoughtful rather than hostile. "I've seen you before, haven't I? At the police station, I suppose, although..."

Rosanna shook her head. "At the funeral of Alison Delaney."

"Ye-es." She nodded. "That was it. I wasn't sure if you were there in an official capacity."

Rosanna didn't correct her. "I attended the inquest too."

"You did? I didn't notice. I had other things to think about."

"I could tell it was very distressing for your daughter."

"For both of us. Look." Dr Rackman stepped back, opening the door wider. "You might as well come in as stand on the doorstep, although, as I say, my daughter isn't here. You can at least tell me what it's about." She led the way into the front room. "Theodora! Not in here!"

The cat had made herself at home on the back of a sofa, but jumped down with a weary swish of her tail and allowed herself to be shooed out. "She scratches the upholstery," said the doctor. "Now. I'm on duty at the hospital at two, so…"

"Oh! A real doctor." Rosanna could have kicked herself for such an inane comment. "I mean—"

Dr Rackman laughed. "Yes, I'm a real one. My husband was the other sort. Classics. Mrs Doctor and Mr Doctor, the girls used to call us."

"Your daughters?"

The smile faded. "Not… Danny is my only child, but I've always thought of Alison as a daughter. And Jude, too. Back then, when they were children. People grow up, of course. Change." Her mouth worked as if she were struggling with words too distasteful to utter. "What am I wittering on about? Sit down, please. Can I get you a cup of tea?"

Rosanna was parched but her guilt at her invasion under false pretences was increasing with every courtesy shown by Dr Rackman. "A glass of water would be nice."

"Just water? Right."

While her hostess was gone, Rosanna launched into an exhaustive study of the room. An academic's room. Comfortable chairs and sofas, all of which had such fraying upholstery that Theodora's banishment seemed quite pointless. Books, of course, on six bookcases, on tables, on the floor. Books in every shape and size, from muscle-straining tomes of reference works to disintegrating paperbacks. Dark red book cloth and glossy dust jackets. Faded orange Penguins, blue Pelicans and the latest Ann Cleeves. Reading lamps scattered around. Pictures – some genuine watercolours, one small oil, a couple of large art prints and an opera poster.

Photographs on the mantlepiece. Rosanna stepped up to look at them. A family group, Mr and Mrs Doctor with Danielle aged about six. Mr Doctor – studio shot, kind and studious. Older couples in the 1950s or '60s. And three girls. Two photos of them, one when they were barely teens, in T-shirts and jeans, laughing and posturing in a garden. In the other, they were older, almost adults maybe, in fancy dress. Two, their fair and dark hair gathered up in elaborate styles, were draped in white clinging gowns pinned at the shoulders and belted with golden cord. The third, under a jet-black wig was dressed in black boots, black leather armbands and a black basque.

"Oh that." Dr Rackman had returned and was setting a tray on the table. Glass of water with ice and lemon, plus a teapot and two cups. She tutted. "Girls. Fancy dress, end of school. They were supposed to be Greek goddesses. Athena, Aphrodite and Artemis, but Jude insisted on Xena Warrior Princess instead. My poor husband nearly had a heart attack."

"Not surprised. It looks uncomfortable."

"It was. Not that Jude would admit it. Now, there's your water. Are you sure you wouldn't prefer tea?" She was already pouring a second cup. She held it out and Rosanna took it. "And tell me why you wish to speak to

Danny. Is it about her wasting police time? We were assured no further action would be taken."

"After she withdrew her allegations."

"Yes. She withdrew them." Dr Rackman stirred her tea vigorously. "So?"

"Why did she withdraw them?"

The doctor looked at Rosanna intently. "Because once she'd calmed down, she realised how ill-advised it had been to make them."

"Why make them then?"

"Because…" The doctor's hand was trembling. The cup rattled on its saucer. "She was upset. We all were. It was a terrible shock. Alison was like a sister to Danny and when something that shocking happens, there's a need to find someone to blame. Difficult to understand, perhaps, if you haven't been through it yourself, and I don't suppose you have. You're too young. But take it from me, when a tragedy like that happens, you don't act rationally or fairly. Simon was Alison's husband, and I don't absolve him of blame. I don't think he was as supportive as he should have been, and he wasn't there for her when she… Well, there you are. Danny just needed someone to blame and who else but Simon?"

"With whom she'd had an affair."

The doctor had to put her cup down, it was shaking so much. She looked sick. "I'm not prepared to talk about that. We all do things we sometimes regret. Or should regret, if we had any decency."

Rosanna nodded, sipping her tea.

Dr Rackman turned her cup in its saucer. "I do know this. Whatever happened between… Whatever happened, I know Danny would never have wanted to hurt Alison. No one with a spark of humanity would want to hurt her. She didn't deserve to be hurt any more."

"I know nothing of Alison Delaney except what was said at the inquest. I know she suffered from depression. How had she been hurt before? Who had hurt her?"

The doctor sat back with a sad smile. "God mostly. Her older brother, James, died of meningitis when she was six and then a couple of years later her younger brother too. Poor little Harry was born with a heart defect. Only lasted a year. Losing two siblings would be more than enough for any child to bear, but then her mother… Laura Greenold suffered from depression too, are you surprised? Emotional causes were quite enough to explain that, but then it was discovered she'd developed a brain tumour.

"I'd treated Harry. That's how I came to know the family. We kept close. The hospital did its best but there was no saving Laura. She was terrified for Alison, of course. I promised I'd look out for her. Someone would have to. Russell Greenold was genuinely fond of his daughter, but not very good at showing it. He was determined to do whatever was best for her, without knowing how. Poor man." Dr Rackman laughed at the memory. "He wondered if he should send her to finishing school. I ask you. Are there still such things? Anyway, I persuaded him to aim for the Royal College of Music for her instead. She was such a gifted musician. A natural. It should have led…" She picked up her cup and took another sip.

"To a career in music?" prompted Rosanna.

"Oh yes, she could have gone so far. She was already being recognised. But then Russell fell ill, cancer. He didn't pressurise her especially, but she felt she should stay with him. She became a music teacher so that she could work locally. A very good one, I must say – I'm not denigrating the profession – but she gave up a great deal to do that. We assumed she'd return to performing when Russell died. She would have done, I'm sure, but love intervened.

"No surprise, of course. Alison was such a beautiful person. In every way. She had those looks, you know, pure beauty from another world. I watched them all grow into women, and I'm Danny's mother so of course I'll be the first to say she's attractive, nice-looking, but I knew she never really stood out. Not like Jude, for instance. Flashy. Every eye would be on her the moment she walked in the room and when she was an adolescent, she really played up to it. But Alison was different. She drew eyes too, but not in lust or jealousy. Just in awe, I suppose; awe that perfection really did exist. And she was never conscious of it, like Jude or like most beautiful people who feel they're entitled to admiration. Alison only saw others, not a reflection of herself."

She's talking about a saint, thought Rosanna. *Is it because Alison's dead and in heaven, or did she always worship her?*

The doctor seemed to realise she was gushing, drifting away from the point. "The point is, Alison wanted love as much as she wanted music. I don't mean romantic love necessarily, but family love, normal family security, everything that had been taken from her over the years. She'd had a serious attachment, but it hadn't worked out. Nothing vitriolic, just not to be. All very amicable in the end, but it left her disappointed. And then Simon Delaney appeared on the scene, on his white charger, ready to sweep her away. Which he did."

"It was a mistake?"

Another long look from Dr Rackman. "How can I judge? We all want perfection for our children, the perfect match, perfect fulfilment, perfect happiness. I thought Simon was too shallow for her, but he did seem to care for her. Allowed her to give up teaching and think about playing properly again. That didn't work out. But he certainly seemed to take care of her. What more could anyone reasonably ask? I know she longed for…" She almost choked on the word, "children. And I expect it was as good a marriage as most."

Dr Rackman had needed only the slightest prompting to talk about Alison Delaney, but now the flow dried up. She stared at the photos on the mantelpiece.

"Did you have any inkling that she might be suicidal?"

"No." The word was wrenched out. "To be honest, we hadn't seen much of Alison for the last year. There was always something getting in the way. I should have made more of an effort." She sighed.

"Your daughter had long phone conversations with her, the day before she died. Do you know what about?"

"Of course not." A touch of anger there. "We share a house but I don't listen in on my daughter's telephone calls. Danny hadn't seen her for some months either, so I expect they were just catching up. Look." Dr Rackman jumped to her feet. "I'm sorry, but I'm going to have to stop now, or I'll be late at the hospital. As I said, my daughter isn't here, so I'm sorry if you had a wasted journey."

Rosanna rose and followed her to the front door. "Thank you for your time. I would like to speak to your daughter, if possible, about those phone calls and other matters, if she would care to contact me." She held out one of the cards she'd had printed with her private details.

Dr Rackman took it automatically, staring down at it before starting to shut the door on her. "As I said, she's not here."

Rosanna adjusted her bag on her shoulder and took a few steps back from the door. No lights in the sitting room but she could just make out the movement of a figure crossing the room, a soft flash of glass catching the light as a photograph was lifted down from the mantelpiece, before being pressed to Dr Rackman's heart.

15. JUDE

"It's not a great time to come, is it?" said Ade, staring through a blur of rain as we left Carmarthen behind and headed off the main road.

"It's December. Wales, not Spain. Anyway, we're here for your muscles, not for sun, sea and sangria."

Ade grinned, flexing his forearm. "Should have brought Tim with us. You don't want to be heaving furniture around in your condition."

"Don't you think a threesome might spoil the illusion that we are Mr and Mrs Camberley?"

"Oh yeah, Camberley. What's my name again?"

"Leo. Like your puppy? And I'm Jayne. With a Y."

"I'll try and remember."

"You'd better. Otherwise I'll have to keep you chained up in the house. Anyway, you'll be too busy doing all the heavy work to talk to neighbours."

"Can't I even tell them about Baby?" He eyed my stomach, which was as flat as a Dutch polder. "They'll never guess from looking at you."

"Women don't suddenly inflate like balloons, Ade. I'm not even due for my first scan for another fortnight."

"Okay, but still, it was very quick, wasn't it?"

"Yes. Took me a bit by surprise."

"Not sorry?"

"No. No, absolutely not."

He glanced at me, slyly. "What does Simon think about it? Jumping for joy at the prospect of being a daddy?"

"More scared, I think. He's very protective, worrying over me."

"So I'm guessing he knows nothing about this trip to Wales with your secret lover."

"Don't talk like that, even in jest. Be serious. But no, he doesn't know. He's in London for a couple of days, with a major client to hook. I didn't want to distract him from his work."

"While the cat's away, you mean?"

"Stop it." I frowned. "I'm a good loyal wife. Okay, for these two days I'm pretending to be your good loyal wife instead, so please get into the part before we get there, or you'll ruin everything."

"Right. Leo Camberley, wife Jayne with a y and baby Adrian on the way."

"No, I didn't say anything about the baby being called Adrian. It might be a girl."

"Right. Phoebe! I demand a say in the naming of our offspring? Head of the Boat Shed household and all that."

"Do as you're told and shut up. And by the way, it's not the Boat Shed any more. Terrible name, sounds like an industrial unit. I've changed it to Bethulia."

"Beth what?"

'Ulia."

"Trust you to go for something Welsh. I suppose you've already mastered the language?"

"Rwy'n meddwl 'mod i'n gallu dweud 'Sut wyt ti.' In this case it means Safe Haven. Is that easier to manage? It's what we want it to be, after all."

"Yeah." He grimaced as a tractor turned out ahead of us, just as two lanes gave way to one. The windscreen wipers started smearing a splattering of brown gunge across the glass. "Nothing safe about it, I reckon. More like a place to catch pneumonia."

"No it isn't. We've had work done and it will be a lovely, comfortable home away from prying eyes. Just as long as you help me shift the furniture into place."

"Yeah."

"You're thinking, Ade. I don't like it when you start thinking. You get all sorts of ideas."

He managed a sad smile. "Just thinking about Danny. Is she really happy about you doing all this?"

I sighed, letting the car slow to a halt. With no chance of getting past the tractor for another few miles, I didn't want to crawl along being sprayed by mud and cow muck. Let it get ahead. "It's difficult. You know how she feels about my marriage to Simon. She can't cope with it."

"You can say that again."

"I know it can't be easy for her. There is too much anger in the mix. I understand what she's going through and I wish I could be with her, like we used to be, but that's no longer an option. Sorting this place out is something that I can do, as my…"

"Penance?" suggested Ade. "Assuaging your guilt?"

"As my contribution. Let's not start doling out guilt. We all have cause for that."

"Yeah. Okay." He stared at the flood pouring down the windscreen.

"All right, Ade. Let's change the subject, before we both shoot ourselves." A car was approaching behind us, so I started up again and trundled back into the slip stream of the tractor.

"Not another word." He kept quiet for about thirty seconds. "Nice long way from Oxfordshire, isn't it? Hey, look!" We had rounded a tight bend and found the tractor executing a sharp turn in through a gateway. "Thank God for that. You can get into second gear."

I even managed fourth. The skies were darkening by the time we arrived, the house a dingy silhouette through the rain. The view across the estuary would be ablaze with the full flame of the evening sun, if there were any, but the icy winter rain continued to fall relentlessly, sweeping in ghostly veils across the grey waters, obliterating the far bank.

I gazed out into the hissing blur, the rain stinging my cheek. Assuaging my guilt. Trust Ade to spell out the truth, in his slapdash way. I couldn't afford his blithe honesty. I had to keep playing a lie. Back at home I acted as if I totally believed Simon's assurances that everything was finished between him and Danny, but I knew the truth. Madeleine had mentioned she'd seen his car hovering near their home more than once. What could Simon have been doing there if not waiting for Danny? I wasn't going to have it. I'd do anything I had to, to keep them apart. Anything.

That was really why I had chosen to come to Bethulia now, while Simon was staying over in London for a few nights. I needed to get my head round the situation, figure out exactly what to do. Would a secret hideaway, 200 miles from Oxford, be sufficient to cut all the ties that had to be ruthlessly severed if I were to rest easy?

"Come on!" shouted Ade, huddled by the door. "I'm getting soaked."

"Wimp." I opened the door and we stepped into gloom and the smell of fresh paint. "Find the light switch."

We were cocooned in bright light, the rain and the cold shut out. The redecorating and revamping had left the house warm, dry, clean and stark. Furniture had been delivered, as instructed, thanks to Mr and Mrs Godfrey, our neighbours up the lane. They had agreed to take charge of a spare key and let people in, but everything was still in plastic wrappings, piled up, waiting for us to organise. I discovered that some had been carted upstairs, piled into one of the bedrooms, which was a bore as we'd need to bring half of it down again. I wouldn't have managed without Ade.

"Kettle here, and it's working," Ade called from the refurbished kitchen.

"Good. Make a pot of coffee then. Everything's in that carrier." I studied the empty bedroom – the one with the view out over the estuary. Or the dark murk where the estuary should be. Blinds had been fitted. I checked that they worked. They did. Not that we'd need to guard our privacy, much. Anyone on the far bank would need high-powered binoculars to look in.

I began ripping plastic off mattresses.

"Coffee's ready!" called Ade.

"Bring it up. Lend me your muscles to get one of these beds back down."

"Down?"

"Yep. The extension's got a bedroom now."

"Another one? Downstairs? But…"

"Just thinking ahead. Stairs aren't great when you're not so fit, Ade."

"Oh. Yes. Of course."

Between us, we slithered a mattress, a base and a headboard down the stairs, and into a newly installed suite with its own bedroom, bathroom and conservatory living room.

"This is great," he said, pressing his nose to the conservatory glass. "She'll be fine here."

Which is more than we were, after struggling down a second time with a wardrobe. When we'd finally manoeuvred it into its new position, Ade threw himself back on the bed, puffing his cheeks out. He had, after all, done most of the work. "Bloody hell. Ever heard of flat-pack?"

"We'd be all day putting them together. Stop making a fuss. Get the chest of drawers down and then we'll head to the pub for a meal, okay? We'll finish the rest in the morning."

The pub was a rash mistake. We returned to the one where we'd eaten before, done up now for Christmas, with lights and a noisy clientele. We ordered food but it was going to be a lengthy wait, so we drank. Or rather, I sipped orange juice and Ade knocked back anything going, like a schoolboy let loose on his parents' drinks cupboard, getting merrier by the minute. I think the locals either saw him as a target for their warped sense of humour or maybe they just embraced him as a new blood brother. Either way, they plied him with more and more when he introduced us to everyone in earshot – *This is my wife Jayne, with a Y* – and explained that we were the couple who had bought a house here in the summer.

"Used to be called the Boat Shed," he explained. "But now it's Bethooja which means—"

"Bethulia," I corrected. "He's never going to get it right, but I'm sure the post office will. This has been our first real chance to return to the property."

"We want to move in properly in time for Baby," Ade declared, clamping his hand on my stomach. "Did I tell you we were having a baby?"

I smiled resolutely and laid my hand on his, digging my nails in till he removed it.

"We're going to call him Adrian after m—"

"*Leo*, darling, we haven't decided a name yet. Yes, maybe, if it's a boy, we'll call him after your *father*, but let's wait and see, shall we?"

"Sorry!" he whispered, with a giggle into my ear, as our new friends bought him another drink to celebrate his forthcoming fatherhood.

I turned to hug him, whispering back "Shut up or I swear I'll drop you in the river and hold you down in the mud."

He just giggled more and we both smiled as another round arrived. Then our food at last, thank God. Once the sea food and burger were consumed, Ade was reaching for the menu again to see which pudding sounded richest and stickiest, but I took it firmly from him.

"We're not having dessert."

"Oh but we need to test it all out so we can tell—"

"You need to get your little wife home. Remember her delicate condition." I signalled for the bill and yanked a handful of his hair.

"Oh, right."

Mostly by leaning on me, he managed to make his way out of the pub without knocking over any tables and a cheer followed us to our car. I got him into the passenger seat and pulled out onto the road back to our cottage.

"That's the last time I go anywhere with you when there's alcohol around," I said, but all I got in response was a burbling snort as he slumped against his seatbelt.

* * *

I was standing out on the patio, looking out into thick swirling mist. I could hear the river, water sifting and slewing, flurries of wings, a curlew's otherworldly call, but I could see nothing. A blanket of tears enveloping the whole world.

The French door opened behind me and Ade emerged, hang-dog, hair tousled. He was nursing two mugs of coffee and handed me one.

"Headache from hell?" I asked.

"Yip." He winced. "You okay?"

"I was on orange juice."

"I mean, your cheeks are wet. Been crying?"

"It's called fog, Ade. Look, your sweatshirt's already sparkling."

"Yeah. Okay."

We stood for a while in silence, staring into the murk. At last, he said "Sorry about last night. Did I put my foot in it? What did I say?"

"Nothing too drastic, but you really are hopeless when you drink, Ade."

"I know, I know. Tim stands over me like a prison warder at parties. I'm sorry. It's just… Okay this is a lark, this play acting, but I keep thinking about what it's really all about, this place. And I start thinking of Danny and what she's going through, and how it's all so bloody… I mean, when you think what a crap time she went through last time on chemo. I just…"

Ade was the only man I knew who could burst into full-flood tears without inhibition. I don't know how Tim dealt with it but I put my free arm around him and let him sob on my shoulder. "Medicine can work wonders these days. And she's got Mrs Doctor looking after her."

"Yip." He sniffed.

I wiped his cheeks and then my own. "Fog," I said.

He managed a smile. "So I didn't mess things up? This will still be the secret safe haven when the time comes."

"Yes, I hope so. In the meantime, though, I think I'm going to have to kill you off." The flash of genuine alarm on his face had me laughing. "Leo Camberley will have served his purpose after this visit." I squeezed his arm muscles.

"You mean you don't want me coming here, getting drunk and blabbing again."

"I mean you and Tim will be off to Spain in a month, won't you? If I need to come here again, it would be more conclusive to say you'd died rather than that you'd run off with your boyfriend."

"Oh, right. So can you give me a dramatic end? Terrorist bombing?"

"No."

"Don't just make it something really naff like me falling downstairs."

"Promise. Now, Let's go in, dry off and get the rest of that furniture sorted."

* * *

When I finally got back to Summervale, Simon's Porsche was in the garage. It was a shock. I thought he'd intended to stay in London for another day at least. No time to think about it; he had the front door open for me.

"Where the hell have you been?"

"Visiting relatives.' I tried to keep it light. 'How was London? Did everything go well? I thought you were going to be there all week."

"Well I wasn't. I wanted to get back to you and you weren't here!"

"When did you get back?"

"Yesterday evening. Any idea how worried I was when you didn't come home? And your phone's still here. Why didn't you take it?" He was seething.

I could see Kathleen Hargreave in her garden across the lane, putting out bird food and listening with all ears. I tried to be conciliatory. "I'm sorry, Simon, please forgive me. I didn't think. I just forgot the phone. Adrian rang."

"Adrian? Who the hell is Adrian?"

"My cousin, Adrian Merriman. Surely I've told you about him. His mother, my aunt, needs to go into a home, and he was worrying about it, so I offered to go and help him choose the best option. He can be hopeless and I didn't want him to mess it up, so I just went."

"You never mentioned this cousin before. You told me you didn't have any close relatives."

"I don't have immediate family. Just Aunty Gwen and my cousin Adrian."

"So where does he live, this Adrian?"

"In Bristol." I was making it up as I went along, because I was determined not to breathe a word about Bethulia. I didn't want give him any clues that would have him trekking out to West Wales to reclaim his woman. "I stayed overnight, just to make sure Aunty was all right. Please, darling, don't be mad at me."

Simon was still angry but relief was beginning to win out.

"Come on," I pleaded. "Let's go inside. We don't want to give the neighbours something to gawp at."

"All right." He ushered me in and shut the door. My case could wait for the morning. "Do you have any idea how worried I was? You can't go chasing off round the country without telling me. You've got to take care, look after my baby, remember?"

"I will." I kissed him, my heart thumping. "I promise, Simon. I will never let anything happen to the baby."

16. DC QUILLAN

Rosanna pulled her sweater tight around her. The flat was warm, but the view through her window was enough to make her shiver. Tiny icicles framed the picture, the sky was heavy with yellowish sacks of the fall yet to come and down below snow was banked up around the block, infilling the narrow paths that had been shovelled out by yesterday evening. A few cars had worn icy ruts in the frost-hardened slush on the road.

It was a day for staying in, under the duvet, with a mug of coffee and hot buttered toast and avoid unnecessary travel, according to the travel reports. But this was necessary. She's lost count of the number of times she'd phoned the Rackman house, asking to speak to Danielle Brightman, only to be told that Mrs Brightman was not at home, or was in a meeting, or hard at work and couldn't be disturbed. All Rosanna's pleas for Mrs Brightman to phone her back had been ignored. So she had decided to attempt one more visit in person, to waylay her quarry somehow and she had planned on doing it this day, her day off. She had psyched herself up for it. She couldn't let a paralysing snowfall across the country put her off.

She'd catch them unawares. They wouldn't be expecting anyone to call today. Determined, she bundled herself into her Michelin Man quilted jacket and pulled on walking boots. Not the best to drive in, but she'd manage. She'd made it into work yesterday through the snow without trouble. Her colleagues had joked she'd coped because she was from Oop North where there was nothing but ice and snow. Ha ha. She'd spent Christmas there with her own supply of northern grit, hadn't she?

No, she hadn't. She had spent it here, in her flat, her own private incident room, mulling over what she knew and what she didn't know. Time to fill in the gaps.

The car didn't want to start. It was spluttering and wheezing, telling her to go back to bed. But then it coughed, choked and sparked into life. She could feel the wheels spinning and slithering as she edged away from the kerb. Not pleasant, but it was easier once she'd turned out of her cul-de-sac. Taking it carefully though. She thought, for a moment, she would have to give up her plans in favour of impromptu policing when the car in front braked but failed to stop at a junction and slewed out into the path of a van. The van swerved, skidded, righted itself, both drivers exchanging words of sympathy rather than anger. The van moved off. The car driver paused for a moment to recover then went on his way.

Rosanna edged round the same junction and every other one on her way, approaching in first gear. She'd have trouble making it to Oxford by nightfall at this rate, but when she finally reached the Oxford road, it was cleared by gritting and, better still, the heating had begun to warm the car. She drove on, staring resolutely ahead as windscreen wipers flicked aside the big fat flakes.

The centre of Oxford was clear enough, but St David's Road was deep in churned snow, lined with cars, some entirely cocooned in white. She decided against attempting it and parked in a marginally more accessible road, tramping back to the Rackman house.

There was an empty parking space at 42 after all, but too late to bother with it now. Someone had cleared the path to the door, opening a narrow avenue of concrete, but leaving a parked Skoda and Clio half engulfed in a drift. The Skoda had a hospital parking permit, so the doctor at least must be at home.

The swept path was rapidly snowing over again. Theodora the cat was in the window of the forbidden living room, watching Rosanna's approach with Egyptian inscrutability. Rosanna rang the bell, stamping her boots clean under the porch, pulling her woollen gloves off and blowing on her fingers. A light flicked on inside, glowing through the stained glass of the door. She heard voices, distant, one coming closer.

"No, you stay."

The door opened and Dr Rackman was there, the questioning look on her face morphing into something like defiance as she recognized her visitor within the inflated jacket and the thick knitwear. "DC Quillan." Her voice seemed unnecessarily loud. "I wasn't expecting to see you back again." The cat brushed past her and padded out into the snow. "Thea!"

"I'm hoping to speak to your daughter, Mrs Brightman," said Rosanna. "I've left five or six messages but no one's got back to me so I thought I'd better try calling in person again."

"Well, you've had a wasted journey, I'm afraid. My daughter was working all night so she'll be in bed and I don't want her woken." The doctor had managed to pull the door half shut, placing herself firmly in the remaining gap, so Rosanna could see nothing of the interior. "I'm sorry." It was clear there was going to be no invitation to tea this time.

Rosanna took a deep breath. "Dr Rackman, please understand, I am not here to challenge your daughter, or threaten her with prosecution. She's not in trouble. I just wish to discover what really happened to Alison Delaney, your daughter's friend, and I think Mrs Brightman understands more than the police… than we were able to establish at the time."

The doctor hesitated, her eyes boring into Rosanna, assessing. For a second her head turned as if she were about to change her mind, but then she straightened and was determined again. "No, I'm sorry," she said, brusquely. "As I told you, my daughter is asleep and she doesn't like being disturbed. Sorry." She stepped back.

"Dr Rackman—"

The door had shut. Rosanna dug her nails into her palms to still her exasperation. Then she stepped back from the shelter of the porch, surveying the house. Curtains had been drawn across a window upstairs. They had been open before. A light glowed behind them. Another light came on, went out. The curtains twitched, a face, pale as the moon, appeared for a second, saw Rosanna and the curtain was jerked back again.

Why? The frustration was driving her mad? Why wouldn't the woman just speak to her? Damned if she'd give up and drive home. Resistance built up within her. She'd stay here until Danielle Brightman changed her mind.

She did stay, for five minutes, by which time the cold was eating into her, her fingers and toes turning numb. This was stupid. She was achieving nothing other than entertaining that enigmatic cat, which sat surveying her from under a bush. Its owners were watching her just as she was watching them. So she'd leave, find somewhere for a coffee and come back when their guard was down.

She stomped back to her car and drove into the town centre, where a frothing cappuccino cheered her up enough to laugh at herself for her obsession with this business. What was she hoping to gain from it? She ordered a bowl of soup as she debated giving up on the whole thing and driving home. But she felt warmed through now, and reinvigorated, so she drove back to St David's Road and cautiously approached number 42. Pointless. The free parking space had been occupied by a dark blue Audi.

It left her no option but to drive on, round the block and the next, eventually finding a free place half a mile away. Once more she set off through the frozen slush and grimy snow, back to 42 St David's Road.

Why show herself just yet? She paused to peer in through a screen of laurel hedging. Nothing much to make out in the windows of the house except the cat, back indoors now at its sentry post, between half-drawn living room curtains. She edged along to get a clearer view through the bare branches of some deciduous shrub. There were figures moving in the living room. Two at least. Were there more? It was hard to tell.

A man, wrapped up in overcoat and muffler, walking a Great Dane, skirted around her, eying her warily. Maybe it wasn't a good idea to be peering through hedges. Neighbours were probably already calling the police to report a suspicious prowler.

She moved on to the open gate, paused for just a second, then strode rapidly across the open garden to the front door. Not rapidly enough. Definitely movement in the living room. Curtains flashed across again, blanking her out. She rang the bell. Waited. No response. Rang again. Knocked. Nothing. They knew she was there but they were determined to ignore her. Apart from screaming at them to open up, what could she do?

She stomped her feet. They were only making her more and more intrigued. Perhaps they didn't care because they had defeated her. Perhaps they guessed that she was acting on her own, with no back-up, no authority.

She stood out in the open for another five minutes, challenging the hidden watchers within, then she gave up. She trudged back to her car, her feet dragging with the weight of disappointment. She started the engine and headed for home.

She was almost at the ring road when her mobile rang. She never answered while driving. Never, except… it would be nothing. And yet… unable to resist, she groped for her phone while steering cautiously around a bus. It would be her luck to be hauled over by traffic police but she'd take the risk, just once.

"Yes?"

"Detective Constable Quillan?"

"Yes."

A pause and Rosanna wanted to scream. Instead, she pulled in to the kerb. "Who is this?"

"I'm Danielle Brightman. You want to speak to me about Alison Delaney."

"Yes." She refrained from shouting, "You bloody well know I do!"

"If you'd like to come to my house now, I can give you half an hour."

"Thank you. Yes. I'll be there in ten minutes."

The phone went dead.

Instead of savouring triumph, Rosanna felt infuriated. She couldn't afford that. She needed to be totally detached and say nothing to send Mrs Brightman scurrying back behind her curtains.

Ten minutes later she was back at St David's Road, determined to leave her car in the middle of the road, engine running, if she had to, but there was no need. A car had gone two houses along, leaving a naked patch of tarmac vacant. She ran, skidding in her haste, and braced herself as she approached the front door of 42A once more. It opened before she could ring the bell and Dr Rackman ushered her in. She didn't waste time on explanations or excuses, just took Rosanna's jacket and pointed to the living room. "She's in there."

"Thanks." Rosanna stooped to struggle with her boots.

"Don't bother!" The doctor was terse. "Just give them a wipe and go through. I'm sure our carpet can take it."

Rosanna wiped thoroughly and went in.

Danielle Brightman was sitting in an armchair with her back to the window. She didn't get up when Rosanna came in, but languidly pointed to a sofa across the room.

Rosanna sat and studied her. The same woman she had seen at the inquest, and yet different. Maybe because she was not blazing with anger but calm. Unnaturally calm, her hooded eyes resting on Rosanna without any obvious curiosity. Or maybe it was because she had taken more care with her appearance. Pure Goth. She was heavily made-up, her pale skin rendered almost white by the thick black eyeliner and the black polo-neck sweater. Lipstick as dark as red could get without quite being black. She was thin. A dark pashmina was casually draped across her from one shoulder and she idly fingered its fringe.

"I'm Rosanna Quillan."

"Yes, I know." The voice was little more than a whisper, as if she could barely be bothered to reply.

"I'm a detective constable. I can show you my warrant card if you wish." It seemed pointless flashing it across the expanse of the unlit room.

"My mother told me. So. You want to talk to me about Alison." Her voice almost trailed away completely.

A creak outside the door told Rosanna that Dr Rackman was within earshot. "You spoke to her, didn't you, twice on the day before she died."

"Yes, we spoke. On the phone."

"Two long chats. It wasn't just idle conversation, was it? What did you talk about? What did she say?"

Danielle took a breath as if about to speak, then stopped. She shrank back further into the shadows, one hand clenching white on the arm of her chair.

"Did she say anything about her husband? About something he had done? Or about something you'd done?"

"Maybe…" Danielle leaned forward slightly. "Maybe you should be asking what I said, not Alison."

"You told her you were having an affair with her husband."

Silence.

"Why did you tell her?"

"Because… because the secrecy wasn't fair on her. She needed to know he was going to leave her."

"And then she killed herself."

"Yes." Very soft.

"You feel guilty about it."

Danielle was almost animated now. "Of course I do! I didn't know she'd take it so bad. I was just tired of all the lies and the prevarication." She stopped. Rosanna waited. "He'd only delayed because she was pregnant. But he still insisted that when the baby was born, he'd… we'd go."

"You and him."

"Yes."

"And the baby?"

"Her baby? He wanted to take it. I didn't want that. That was cruel. She should have been allowed to keep her child. After all…"

Rosanna waited, but nothing followed. "After all?"

"After all, I could give him a child if he wanted." Danielle let the pashmina fall back. She wasn't as thin as Rosanna had thought. Not quite. "Or even if he didn't want."

"You are pregnant."

A shrug and a hint of a smug smile. Rosanna calculated. It was nine months since Alison Delaney had died. Danielle's pregnancy was beginning to show, but it was nowhere near full-term.

"So you are still having an affair with him?"

Another shrug.

"Even though he married another woman."

"Jude!" Another spurt of animation. "Judas! It was all..." Danielle sank back again, her face turned even further from the light, her silhouette quivering. Behind her, Theodora rose and stretched on the window sill, warning Rosanna to back off, but Danielle had already recovered her self-control. She turned to face Rosanna again, chin raised. "He phoned me, you know, after he found Alison. You know what he said? 'Why didn't you keep your mouth shut? You can forget about us now. If they get a hint that we're connected, I'll be in the frame for her death.' He was wild of course, but then so was I. I couldn't believe he meant to throw me over like that. So I went to the police. Stupid. I withdrew my statement later. Of course he couldn't have killed her. He was in London, wasn't he?"

"Yes. Apparently. Do you think she challenged him about the affair? Do you think he got angry, told her it was true and he would be taking the child?"

"I don't know, do I?"

"Perhaps she threatened to fight him over it, to leave him while she was still pregnant, and deny him any access to his own daughter."

"It's possible, I suppose."

"That would be an explanation for what occurred. Because I believe he locked her in the room where she died while he went to London. To prevent her leaving."

A gasp. "How… Rubbish. I don't believe it."

"You don't want to believe it, you mean, because you are still having an affair with him. Carrying his child. And at the same time, he's married to your other friend Judith."

"Jude had no business coming between us. He doesn't love her, you know."

"Is that what he told you?"

"He doesn't have to!"

"Why did he marry her then?"

"She tricked him probably. She came home from abroad when Alison died. I was mad. I told her Simon had killed her. Jude just brushed it off. 'Poor Simon. Don't say things like that.' She'd always fancied him. I should have guessed she was already planning to snatch him up for herself. Well, she's not keeping him."

"But you think you are."

The dark lips smiled slowly. "I know I am. Jude may have forced his hand by getting him to get her pregnant, but—"

"Judith Delaney is pregnant too?"

"Yes. But I'm sure Simon knows how to deal with that."

"Deal with what? Her baby, you mean?"

"It might come to nothing. Accidents happen."

It was Rosanna's turn to be silent. A clock ticked.

"If that's all?" Danielle spoke up at last, her voice louder than it had been. On cue the door opened and Dr Rackman stepped in.

"I'm sorry but I'm going to have to ask you to leave now. Would you mind…" She was shooing Rosanna from the room like a determined sheepdog, thrusting her jacket at her and bundling her out of the front door. "I'm afraid I don't have time to offer you tea. I don't approve of what's going on, but my daughter has answered your questions, I trust. I'd be grateful if you do not attempt to communicate any further. Thank you." Once more she was shutting the door in Rosanna's face.

Rosanna didn't wait this time. She turned on her heel and headed for her car. She had one answer at least: a possible explanation of why Simon Delaney had left his wife imprisoned on the day she died. Other questions remained. She couldn't decide what to make of Danielle Brightman, heartless bitch or self-deluded fantasist. Was she genuinely expecting Delaney to leave his second wife for her, just as she claimed he'd been going to do with his first? Was the child she was carrying even his? She was obviously unbalanced. But suppose she was telling the truth, suppose they still intended to be together… He had already driven one wife to suicide. What would happen now?

17. JUDE

Simon had another overnight stay in London planned, so I took another trip to Wales. I wanted everything settled, I wanted Danny safely out of the way and I wanted Simon to know nothing about the cottage, so secrecy was the only way. It was risky, especially after the last trip when he'd come home early, but this would be the last time, just to make the place ready for occupation.

I made sure to take my phone and in the course of the journey I sent Simon various texts to reassure him I was thinking of him. He had been very solicitous over the last few months, fretting over the thought of me driving myself to the shops or the doctor or the book club, convinced I wasn't up to it anymore. He'd have been appalled at the idea of me driving all the way across Wales.

My bump was showing now if people chose to notice, but driving really wasn't a problem. I was still keeping fit and as active as Simon would allow. He'd lost one baby, so I understood his paranoia about this one, but I was more sanguine. My maternal instincts had taken hold of me now and I just knew I was going to carry this child to full term and give birth to a beautiful baby. My second scan was coming up soon, and Simon had murmured that we would soon know if I was carrying a girl or a boy. He was almost giddy about it. He insisted that he didn't mind either way, but it was obvious that he longed for a son, a mini-Simon, and I hoped it would be a boy. I wanted him to know it was a boy.

We'd had horrendous snow and ice at the beginning of February, but it had cleared away and the weather was warming up nicely, so the roads were no problem. I made good time. I stopped just short of my destination to make adjustments. The house needed to be prepared, of course, but I also needed curious neighbours to be warned that occupants of Bethulia might not be as expected. Ade and Tim were safely in Spain now, though they kept in touch. Ade was having a wildly exuberant time by the sounds of it and asked me, in occasional texts, if I'd killed him off yet. It really was the best solution to the Jayne and Leo Camberley scenario. Divorce is complicated. There's nothing complicated about death.

I rummaged in my bag, found a black sweater and put it on. Sorted out my hair, wiped off my makeup, leaving a tearful smudge of mascara, and let my shoulders sag. Then I drove on, the last half mile to Curlew Cottage.

Mr and Mrs Godfrey saw my car turn in at the gate and were out to greet me. They waved, so I politely stopped before turning down the lane to Bethulia and wound the window down, taking a deep gulping breath.

"Hello, my dear, you're looking very…" What had Mrs Godfrey intended to say? Blooming? Instead, she asked, "Are you all right, dear?"

I nodded, struggling to speak. "Yes, thank you. No. Actually, not really. I lost… Leo… my husband died." I sniffed and urgently wiped my cheek, smudging the mascara further.

A noisy intake of breath from both of them. "No! Oh, goodness me, how awful! You poor poor thing. Come in, come in, let me make you a cup of tea. You don't want to be all on your own down there in that cottage."

"Thank you but… If it's all right with you, I would rather be on my own just now. Because I don't really feel as if I am. I feel as if Leo is still with me."

"I understand. Of course you do. But what a terrible tragedy. And he was so young, such a nice friendly man."

"Yes, he was." My voice was breaking.

"Was he ill? We had no idea. He looked so well."

"No, it was an accident, on the way to work. A sheet of glass." I was thinking of a scene in The Omen. "Instant." I stopped short of mentioning decapitation.

"Oh dear Lord, how horrible. But, well, I mean… At least it was quick. Not long-drawn-out suffering." They were struggling to find something faintly positive to say, and I felt guilty that I was putting them through it, but better to get it over with now.

"Yes. I keep telling myself that. Although I hardly know what I'm doing from one day to the next."

"Poor poor thing! And with a baby on the way too!"

I laid a hand protectively on my stomach and bit back tears. "Yes. His baby. I must take comfort in that. I came to check everything was all right here. Something to do, to take my mind off it, but I don't know what I'll do with the place. It was going to be our home but… I don't know whether to sell up or let it or what. I haven't decided."

"Of course not. And you don't need to rush into anything now, do you? You just concentrate on looking after yourself and baby."

"Yes, I will. I know Leo has gone to a better place." Warmer, anyway.

"Amen," said Mr Godfrey devoutly. He and his wife stood hand in hand, watching me drive on down the track. Shame was prickling up and down my spine. How could I have done that to them? My turn to look for the positive. It was good, wasn't it, that Bethulia had such kindly trusting neighbours? They would be needed in the months to come.

My wickedness did not go unpunished. I had some work to do in the house, the little extras to be unpacked, the freezer and larder to be stocked with basics, but I was finished by the evening and what I really wanted then was to go out, find a place with decent food at least since I couldn't drink, have a little human warmth. But I could hardly be seen hitting the nightlife when I was supposed to be a grieving widow, so I had no option but to stay in with my own thoughts and the sound of rain beginning to patter on the windows. I checked on the logs that had been ordered and tried out the wood-burning stove, to cheer the place up, but as the evening progressed, my guilt progressed with it.

The flickering light conjured up memories of sitting around a similar stove in Oxford, three girls, watching the dancing flames and the glow of the logs.

"What do you see?" Alison is hugging her knees.

"Flames," I say.

"No, what do you see in the flames. Look!" She points at the sparks shooting upwards. "Fairies! They're trying to get to the stars. Maybe that's what stars are. Fire fairies."

Danny opens her mouth and I know she's going to start on astrophysics, so I jump in. "A dragon. Definitely a dragon. Look, it's coiled round and there are its wings. It's just snoozing but any moment now…"

Danny's got the message. She smiles, cocking her head on one side. "I see… a phoenix! Burned to ashes and then bursting back into life."

"Yes!" says Alison.

A bird reborn to glorious gilded life. But the truth was, birds that burned to ashes didn't come back to life. No one did.

I thought of Ade here, playing the fool because he was trying to stifle his distress for Danny. I shouldn't have killed off Leo Camberley. There was already too much death in the world, and there'd be more, always more. No stopping it, however hard I tried. I sat enveloped in gloom, letting the fire die, sipping my decaffeinated coffee and aching for a G&T.

* * *

In the morning, early, before leaving, I swept out the stove, gathered up the ashes into a box and padded down to the creaking jetty below the house. I stood at its end, head bowed, listening to the incoming tide surging beneath me. Then I tipped the ashes out onto the lapping water. A fisherman, barely visible in the half light and drifting mist, was watching. Word had spread. I think he removed his cap.

Performance over. Guiltily, I hurried back up to the house, locked up and drove away.

I was determined to be home before Simon this time. He had a meeting at three, I knew, so there should be no problem. I'd already been on the road an hour and a half when I phoned him to say good morning and how are you, darling? He was fine, kissing down the phone and promising not to be late. All was well, I was safe. Except that I was barely past Swindon when he phoned me back.

"You okay? Not overdoing things, I hope."

"Not at all. I had a lie down, but I'm up and about again now."

"Good, if you're sure… Can you check something for me in the office? A file. For Cuthbertson, Andrew D. I don't know why it hasn't transferred here. No need for a password, it's a old paper one. Should be in the filing cabinet by the door."

"Cuthbertson," I repeated slowly, putting my foot down. "Let me make a note of that. Right." A lorry rumbled past me in the opposite direction.

"What was that?" he asked. "Traffic?"

"A tractor or something in the field," I said. "I've got the windows open to air the place. Right, I'll go and have a search for this – ah, damn. Someone at the door. Look, I'll deal with them, then I'll scan this file and email it to you ASAP. Love you." I rang off before he could answer, overtook a tedious little hatchback and headed for home like a vampire bat out of hell.

When I got there, wheels squealing on the gravel, I left the engine running and flew indoors, into the office, switched everything on, found the file, scanned and emailed it through, sent him a text – *sorry, Mrs H called. Couldn't stop her talking. Got the file? XX.*

I sat back, breathing heavily, feeling my heart racing and a queer flutter in my stomach. I wasn't going to risk any of that again. I wouldn't have to, anyway. No more surreptitious trips to Bethulia while Simon was away. The house would be properly occupied soon.

When I went back out to the car, Mrs Hargreaves was peering in through the gate, looking worried.

"It's all right," I called. "I was caught short, needed a pee urgently. I'll just put the car in the garage then why don't you come over for a coffee?" It didn't hurt to cover all the bases.

18. DC QUILLAN

By the time Rosanna got home from Oxford, she had decided she was going to speak to Mrs Judith Delaney.

The following morning, she wasn't so sure. She spent the weekend prevaricating. Should Mrs Delaney be warned? Of what? Of her husband's part in the death of his first wife? Of Danielle Brightman's claims that he was still seeing her? That he was the father of her child? That accidents could happen? She really had nothing concrete to say. Someone else had been in the Oxford house, she was almost sure. Had she nearly caught Simon visiting his mistress? No wonder Dr Rackman had been so cagey about letting her in and so cold about her daughter's claims. She didn't approve.

Would the second Mrs Delaney be happier left in ignorance? Ignorance of adultery maybe, but the implied threats in Danielle's words couldn't be ignored. Policing wasn't just about picking up pieces after disaster had struck. Rosanna had a moral duty to prevent disaster striking in the first place.

She'd do it. She was on early shift, so she drove out to Soweridge on Tuesday after work. No Luke waiting impatiently for her return. He'd moved out just before Christmas, unable to cope with her obsessive fixations any longer. She didn't blame him.

A useless journey. She followed a silver Porsche down Tork Lane and recognised it as Simon Delaney's.

Two people in it, one with red hair. She watched it turn in through the gates of Summervale and she drove on. No point trying to speak to his wife if Simon was at home, which he obviously was, that day.

She tried again on Thursday. Nothing stirred at Summervale. No one answered when she rang the bell. Simon Delaney was safely out of the way, but so too was his wife. Rosanna parked up in the lane and waited to see which would come home first. Neither. Darkness fell, lights came on in houses, dinners were eaten, a car turned out further along the lane, heading for the village, but Summervale remained silent and dark. By midnight, Rosanna accepted that neither of the Delaneys were going to appear.

She drove home, ate a bowl of Shreddies because it was the simplest way to settle her growling stomach, and went to bed. This wasn't going to work. She had to do better.

No point trying at the weekend. On the Monday, she made another attempt.

Her shift had changed, so she arrived at the house at ten in the morning and rang the bell. This time there were footsteps in response, but not the ones she wanted. A man's voice called "It's all right, I'll get it," and a second later Simon Delaney opened the door.

Why wasn't the man at work? At least the second's warning meant Rosanna wasn't caught totally by surprise. She pulled out her warrant card and held it up. "Good morning, sir." She had an explanation on the tip of her tongue, but it evaporated at the fleeting horror on his face. He quickly recovered himself. Almost. His left eyelid was twitching.

"Yes?"

"Just letting you know we've had reports of break-ins in this area and we're warning residents to be on the look-out."

He shrugged, his attempt to look nonchalant almost hitting the mark. Did he recognise her? Was that it? So he had been at St David's Road, listening. Hearing her accuse him of holding Alison prisoner, and Danny suggesting that he was going to see that an accident happened to Judith. He cleared his throat. "Okay."

"What is it, darling?"

Delaney glanced over his shoulder at the red-haired woman who had stepped into the hall behind him. "Just a warning about burglary." He turned back to Rosanna. "Thank you for taking the trouble, but I think our security is tight enough."

"You work from home?"

"Sometimes. Why?" He was just a little too defensive.

"If you do, and the house is seldom left unattended, it's unlikely a burglar would attempt anything."

His wife had stepped up to join him, smiling tentatively. "And even when my husband's in London, as he will be from Wednesday onwards, I'm always here, aren't I?" She looked to him for confirmation.

"That's right." He kissed her cheek, seeking to turn her away from the door. "So… Is that all? Thanks for letting us know, Constable."

Rosanna nodded, backing away. "Sorry to have bothered you then. Good morning."

She wondered if he was sweating as much as she was. She had no authorisation for the enquiries she was making – but if he did recognise her from Oxford, would he dare report the matter to her superiors? At least there was no risk of running into him again. From Wednesday onwards, Delaney would be in London.

On the Wednesday, Rosanna was back, confident that Mrs Delaney would definitely be home alone. As confirmation, the garage was open and the Porsche was missing.

Sure enough, Judith Delaney answered the door when Rosanna rang the bell. Unbelievable. She was wearing a frilled apron and rubber gloves, housewife par excellence, and still glamorous with it. She would never look ordinary.

"It's you again, Constable." She seemed nervous. "Have you caught the burglar?"

"Not yet, ma'am. I was hoping to speak to you on another matter."

"Well…" She hesitated, concentrating on ripping the gloves off. "My husband doesn't really like me letting strangers into the house, but you are police, so I suppose that's all right. Come in, please." Hands clasped, she led Rosanna through to the drawing room where Ben Morgan had interviewed her husband the day Alison died. Nothing much had changed. The grand piano was still there but closed. A huge vase of white lilies stood on it as if it were an altar, a few grains of yellow pollen sprinkling its polished lid.

Judith Delaney indicated a chair, and seated herself on the edge of a sofa, hands clasped around her knees. "What can I do for you?"

Rosanna had been so intent on getting this woman alone that she hadn't really worked out how to begin. "You're Simon Delaney's second wife, I believe." Believe? What a stupid thing to say.

Judith was still for a second then smiled politely. "Yes, his first wife, Alison, died last year. But I'm sure you know that."

"Of course."

"If you've come to talk about Alison, I should tell you I was a very good friend of hers, long before I met Simon. And just to set the record straight, Simon and I didn't start seeing each other until after Alison's death."

"Are you aware of the circumstances of her death?"

"You mean her suicide. Yes of course he's told me all about it."

"You know she died alone, in the back bedroom?"

"Yes, yes. I have no idea why, but it must have been horrible for Simon. It affected him badly. He doesn't like dwelling on it."

"Do you know where the keys are to that room?"

"The keys? Of course. They're in the room. I know because we had to replace the locks. The old keys were missing. It worried me and I mentioned it to Simon, so he had a locksmith come and change them. Why on earth are you asking about that? Is it because of this burglar?"

Mad, but Rosanna felt impelled to charge straight into the fire. "No, it's because I believe those earlier keys were removed on the day Alison Delaney died."

Judith looked bewildered. "Why?"

"Because I believe your husband locked her in there, while he went to London."

"No!" It was a whisper, her hand to her throat. "No, that's nonsense. He wouldn't. He says these things but it's just words. He... wouldn't."

"Do you know that the day before she died, Alison spoke to Danielle Brightman?"

"Danny? I'm sure she and Danny spoke all the time. They were friends."

"Danielle was having an affair with Simon. Did you know that?"

Judith took a deep breath. "Yes, I know. I've known all along. Not that it's any business of yours."

"Mrs Brightman claims she told Alison about the affair the day before Alison's suicide. Told her that Simon Delaney was intending to leave Alison."

"That's... no. Simon wouldn't. That's Danny, she exaggerates. I mean, she fantasises. I know about the affair but it was nothing. It's finished. I don't want to hear any more about it." She was a shade too insistent.

"I've spoken to Mrs Brightman. She claims it isn't finished at all."

"No!" She blurted it out too quickly, too definite. "No, that's a lie."

"Are you sure?"

"Yes!" Judith was compulsively working her apron into pleats.

"Danielle is pregnant."

"No!" Judith gathered her hands over her belly. "I don't believe it. Or if she is, it's not Simon's. He said... He promised... It's not true. Why are you doing this? What are you trying to achieve, coming here like this, telling me all these lies?"

"Mrs Delaney, I believe your husband was responsible for the death of his first wife, and I don't want the same thing happening again."

"It won't! It won't because none of it's true. You're making all this up." She was on her feet, angry. "I'd like you to leave now."

Rosanna rose too. "I'll go, Mrs Delaney, but I want you to know…"

"I'm not listening! Go! Please, just go."

What could she do but obey? Before Judith could close the front door on her, Rosanna tried once more. "The last thing Danielle said to me was 'accidents happen.'" Judith blanched. "I don't want an accident to happen to you, Mrs Delaney."

"It won't." A whisper again. "It can't. It can't." The door slammed shut.

Rosanna turned, surveying the garden while her pulse slowed – the dark shrubs, the gravel drive, the clumps of daffodils, the remaining car in the open garage. Then she walked slowly back to hers, got in, sat there, thinking, thinking, thinking.

Something was going to happen. Something bad. Something very bad. The question was, what was she going to do about it? Where was she to go from here?

19. SIMON

Simon had a dream, a nightmare so vivid it woke him up, sweating. Had he been shouting? Jude was still asleep beside him.

He had been hauled before the headmaster who was holding his exam results and telling him he'd failed. Failed everything. The Head was yelling *Fail! Fail! Fail!* in his face and all Simon could think was *no, it can't be. It's not how it was meant to be. I couldn't have failed.*

Everyone was laughing as Simon was dragged into the headmaster's office, the door slamming behind him. There was a table with a box on it. A box wrapped in gift paper and tied with a bow. It had his name on it, and it filled him with both dread and excitement. He had to see. He tugged the ribbon, and the box lid shifted up and he could see a woman's arm. A hand. The fingers moved, and he didn't know which woman it was, trapped inside, but it was reaching for him.

That was when he woke, in a sick wave of terror.

Which woman was going to come crawling out of that box to claim him? Jude or Danny? Or Alison? He got up to shower, swilling mouthwash to take away the taste of bile. Facing himself in the misted mirror, he knew he had to wrench himself free of this weight of anticipation and indecision that was dragging him down into insanity.

He was married to Jude. What was there to complain about? Quite apart from the sex, which was incredible, she was charming, proficient, quick-witted. She had talents, but they weren't the sort that left him in the shade. Not like Alison. They were talents he could appreciate and use. She was organised and efficient. A perfect help-meet.

Too perfect, that was the trouble. Too involved in him, in his life, in his business, in his thoughts. He had this need to be in control, the one making the decisions, winning – always winning. He wasn't made to be a mere half of a partnership. He couldn't deal with it. He thought of it as his strength, but he knew, deep down, it was his weakness. It was what had pushed him into so many pointless wrong steps. His agonisingly petty mistake with Alison that he had made worse and worse, even when he'd tried to correct it. His terrible mistake with Danny that haunted his nightmares still and always would. The moment he'd turned that key in that lock just because he'd snapped at Alison's challenge, only to find he had no way back. He couldn't let more stupid mistakes pile up to ruin things once more. It would be all right if he didn't let the wrong button be pushed. Soon enough, please God, Jude would be occupied with the baby instead of him.

As long as it survived. As long as she got through the nerves and endless mood swings that were beginning to grip her, brimming over with energy one moment, a tearful kitten the next. Worry about it gave him palpitations, fearful that somehow life was determined to run in an endlessly repeating circle. He'd never craved children, putting it off and off although Alison had been desperate for a baby. But when he'd finally got her pregnant – when he'd been forced to get her pregnant, just to keep control of the chaos he'd created – something weird had flipped inside him. His child was coming into being. His creation, his son and heir, his legacy. He'd become obsessed with the idea. Even when he found Alison was carrying a daughter, still he was obsessed with this new need to protect his little girl. To be in command.

Now it was happening again and he just wanted it to be over with, everything to be all right. But there was Danny, always, waiting in the wings, dominating his life again, occupying his mind, devouring his soul. Irresistible.

He'd lost count of the number of times he'd spent mornings or afternoons in Oxford, while Jude thought he was in London. The number of times he'd lurked in St David's Road, watching for Dr Rackman to leave, waiting for his chance to approach the house. Was he mad to be playing such a game?

Then the policewoman was standing on his doorstep, flashing a warrant card. The woman he'd seen in Oxford, calling at 42A, and now she was in Soweridge, at his door. He'd nearly soiled himself. It had all dissolved into a inane chat about burglars, but he hadn't known whether to breathe easily again or pack his bags and leave.

He just wanted to be out of this, but he was in too deep. He had to resolve things or go under.

He glanced at the last text message Danny had sent. "Soon, Simon! Soon!" How soon? What was he to do? Enough. He was tired of waiting. It was time to start afresh, do what he should have done long before now. No point in being squeamish. There were two women ruling his life and it couldn't go on. One of them had to go.

20. JUDE

I won't lie. The visit from DC Quillan had me deeply disturbed. How was I to respond? The police hadn't come up with any of this at the inquest. What was going on?

I was on edge when Simon came home that evening, and he could sense it, though I tried to hide it.

"What's up, darling? Are you not feeling well? Is it the baby?"

"No." I couldn't tell him about Quillan's visit, or the suspicions she had tried to plant, but I had to account for my nerves. "It's a stupid phone. I bought a new one for the office. I just…" I managed a laugh. "I just can't get my head around setting it up. Silly, I know. I want to deal with it and I don't want to deal with it and it's argh! A pregnancy thing, I expect. I'm up and down like a yoyo." It was true, more or less. The phone had arrived, but it was still sitting in its box by the drinks. I knew he would love the opportunity to take charge, a nice definite action.

"Silly girl." He put his arm round my shoulders and kissed my forehead. "I'll fix it. Can't have you worrying over things like that."

I sat back and watched him rip open the packaging and set up the phone for me with deft thumbwork. "It's happening all the time, these days. I get het up over nothing. Sorry. How did things go in London?"

"Fine. Colby's happy. There you are. All done. You want it?"

"Oh, not now. Leave it there. I'll start afresh in the morning when my brain is back on track. Let's have dinner." I escaped to the kitchen, DC Quillan's visit still nagging at me; her belief that Alison had been locked in that room by Simon. Where had that come from? What was I to believe? I knew what I wanted to believe, but that was another matter. Sometimes it's just better to trust.

Dishing up the dinner, I made my choice. I was going to plough on and trust.

Easier said than done, of course. Simon could tell I was still on edge, but he took it as a part of the great mystery of pregnancy. On his insistence, I gave up my yoga class, although I am sure it was doing the baby no harm. He suggested I skip the next book club meeting since I was so fraught, but I perversely insisted. He was equally perverse in his determination to drive me the mile to the house of the club's host, Jenny Parker, as I couldn't be trusted behind a wheel in my present emotional state. I didn't tell him that our latest book, *The Flight of Cornelia Blackwood*, was about post-natal psychosis. If he thought I was emotionally unstable now, just let him see what I might be like after the birth.

Jenny was concerned. "Have we chosen the right book, do you think, ladies, with Judith being pregnant? Not a bit too insensitive?"

"I'm fine," I insisted. "Please don't change anything because of me."

"The last thing we want to do is upset anyone."

187

"She's not upset," interrupted Barbara Isaacs, who never noticed that she regularly upset everyone. "It's only a bloody book. So, come on, Judith. Any good tips for us this week? Any investments we should know about?"

"No!" Same thing every week. I was getting tired of it. "I told you. Simon doesn't let me have anything to do with his business." The lie was now well established, but it still didn't shut her up.

"Surely you can drop us a hint or two?"

"No I can't."

"Well, I must say, I'd be ashamed of myself if I couldn't wheedle a few secrets out of my Derek. Doesn't he tell you anything?"

I shook my head, feeling the tears brimming again, which was embarrassing but that was how it worked.

"Leave her alone, Barbara," said Jenny. "Why don't we have a tea break and then we'll get back to the book."

Tea break meant tea and coffee and sticky cream cakes, and a G&T for anyone who wanted it. I wanted it but stuck resolutely to my tea. We'd barely got through the bun-fest and back onto topic when I saw Simon's Porsche pull up at the gate.

I leapt up. "Sorry. I'm afraid I've got to go." I was scrabbling for my coat.

Barbara turned to peer out of the window. "Oh, let him wait, he won't mind."

"Yes, he will. He'll be furious if I keep him waiting." I gripped Jenny's hand in thanks and hurried out before Barbara could rugby-tackle me.

PART TWO: THE LOVERS

I almost ran to the car and leaped in. "For God's sake, get me out of here."

Simon smiled. "Not a good meeting?"

"There's only so much I can take of that bloody Barbara Isaacs. Here." I reached for the fedora, tucked behind his seat and rammed it on his head. "Be an Indiana Jones and rescue me. She's utterly impossible."

"I could have told you that. She's the queen bee round here, so no chance of kicking her out of the book club. If you want to talk books, you're stuck with her."

"Not sure I want to go again."

"That's fine by me." He shifted into first gear and we rolled forward. "I'd rather have you home with me, any evening."

* * *

So I was home every evening. And every day. It didn't help. I was perpetually on edge, wanting to cry. There was plenty to distract me in the office, calls to make, things to book, accounts to check, business to organise, even though Simon kept suggesting that I take the next few months as maternity leave. I wanted to carry on as if everything was normal.

Which it wasn't. Simon was home on the Wednesday, preparing to see a local couple. Most of the clients who came to see him at Summervale were male, retired businessmen, ex-army types or elderly dons, worrying about their stocks and shares. Very few women. I took it into my head that Mr and Mrs Philby would need extra-special treatment and that it was my personal job to impress the wife.

So I left Simon to greet them on his own and concentrated on making the tea tray spectacular. I brought out Grandad Greenold's antique silver teapot. I laid out the best gilded porcelain cups and saucers. Sugar lumps with tongs. The Viennese fingers didn't seem adequate, so I made a plate of wafer-thin crustless cucumber sandwiches, and then I dashed out to fill a cut-glass posy vase with miniature narcissi – it had turned incredibly warm for a February and the garden was full of them. I washed my hands, smoothed down my vintage dress, rearranged my hair and carried the tray through to the office.

Needless to say, I'd taken far too long. Simon was already in mid-flow, explaining finance to his rapped audience.

"Oh! I'm sorry. I'm so sorry. I didn't mean to interrupt you."

"That's okay," said Simon with more than a hint of impatience. It was understood that I didn't disturb his consultations.

"Shall I… should I go?" I hovered by the elegant little Regency table where I usually poured the tea.

"Just leave it there," said Simon.

"I'm sorry I was so late. Do you want me to…"

"Just leave it, Jude. We'll manage." He gave a bright artificial smile. "My wife, Judith."

Mr Philby had half-turned to acknowledge my presence. Mrs Philby rose with a smile to take the tray from me. "I'll see to it, my dear. It looks lovely."

"I'm sorry," I whispered again, feeling tears prickling my eyes, and I fled.

A hour later Simon opened the bedroom door to find me lying with a pillow over my head. I could hear the Philbys' car leaving.

"Jude, what the hell was up with you down there?"

"I don't know!"

"You know the rules. Don't interrupt a consultation."

"I didn't realise I'd taken so long. I'm sorry."

"Don't keep saying that. Come on. You've been crying, haven't you?"

It was true. I had. The pillow was damp. "I can't help myself."

"Oh poor old Jude. I think you'd better leave the clients to me from now on. Until those hormones settle down. Mrs Philby was quite concerned about you."

"Maybe I should phone her, just to reassure her I'm all right."

He kissed me. "No need for that."

I did phone Mrs Philby though, the next day. I didn't want her to get the wrong idea. But I agreed that I'd leave the clients to Simon from now on.

The next day, first of March, my scan was due and Simon accompanied me, his turn to be the one in a hurricane of nerves. This was the stage he and Alison had reached and he was terrified that something terrible would happen again. For once I was totally calm. Matters were out of my hands and there was nothing for me but to let it happen. Simon clasped my fingers throughout the procedure, not daring to look at the screen.

I watched it while my naked belly was being ironed with cold gel and an ultrasound probe. "Everything's all right?"

The doctor smiled reassurance. "A OK. Size, position, everything's where it should be. No abnormalities evident. Your baby looks fine."

"Thank God," I said, and I found myself almost in tears with relief. The baby was fine.

"Can you tell the sex?" asked Simon. He was trying to sound off-hand, though I knew that it mattered to him.

"Do you want to know?" The doctor looked at me, assessing my reaction.

"He's desperate for a boy," I said, then hurriedly added, "but we don't mind which, do we, Simon?"

He nodded. "Just curious. That's my son or daughter. Either's fine but I just want to know."

"Well then, it's a boy. You are going to have a son. Congratulations. I hope you enjoy the rest of your pregnancy and experience a happy birth."

"I'm sure it will be wonderful." I smiled with heartfelt relief.

Simon was quiet for a while on the journey home. Then he said, "There we are then. Everything's fine and it's a boy."

"Your son."

"Yes!" Suddenly he was hooting his horn, to the alarm of other motorists. After that, he kept his excitement within the car. "So we can choose a name now. Randolph?"

"No!"

"Titus." There was something slightly forced in his gaiety.

"Not Titus. What about Simon?"

"Not for the first name. Something more significant. Boris!"

"Over my dead body. What about Philip, after your father?"

"No," said Simon firmly.

"Strange to think I've never even met him." It wasn't strictly true. His parents had been at Alison's wedding, an affable, unassuming couple who had gushed so enthusiastically about Simon's lovely bride that it dawned on me they'd never met her until that day. "What a lovely lass, beautiful inside and out," Philip had said. "Well at least she'll want for nothing with my boy. Got his head screwed on firmly, has Simon, when it comes to money. Not like me. I'm a bit of a Mr Micawber, I'm afraid." We'd spent the next quarter of an hour talking about Persian poetry, with Philip apologising that the only Persian poet he'd read, apart from Omar Khayyam was Rumi. Which amused me because that was at least one more than most people. I didn't notice Simon saying more than two words to him in church or at the reception, though Alison had made a fuss of them. She told me later that she had invited them herself when she'd realised that Simon had inadvertently left them off the guest list. Only Alison would assume it was inadvertent.

"What does he do, your father?" I asked.

"Why?"

"Just curious. All I know is what you put on the marriage certificate. "Marketing." You never talk about him."

"What's there to say?"

"Didn't you get on?"

"We've nothing in common, that's all. He was in retail, okay?"

"What does that mean? Was he a managing director of Harvey Nicholls or did he have a barrow at the local open-air market?"

"You're mocking me."

"No I'm not. I just wanted to know. You know my father was a humble clerk in the civil service. So, what did yours do?"

"All right, if you must know, he worked for Massey Ferguson, on the production line, got laid off, retrained, finished up in charge of the cheese counter at Sainsburys. He was proud of that. Can you believe? In charge of cheese. And always, always in debt. He used to give me pocket money on a Saturday and borrow it back on the Monday. Hopeless. Never understood I might be aiming for more. He thought he was doing me a favour by offering to get me a job in the store."

"Ah. But my Simon had bigger plans."

"Yes. Much much bigger. And we'll have bigger plans still for Baby… Alexander?"

"Whatever, as long as it's not Ronald after my father."

"How about Jude, after his mother?"

"You know, I think it would be a wonderful idea to name him after his mother and his father. I can't wait to see the nursery again.'

"The nursery." He repeated the word as if its existence came as a shock to him. Had he forgotten it?

"Just picture it, Simon; that pretty nursery, behind that shut door, waiting and waiting for this day. All set up and ready; Alison's gift to us. There'll be a baby in there at last."

That evening, I found him at the nursery door, staring in. I don't think he had trusted himself in there since Alison's death. Everything was exactly as it had been on the day she died. Pink walls, pink rug, a frieze of Beatrix Potter characters, white cot, pink quilts and blankets still in shop wrappings.

The tic was there, in his left eye-lid; always a sign of stress. It must have been a torture to face that room, enshrining all that hope and despair. "We'll strip all this out, chuck everything, start again," he said. "I'll call the decorators tomorrow."

"Must we, really?"

"Why not?"

"Can we at least keep the cot, since it's white? Just to remind us of Alison."

"What?"

"I'd hate to waste it. Don't call the decorators yet, please, Simon. I don't want strange men tramping all over the house just now. I'm not sure I could cope with the smell of wet paint. Let's leave things for a bit longer. We still have months to get things sorted. Leave it exactly as it is for now."

He agreed – reluctantly. He was already thinking ahead. I found him, the next day, on the computer, scrolling through lists of public schools.

"You're joking," I said, peering over his shoulder. "Still more than four months to his birth and you're organising his education?"

"Just day-dreaming about what might be. Why should my son have to go to some crap comprehensive like me?"

"You went to a perfectly good comprehensive and you did extremely well. Do you seriously think you'd have had done better in life if you could quote Cicero? Come on, admit it, Simon: you've made the right decisions all along, haven't you? Well? Do you really think your life have been so much better if you'd made different choices, done anything differently, taken a different route along the way?"

He switched off the screen. "Like I said, I was just day-dreaming." He got up abruptly and walked out of the office. I found him back in the nursery, dismantling the cot.

"But I thought we'd agreed to keep Alison's cot."

"No, I can't. I'm taking it to the tip."

"But it's perfectly good, Simon."

"I told you. I want us to start afresh. I want this all ripped out."

"Oh, but it has her style, her taste. You can't just destroy it. At least take it to a charity shop."

"No, no. I want it gone. Wiped out."

He meant it. I came out onto the drive to watch him load it into the Porsche with a struggle. Then the bedding.

"Does that really have to go, too?"

"Yes! Everything."

Kathleen Hargreaves, topping up peanuts at her bird table, watched as he drove off, then glanced at me anxiously.

"He's taking them to the tip," I explained.

"Oh dear," she said.

I sighed and retreated indoors, to give vent to my own feelings. I stared at what was left of the little pink nursery, aching with a renewal of grief, memories of Alison welling up. I wanted to talk to Danny and I couldn't, not any more. It was all such pointless, stupid, futile waste.

The trip to the tip failed to calm Simon's nerves. Or mine. What should have been a weekend of celebration was instead a weekend of silent distress for me and irritation for him. I was grateful when he set off for work on Monday. Once he was in his office, dishing out the obligatory champagne, the lure of high finance would take over and his equilibrium would be restored.

It worked. In the evening, as he strode back from the garage to join me on the doorstep, I could see he was in good spirits again.

"Good day?"

"It certainly was. What are you looking at?" He followed my gaze up to the darkened sky. "Checking the baby's astrological expectations?"

"Sorry, far more prosaic. Just checking for rain?" I'd been watching a couple of pinpoint lights work their way across the heavens. Planes heading off to who knows where, taking people beyond and beyond and beyond. It was such a wide world. I was remembering my flight back from Seoul, to be greeted by the news of Alison's death. Less than a year ago and yet it seemed like a previous life. "Come on in. I'll pour you a drink. Tell me about your day."

"Took a client out for lunch. Ate far too much, of course."

"Anywhere nice?"

"Otto's. His choice and I paid. Seemed to do the trick. He'll be paying me from now on."

"No such thing as a free lunch?" I laughed. "Yes, we all pay in the end."

I let him talk on, working his way through a couple of glasses of Shiraz while I prepared us a quick supper. If he'd had his fill at lunch, I knew he wouldn't be needing much. A fillet steak and salad. I had no appetite and merely picked at mine.

"I've left Chloe dealing with the rest of it," he said, pushing his plate back, replete. "She can sort it with her eyes shut. And Rogers is happy with the arrangements for Thursday." He looked quizzically at my barely touched dinner. "You okay? You're very quiet. Something on your mind?"

"Simon." I placed my knife and fork carefully on my plate. "I'm leaving you."

"What!" His face froze as he stared at me.

"I've had enough."

It was as if a pin had been pulled in a grenade. He exploded. "What the hell do you mean, you're leaving me? You don't bloody well walk out on me. I won't let you. What the fuck are you talking about? You're not going anywhere!"

For a moment I could only stare back in astonishment.

He reached across and gripped my hand. Hard. "Are you mad? That baby you're carrying is my son! How can you talk of leaving me?"

"Simon!" The initial shock had worn off. I managed a laugh. "I only meant I'm going upstairs, I'm leaving you to finish your dinner. I've got a bit of a headache and I want to lie down."

His face, which had been taut with fury a moment before, melted into a blubbery mess. His hand released mine. It was shaking. "For God's sake, don't do that to me, Jude."

"Sorry, I had no idea you'd take it that way."

"How do you expect me to take it when you say you're leaving me? You'd had enough. Christ!"

"I meant that I'd had enough dinner."

"Well for God's sake, why couldn't you have said that?"

"Sorry. This headache. I wasn't thinking.' I poured him another glass of wine. 'Simon, as a matter of interest… What would you have done if I had been going to walk out on you?"

"Lock you up!" he snapped, the anger brimming again, and then he realised his response was at best inappropriate and he laughed, unconvincingly. "Or put you on a lead."

"Oh Simon, you were thinking of Alison, weren't you?"

"What?" He was so jumpy. I'd really upset him.

"I mean you were thinking of her leaving you like that. By dying."

"Yes. Yes, I was thinking of Alison."

199

"I can be so crass at times." I needed to soothe him but there were DC Quillan's allegations jangling in my head. Had they been put to him by the police? How had he answered? "Simon, what you said – did you lock her up?"

"What are you talking about?"

"Alison. It couldn't have been out of malice, I know that. Were you afraid for her, is that it? You suspected she might be suicidal and you locked her in for her own protection?" He was staring at me in horror. I reassured him. "You can tell me if that's what happened, if you were just trying to protect her from herself. I was wondering why we had to get those locks replaced. I thought… Please, don't torture yourself over it. Did you?"

He swallowed. "Yes." It was a whisper. "For her own protection."

"Oh God, and she still managed to kill herself. You poor thing. You've had to nurse an awful secret like that all this time."

He bowed his head, his hands still shaking.

"Isn't it better now you've told me? Because I understand, my darling. You don't have to keep any secrets from me."

"No. Of course I don't. I know that." He was trying to get a grip. "Look, you said you had a headache. Go on up and have your lie down. I'll sort things out down here."

"If you're sure?"

"Positive."

I made my way upstairs. I could hear him, in the kitchen, bringing up his steak.

* * *

He was in half a mind to stay home the next day, because of my headache he claimed, but I suspected he was still nursing the nightmare that had disturbed him most of the night. I did my best to reassure him that the past was the past and I would never let him go. When he came home, earlier than usual, that look of relief on his face when I was there to greet him persuaded me to be more loving still. We forgot about dinner and went to bed.

Much the same happened the next day. "A second honeymoon," I whispered, although we'd never had a first. The following morning he was reluctant to rise. "Not sure I should stay over tonight. Maybe I'll cancel, come home after all."

I laughed softly, putting my arms round him and nibbling his ear. "Now, now. Business first. You'll be home tomorrow night and then we'll have all the weekend to ourselves. No need even to get dressed."

"That sounds like a very good idea."

"I'll be waiting for you."

"And I'll be ready for you!"

I made him some toast and poured his coffee, brushed his shoulders and kissed him once more. "Now off you go. Fingers crossed that everything goes perfectly with Rogers. He'll be a serious catch."

"I'll land him okay!"

I stood on the doorstep watching as he started to reverse the Porsche out the garage – and ground to an abrupt halt. He got out, staring down at one rear wheel, and thumped the roof of the car in fury. "I don't fucking believe it! A sodding puncture! How did that happen. Oh for fuck's sake!"

"Calm down. It's not that hard to change the wheel."

"Oh great! Thank you. So I'll miss the train, get in late, find that—"

"Hush." I reached for my car keys hanging by the door. "Take mine. You'll be fine. I'll get someone out to change the tyre."

His anger made him hesitate for a moment. Simon was like that. When everything was going according to plan, he was king of the world and graciousness itself, but when the slightest hiccup interrupted the flow, he'd erupt. He needed one more second of grinding fury and then he calmed down, nodded and took the keys from me.

"Okay. Thanks. Where would I be without you?"

"Calling a taxi? Off you go now."

I waited until he'd driven my car out onto the gravel. He wound down the window. "Go on in, before you get cold. And you take care while I'm away. I'll be phoning to make sure you're okay."

I waved him away. "Goodbye, Simon."

PART THREE
JUDGEMENT

1. DC Quillan, Oxfordshire
8th March 2019

Rosanna had been expecting it and yet it still caught her by surprise when it happened. Ben Morgan, detective sergeant now, saw her coming and waved from the window, mouthing something but she couldn't tell what. By the time she'd come in through the station doors, he was bounding down the stairs to greet her.

"Soweridge. Tork Lane."

"Yes."

"Sounds like trouble at the Delaney house. Neighbour's called."

"What's happened?"

"No idea yet, but—"

"Quillan." DI Stansford was at the top of the stairs. She beckoned Rosanna.

"Disturbance reported at the Delaney house," said the DI crisply. "Possible assault. Can you deal with it objectively?"

"Yes, ma'am."

"Then come with us."

It was a silent journey. DI Stansford was occupied going through records, while Ben drove. Rosanna was happy to be left alone with her thoughts – although she had no idea yet what direction those thoughts were heading. A disturbance reported. A possible incident. That was all the information so far, so it could be anything.

They turned in through the gates of Summervale. Cool March morning light, contrasting with the June twilight of her first visit, and no ambulance on the gravel, just a couple of police cars and the grey Porsche. It was half out of the garage, one tyre flat. A uniformed sergeant was waiting for them. He leaned over their car as Stansford wound her window down.

The DI snapped her notebook shut. "So, what's gone on?"

"Neighbour contacted us this morning, reporting a commotion in the night. No response from any occupants of the house, so we effected an entry. No one inside but definite signs of disturbance. Broken glass with what looks like blood on it, and possibly blood on the gravel by the door. Waiting for SOCO now."

"Neighbour who made the report?"

"A Mrs Kathleen Hargreaves." The sergeant nodded towards the house opposite. "Likes watching her neighbours. She's got a friend with her, who persuaded her to call us this morning."

"Any reason why she didn't call us at the time?"

"Didn't want to make a fuss."

"Right." Stansford was out of the car, buttoning her jacket. "Morgan, take charge in the house. Deal with

Crime Scene when they arrive. Quillan, come with me. I'll speak to the witness."

Mrs Hargreaves' house was the only one in Tork Lane not hedged in by impenetrable shrubs. Her low front hedge gave her an uninterrupted view of the lane and all who passed along it. No gnomes in the garden but two stone rabbits and a thatched bird table amidst daffodils and crocuses.

A PC opened the door and showed them into a front parlour, cluttered with china and chintz. A twittery old lady rose to greet them, one nervous hand to her throat. She was backed up by the friend, a woman of a similar age but one more likely to maim if they disturbed the antimacassars.

While the DI introduced them, Rosanna checked the view from the window, under its swathes of lace curtain. Sure enough, straight through the double gates opposite to the front door of Summervale. A copy of British Garden Birds lay on a dainty little round table, an innocent excuse for the pair of binoculars on the sill.

"You don't mind my friend staying with us?" asked Mrs Hargreaves.

"Not at all. You are?"

"Barbara Isaacs. You are a senior officer, are you?" The friend was not going to be fobbed off with inferior goods.

"Detective inspector, Mrs Isaac. So, Mrs Hargreaves." Stansford glanced at Rosanna to make sure she was ready to take notes. "Can you tell me what you saw and heard… last night, was it?"

"Yes, oh, um, well…"

"Take your time."

"Go on, Kathleen," ordered Mrs Isaacs.

"It was the car, you see. That's what woke me."

"The Porsche?" Seeing Mrs Hargreaves' blank face, the DI corrected herself, pointing to the nose of the Porsche just visible beyond a laurel. "That car?"

"Oh! No. No, that's Mr Delaney's car, the one he usually drives."

"And a bloody ridiculous car it is too," interposed her friend.

Mrs Hargreaves smiled apologetic agreement. "But I think there was a problem with it. Yesterday morning. Mr Delaney was shouting at his wife and she gave him the keys of her car, so he took that."

"I see. Do you know the make and… do you know what sort of car it was?"

"Well, no, I'm not very good with cars. It's blue, though. Dark blue."

"Audi A5," said Mrs Isaacs, decisively. "She sometimes drives to my book club in it."

"Thank you, yes, that's very helpful. And so, Mrs Hargreaves, you heard the Audi return in the night."

"Yes. I'm quite a light sleeper you know, so the noise of the engine woke me. And the wheels on the gravel. And the car lights, of course. So I got out of bed to see, because, well, it can be quite alarming. And after last time, with his other wife, you know…"

"Alison Delaney, yes of course. Do you have any idea what time the car arrived?"

"Oh yes, I have a clock radio by my bed. It was just half past one."

"And did you see anything after that?"

"By the time I got to the window, he'd already gone in. There were lights on. A bit of shouting. I couldn't really hear what. Anyway, I decided to go down and make myself a cocoa, help me get back to sleep, and that's when I saw her. She opened the front door. She had a suitcase, I think. She looked really quite upset. He pulled her back in and sort of pushed the door but it didn't quite shut. He was shouting, things like "You can't leave me, I won't let you.""

"You can't leave me?"

"Yes. Well, I mean, husbands and wives do have rows, don't they? Shout at each other."

"Do Mr and Mrs Delaney often have noisy rows?"

"Well, no. Not very often."

"Huh." Mrs Isaacs grunted. "Too much of a mouse, that woman. Scared of him if you ask me. Should have seen the way she ran from our last book club meeting because she was terrified of keeping him waiting. And he doesn't let her have anything to do with money or business, which, if you ask me—"

"So it was unusual, was it, Mrs Hargreaves, to hear them shouting? Was it just shouting?"

"Well, yes, at first but then... I heard... I don't like to—"

"Come on, Kathleen," ordered Mrs Isaacs. "Buck up. Spit it out."

Mrs Hargreaves gave a shuddering sigh. "I heard a sort of crash and then..." She looked hopefully at the teacup at her elbow but it was empty.

The DI glanced at the PC, who sidled off to make a fresh cup. "You're doing well. What then, after the crash?"

"I heard a scream."

"A scream? You're sure?"

"I think so. It started and then it stopped. But I might be wrong. It might have been nothing. I mean, I was a long way away."

"Very well, we'll say you thought you heard a scream. And then what?"

"Well, nothing for a bit. Everything was quiet, but there were lights going on and off and then I saw Mr Delaney."

"It was definitely him?"

"Well, I thought so. He was wearing a coat with the collar up, and his hat."

"Ridiculous thing!" Barbara Isaacs butted in again. "Saw him wearing it last week in the car. Suppose he thought it made him look dashing, but if you ask me—"

"So he was wearing his hat?" prompted the inspector.

"Yes. The brim was pulled down low so I couldn't really see." Mrs Hargreaves seized on a happy thought. "Perhaps it wasn't him after all? It might have been a burglar."

"Possibly. What did he do?"

"He came out. Carrying something. Well, not carrying, exactly. Dragging. I couldn't see at first because the car was in the way. He must have put it down, because he came round to open the boot and then he went back for it."

"What was it?"

"I really can't say for sure. Their security light was on, but even so… It looked like, maybe, a carpet? Rolled up. He had to struggle to get it into the boot. He slammed it shut and then he drove off. Well, I didn't know what to think. I mean, I don't like to go accusing neighbours. There might have been a totally innocent…"

"Innocent, my eye!" declared Mrs Isaacs. "Isn't it obvious, he killed his wife and he was getting rid of the body? Clear as day, isn't it, Inspector?"

Stansford turned her head in a gesture that could have been a shake or a nod. "We don't know anything for certain yet, Mrs Isaacs. I'd advise against speculation until we've examined all the evidence. But, Mrs Hargreaves, you must have suspected something untoward had happened. Why did you wait until…" She checked. "7:47 to call us?"

Mrs Hargreaves flapped. "I thought he'd come back, you see. And she'd open the door and it would all have been nothing and I didn't want to call the police in case I was just imagining things."

"Silly, Kathleen!" scolded Mrs Isaacs. "So this morning, she called me in a state and I came over."

"And Barbara said I should call 999, so I did."

"I'm very glad you did, Mrs Hargreaves. You say you thought the driver might come back."

"Well, yes, Mr Delaney usually gets home quite late, after seven, but if he's not home by ten, that usually means he's staying over, in London. His office, you know. So I thought, if he had come home, he'd be back. Maybe he just drove out to the tip."

"At, what, two in the morning? Does he often drive to the tip then?"

"No, but… He went there the other day. With all the baby things. The cot, you know. Mrs Delaney was quite upset about it."

"He took the cot to the tip?"

"Yes. I hope I'm not speaking out of turn."

"Damned silly," said Mrs Isaacs.

Mrs Hargreaves looked ready to agree, but instead she jumped up, as the PC returned to the room with a tray. "Oh no, no, no! Not the packet. I have a biscuit barrel. And nice plates."

* * *

Marching back to Summervale, DI Stansford glanced at Rosanna. "God bless old ladies who have nothing better to do than collect bone china and spy on their neighbours, but what a difference it might have made if she'd called us at the time."

"She was afraid of upsetting her neighbours."

"Not something that Mrs Isaacs would worry about. So what are we to make of her story, do you suppose, Quillan? Sounds like a classic case of a domestic argument taken too far and a hasty effort to cover it up."

"Yes, ma'am."

"Almost too classic, you might say."

"Predictable, yes ma'am, but people do behave in predictable ways."

"Indeed they do. Let's see what they've found in the house."

The senior scene of crimes officer met them at the door, pulling his mask down. "Got blood traces here in the hall. Smears. More in the dining room – blood splatter and pooling on the carpet. Someone's attempted to wipe it all clean, but not quite well enough. A hasty job." He waited for them to don their protective gear and led the way through to a room with French windows opening onto the back garden. Modern dining furniture in a room designed for French-polished mahogany.

"Splatter here." He pointed to almost invisible drops on the carving of the ornate fire-place. "And pooling here." He indicated an area of the pale fitted carpet that was slightly different in colour to the rest. There were faint stains in the middle of it. "I'm guessing there was a rug here, which probably absorbed most of the blood but some seeped through. We haven't found a rug to fit, so far. Upstairs, a broken window on the landing – pane cracked, very recent. And there's a suitcase containing women's clothing in the master bedroom. Thrown on the bed, by the looks of it. It's knocked over a lamp on the bedside table."

The DI nodded. "Thank you. Morgan." Ben was coming down the stairs, jotting in his notebook. "You'll bring me full details of their findings when they're done. Our next step, obviously, is to speak to Simon Delaney. Assuming we can find him. Any thoughts, Quillan?"

"Find the blue Audi? And check with his office?"

"That would be a start."

2. DC Quillan, Oxfordshire
8th March 2019

Rosanna stood at the DI's desk, waiting for Stansford to put the phone down.

"Okay, Quillan. What have you got?"

"Delaney did go to his office yesterday, had dinner with a client, came in first thing this morning, but left again, saying he had some domestic business to deal with. One of his people, Chloe Harper, thought he looked stressed. She says he never drives into London. He catches the train. Mrs Delaney's Audi, registration number—"

"We have it. It's parked at Oxford station. Forensics are giving it an initial examination now and we're checking CCTV. Right." Stansford jabbed a finger at a chair. "Sit."

Rosanna sat.

The inspector leaned back. "I know you've been secretly digging into everything about Simon Delaney ever since his first wife killed herself. What have you got on him, precisely?"

Rosanna didn't bother denying it. "He's driven. Wants to succeed, to climb."

"Not necessarily a villainous trait."

"A levels in Maths, Economics and Statistics, degree in Investment and Financial Risk Management from—"

"Thank you, Quillan. Never mind his full educational history, unless it involves violence against his teachers."

"Worked for one of the City finance firms, Ellcon Capital. He quit them about six years ago and concentrated on expanding his own business, Delaney Asset Management and Financial Advisory Services. Opened his office in London. This was all at about the time he met and married Alison Greenold."

"Using her money?"

"It gave him the capital he needed to take the risk."

"Anything fishy about the company?"

"Not that I could tell, but I'm not an expert."

"No, but we have people who are. So, go on."

"His team had nothing negative to say about him. They appreciate him. They're doing well out of the firm. Doesn't mean they like him personally."

"It doesn't mean they don't, either. Don't let your own prejudices colour this account, Quillan."

"No, ma'am."

"So what about his personal life? I'm sure you've fished in that pond."

"He has a brother who's a teacher in Coventry. Parents live there too. Father is now retired. Simon seems to have cut his old family ties. He has business colleagues with whom he socialises, but no obvious close friends that I'm aware of. But…"

"Aha. The but. But what?"

"Danielle Brightman. She was the woman who accused him of murdering his first wife. She later withdrew the allegation, but he acknowledged that he had had an affair with her."

"Yes, I remember. I spoke with her myself and she confirmed it. I presume you have hunted her down, to satisfy your own curiosity?"

"Yes, ma'am. She claims that the affair is still ongoing. She resents the present Mrs Delaney for stealing him from her, but she's convinced he would 'sort it out' in her words. She said 'accidents happen.'"

"Did she, indeed? Perhaps, in that case, we need—"

"Ma'am." Ben interrupted abruptly. "Delaney's turned up. Just off the train, in Oxford."

Stansford pushed her chair back. "Good. At least that means we don't have to waste our time sweeping the country for him. Bring him in."

* * *

Simon Delaney was sweating, his eyelid twitching as he nervously tugged at his tie and cuffs. He jumped up like an electrified frog as the DI came into the room.

"What's going on here? What's happened to my car? There were policemen all over it."

"Yes, Mr Delaney, they were looking for evidence."

"Of what? Has someone vandalised it?"

"Not that I know of."

"Then let me get back to it. I need to get home."

"I'm afraid it will have been towed to the station by now, Mr Delaney. Forensics are probably taking it apart."

"Why?" He was waving his hands around. "Why? Did someone take it or something? Carry out a robbery?

No, it's exactly where I left it, yesterday. And now I need to get home to my wife."

"She isn't at home, Mr Delaney."

"Where is she then?"

"I was hoping you could enlighten us on that point."

"What do you mean? I don't get it. What's happened?"

"Sit down, Mr Delaney."

"Not until you—"

"Sit down!"

Delaney sank back into his chair, terrified.

"Now. Before I question you further, I believe you declined the offer to have a solicitor present? Would you like to change your mind?"

Delaney stared at Stansford for a moment, trying to grasp at facts that weren't there. "Yes. Yes, I want a solicitor."

"Good. Fortunately, we anticipated your request and advised Mr Wicks that you might be requiring his services. He's in the building now, so we won't have to delay."

A very brief delay. Delaney's solicitor was shown into the interview room and Delaney was immediately out of his chair again. "God knows why they've got me here, Kevin. I don't have a clue what's going on."

"All right, Simon." Wicks looked as calm and authoritative. "Perhaps you would be so kind as to tell us, Inspector, why you have brought my client in?" He seated himself and gestured to Delaney to do the same.

"Certainly. First of all, we would like Mr Delaney to tell us where he has been for the last twelve hours."

"Simon?"

Delaney looked exasperated. "I was in London. I had dinner with a client last night, then I was at my flat, in Harbour Way, from about ten I suppose, until seven-thirty-ish this morning, when I went to my office to deposit some papers, then I took a tube to Paddington and a train to Oxford. Came to pick up my car and I was hauled off here by a couple of police heavies, and now I want to know what the hell is going on."

"So you didn't return to Soweridge in the night?"

"No, of course not. I stayed the night at the flat. What is this all about?"

Wicks butted in. "Yes, Inspector, you haven't yet given us any idea what Mr Delaney is supposed to have done. He has informed you where he was."

"We are more concerned about where his wife is. She is not at their home. If we can just establish her whereabouts...?"

"Jude?" Delaney spluttered, speechless for a moment, then he collected himself. "That's it? That's the great puzzle? Right. I can tell you. She's in Bristol." He sounded both aggressively certain and profoundly irritated.

"Bristol?"

"Yes!" He sat back, folding his arms. "If she's not at home, she's in Bristol. With her cousin. She phoned me last night, at the flat. That's why I came home. Stupid woman!" He ground his teeth with frustration. "I told her not to go."

"Explain, please?"

"I told you, she phoned me. Must have been gone eleven. She said her cousin had called to say his mother had been rushed to hospital, he was in a state and she needed to go there. She was going to call a taxi. In the middle of the night! I told her to wait. I'd come home first thing in the morning and I'd drive her to Bristol if she was so determined to go, although I couldn't see how that was going to help her cousin. She agreed. She said she'd wait for me. Obviously, if she's not there, she must have called a taxi after all and gone."

"To see a cousin in Bristol?"

"Yes. As I said."

"The name of this cousin?"

"Adrian something. Merriman, that's it."

"And his address?"

"I don't know! I never met the man. All I know is he lives in Bristol."

"Very well, Mr Delaney. We'll see if we can find your wife in Bristol."

"But what the hell do you want with her? What do you think she's done? She's pregnant. She can't have done anything."

"Yes, she's pregnant. How do you feel about that? Annoyed?"

"No. Of course not. What do you mean? What's happened?"

"Mr Delaney, we have had reports of a disturbance at your house last night."

"Reports? What reports?"

"A neighbour witnessed a man arriving in a dark blue car, in the early hours, there were sounds of an argument and he left again, carrying a large bundle. Upon investigation, we found signs of a struggle and blood."

"Blood?" It was almost a scream.

"But no sign of your wife. You'll understand, Mr Delaney, why we urgently need to find her."

Delaney had turned a pale grey. He was gripping the desk to keep himself upright. Rosanna wondered if he would actually faint.

3. DC Quillan, Bristol
9th March 2019

The Sold sign at the gate of 153 Lemmingford Road in Bristol confirmed what Rosanna could see for herself through uncurtained windows: the place was empty. It had been simple to track down Judith Delaney's cousin. The electoral register gave this as his address, along with a Timothy Draycott, but it seemed both had moved on.

Rosanna knocked once more, to be quite certain.

"Are you the new lady?" A lisping voice addressed her from the hedge separating 153's tiny front garden from the next.

Rosanna peered over at a small girl. "Hello. Are you looking for a new lady?"

"Are you going to live there now?"

"I'm afraid not. I'm just looking for the man who used to live here."

"Ade and Tim."

"Yes, that's right. I'm looking for Ade."

"I like Ade. He's gone away. They live in Spain now. They've both got willies."

Rosanna swallowed a cough. Fortunately, before she could think of an adequate reply, the front door of 155 opened and a woman looked out. "Lulu, what are you doing out here? I said play in the back." She peered at

Rosanna across the hedge. "Are you our new neighbour? Moving in?"

"No, I'm just looking for Adrian Merriman."

"Oh well, missed him by a couple of months, I'm afraid. They've bought a bar or something in Spain. Right down the south somewhere. Packed up and went just after Christmas. I've got their address, if you like."

"Please, yes, that would be helpful. So neither of them have been back since?"

"No, the estate agent's been handling the sale for them. They couldn't wait to go. A pity. Lulu misses them. And they were nice neighbours, though I won't miss the clarinet at seven in the morning."

"They're musicians?"

"Tim is. Ade is supposed to be some sort of writer. Nice men both of them, even if they did prance around stark naked in that conservatory of theirs. Didn't know where to look sometimes. So you don't know them then?" The neighbour was suddenly wary.

"No." Rosanna produced her warrant card. "Detective Constable Quillan."

"Oh my God, what's he done?"

Rosanna laughed reassurance. "I have no reason to believe he's done anything. Sorry, you are–?"

"Purley. Geraldine Purley."

"Well, Mrs Purley, I'm looking for a cousin of Adrian Merriman. Judith Delaney? It was suggested she might have come here. You haven't seen her?"

"Oh. Jude, you mean. Well yes, she's been here a few times. Is she Ade's cousin? That would explain it, them going off together. Did seem a bit weird, with him being, you know, with Tim."

"She's gone off with him?"

"Not now. Just for a couple of days once or twice. Look, don't stand there in the cold. Come on in."

So Rosanna joined Geraldine Purley in her kitchen, where Geraldine put the kettle on within sight of Lulu, now playing in the back garden.

"Have to get her tea soon. Sorry, what were we saying?"

"Mr Merriman and Mrs Delaney going off together. We are very keen to find her."

"Oh Lord, that sounds bad."

"We were told she'd come here yesterday to see Mr Merriman and his mother who had been taken ill."

"She didn't come here. Perhaps she's gone to Spain. No, but wait. That doesn't make sense. Ade's mother passed away a couple of years back. He was terribly upset about it. Tim took him off to Spain afterwards for a break. I think that's when they decided to move out there."

"I see. So, you think when he and Mrs Delaney sometimes went off together, it was to Spain."

"Oh no, Wales."

"Wales? Are you sure?"

"Well they'd only be gone a couple of days. Last time was just before Christmas, I think."

"And it was definitely Wales."

"He sent a postcard to Tim. Daft really because he was back before it arrived. The post got mixed up – all those Christmas cards, I suppose. It came through our letterbox by mistake, in a bundle of other stuff. Picture of a weird statue of a beaver or something. No, that's right, an otter. It said 'Beth Julia's arms are open. Wales is ready and waiting.' Not signed or anything. I thought it was a bit odd until I realised it was addressed to Tim, so I took it round."

"Beth Julia, did you say?"

"Yes, I think that's what it said. Because I asked 'Who's this Beth Julia then,' and Ade laughed and said she was his secret mistress. Which she isn't, obviously."

"I see. Well, that's… interesting." Rosanna took the proffered mug of tea. "You say you have their address in Spain."

"Yes, I'll fetch it for you. And Ade's phone number, if you like."

"Please."

Geraldine led the way into the living room and shuffled through a pile of bills and envelopes on the mantlepiece. She extracted a photo and flipped it over. "Tim wrote it on that."

Rosanna noted down an address in Nerja, and two phone numbers. Then she turned the photo over. Two men, one dressed in a straw hat and lurid Hawaiian shirt, the other in something vaguely Arabic, raising glasses outside a whitewashed building with shutters and red tiled roof, vivid against a burning blue sky. "Are these them?"

"What? Oh yes, that's Ade and that's Tim and that's the place they've bought. They said we could come over and stay, but maybe not."

Rosanna took a long look at the photo, then handed it back. "Thank you. So, you are quite certain you haven't seen Judith Delaney in the last day or two?"

"Not since before Christmas. She'd have no reason to come here, would she? Unless she knows the new owners and they're not moving in until next weekend. Mr and Mrs Price, if that's any help."

"Thank you. Any information is useful. Now I'd best leave you to see to Lulu's tea."

Back in her car, Rosanna sat staring at the Spanish address she'd written down, her inner eye seeing instead that photograph. Two men that she had seen before at Alison's funeral, sobbing and talking to Dr Rackman.

"Beth Julia," she murmured as she started up the engine.

4. DC Quillan, Oxfordshire
10th March 2019

When Rosanna came into the station, she could tell that it had been humming overnight. Ben Morgan strolled over and leaned on her desk as she wriggled out of her coat. "So Bristol's a blank?"

"The neighbour says Adrian Merriman moved out just after Christmas and hasn't been back. He's been living in Spain ever since. I spoke to him on the phone and he claims he's been at his bar for the last eight days without a break, supervising alterations. We could ask the Spanish police to confirm that."

Ben nodded. "I'll sort it."

"I'm inclined to believe him. He sounded genuinely upset when I told him Judith Delaney was missing. And he did confirm his mother died a couple of years back."

"So Delaney's account of the eleven o'clock phone call sounds like bullshit."

"Yes."

"She did phone him though. We've checked. Eleven twelve, lasting nine minutes. A row? She tells him she's leaving him, maybe? He's determined to stop her. It would have given him time to catch the train that gets into Oxford just after one. Pick up his car, drive to Soweridge… it fits with the neighbour's account. We're checking CCTV now."

"Good."

Ben grinned. "And… we've had a rummage in his safe. Want to guess what we found?"

The answer was on the tip of Rosanna's tongue, but she bit it back. "What?"

"A couple of keys. Look like bedroom door and window? They don't fit, unfortunately, so it's not conclusive proof, but..."

"She told me they'd had the locks changed, because the keys were missing. Well."

"And there was more in there. Lots of paperwork, mostly financial – the fraud guys are going through it. Dynamite, apparently. Plus there was a phone. A million and one calls and texts to and from a particular number."

"Danielle Brightman?"

"You've got it. And an email printout confirming a booking of a flight, tomorrow, Heathrow to Cape Town. One way, in the name of Simon Philip Delaney."

"Anyone spoken to Danielle Brightman?"

Ben shook his head. "No go. The local guys tried her address and her mother claimed she'd gone abroad. More than a week ago. We're checking that, but I'm driving over now to see if we can get any more from the mother? The DI thought you might know her."

"I have met her."

"So come with me now."

* * *

A supercilious feline head stared them down from the window as they walked up to the front door of 42A St David's Road, crunching on the gravel.

One ring of the bell was enough. Dr Rackman opened the door and stood back as if she were expecting them. Rosanna winced involuntarily with sympathy. The doctor looked ill, aged by a good ten years. Her eyes were red.

"DC Quillan, isn't it?"

"Yes, and DS Morgan. We'd like to ask you, if it's —"

"Yes. Go on through." She followed them into the living room, gestured to the empty sofas and sat herself down on the edge of an armchair, tense, holding herself together, ready to disintegrate at any moment. "You want to ask about my daughter."

"I'm sorry. I can see it's painful for you."

"Painful for everyone, I imagine. Has Judith been found?"

"No, not yet," said Ben, but then he sat back, leaving the field to Rosanna.

Dr Rackman turned her head away, staring at the empty fireplace. "I suppose he's already flown."

"Simon Delaney is being questioned at the station."

Dr Rackman looked up sharply. "Is he? I thought he'd be with her by now."

"With your daughter, you mean?"

"Yes." She looked sick as she said it.

"In Cape Town?"

"Cape..! No. At least, I don't know. My daughter flew to Zurich. That's all she would tell me."

"Zurich, you say? But you were expecting him to join her?"

"She was certainly expecting it." The doctor's inner anguish became a surge of anger barely under control. It was a grand display of indignation. "I can't believe she would be so utterly unprincipled. She says she loves him! How is that an excuse? She told me he was leaving Jude for her and I thought she must be fooling herself. He wouldn't be so cruel. But now… they tell me Jude is missing and something about blood and… Listen. Danny told me he was leaving Jude, that's all. We had a terrible row but she was determined to go. Just to join him, that's all. If he's hurt his wife, it had nothing to do with Danny. She wouldn't be involved in anything like that. I know she hasn't forgiven Jude for marrying him, but she wouldn't… They're practically sisters. If she even suspected that Simon—"

"She accused him once before."

"She was upset about Alison. She didn't mean it."

"No? No." Rosanna could sense Ben urging her on. "So, your daughter told you she was flying to Zurich. Did she give you an address where we might find her?"

"No. She wouldn't. I only knew about the flight because I picked up her phone and there was a booking confirmation. That was when the argument started. She already had her bags packed." The indignation suddenly dissolved. "She was determined to go and I couldn't stop her." Dr Rackman burst into tears, her shoulders heaving as she struggled to control the sobs. She clenched white knuckles to her mouth until she had the convulsions subdued. She breathed deeply a few times, then raised her head, blinking away the last of the tears as Theodora the cat jumped down from the windowsill to slink across the room and wind herself around the doctor's ankles. Dr Rackman leaned down to fondle one grey ear, then looked at her guests.

"I am so sorry. I should have offered you tea."

"Thank you, but we won't bother you any further, Mrs Rackman." Ben had risen to his feet. "Unless you can give us any further idea of your daughter's whereabouts or intentions."

"No." The doctor rose too. "I'm afraid my daughter is lost to me now." She shut her eyes for a moment.

"Then we'll leave you in peace."

She followed them to the door. Rosanna paused to shake her hand. Their eyes met. "My condolences," said Rosanna softly.

The doctor's grip tightened slightly, before she let go. "Thank you," she said, and stooped to pick up the cat.

"What do you make of it then," said Ben as they returned to their car. "Zurich? Why Zurich, I wonder."

"Trying to confuse the trail, perhaps?"

"Or there was something she had to do in Switzerland. Let's see if the guys from fraud have turned up an explanation. Meanwhile, I'll check the flights, just to confirm the mother's story." He glanced at the radio. The station was calling. "Morgan. What is it?"

Report of a possible sighting, Sarge, since it's been on the local news. Driver on the bypass near Iffly, some time after two in the morning. Saw a dark car parked in the layby on the bridge and a man leaning over the parapet.

Driver slowed, worried about a suicide, but the man returned to his car, so he drove on.

"Leaning over the parapet?"

Over the river, yes, Sarge. The DI's requested a search.

"On my way now." Ben started the engine, grinning at Rosanna. "Sounds like the game's afoot."

"Yes, it is," she said quietly. "The game."

5. DC Quillan, Oxfordshire
11th March 2019

Great excitement at the station. Rosanna thought, for one confusing moment, that they'd found a body. No, but they had dredged up a rug, snagged on a tree. Quite a sizeable one, matching exactly the pale patch on the Delaney's dining room carpet and, despite the soaking, it was stained with blood. Forensics had already established that the blood traces found in the house, on the gravel and in the Audi's boot were a match for Judith Delaney. Meanwhile, the fraud team had been hard at work on Simon's accounts and the contents of his safe.

"They reckon he did a pretty good job of hiding it, but he's been filtering off chunks of his clients' money for months," said Ben, perching on the corner of Rosanna's desk and taking a swig from his water bottle. "About six million in all. And transferring it all to..."

"Let me guess. A Swiss bank account?"

"Of course. But not just that. An account in the name of Danielle Brightman."

"Yes, I'd have guessed that too."

"So, since I've already checked the flights and confirmed that Brightman flew to Zurich on the twenty-eighth of February, they're checking with the bank now."

"I thought Swiss banks refuse to disclose clients' business?"

"Not when serious crime is involved. And seeing as how Brightman flew on to South Africa two days later, I think we can guess what she was doing in Zurich. Which confirms what the text messages were saying."

Ben screwed the lid back on his water bottle, grinning with satisfaction. Unsurprising, really. Everything was falling so neatly into place. Simon Delaney's safe contents alone would have been enough to justify his arrest. Apart from details of dodgy dealings, there was the phone, choc a bloc with calls and texts from Danielle Brightman, loving and threatening at the same time, and a letter from her, with a confirmation of a DNA test, demanding that he "go through with it." And there were the two keys.

"No fingerprints on them except Delaney's," said Ben. "Like everything else in the safe. It's pretty damning support for your theory that he locked his first wife up."

"Yes."

"And now the CCTV… They've strung it all together and he's there, the whole way, London, Oxford station, back at the Docklands again. I ask you, did he seriously think a hat would be enough to disguise him?"

"It means you can never see his face. Enough to cast doubt, maybe?"

"But he had the keys to the car. Who else could it be?" Ben looked up as DI Stansford approached. "Anything new?"

Stansford smiled. "We have a finger."

"What?"

"It bobbed up at the lock. Ring finger, complete with wedding ring, sliced clean off." Stansford glanced at Rosanna. "I thought you'd like to know."

"Yes!" Rosanna was impressed.

"I'm afraid your part is limited now. It means Major Crimes will be taking over."

"Yes, ma'am. I suppose they will."

"Good, well, get your notes in order."

When the DI had gone, Ben pulled a face. "Great, but a pity that we don't get to see it through."

"It was bound to happen."

"You're bloody calm about it all. Come on, Ros, you've been itching to nail this guy from day one. Don't tell me you're not a tiny bit disappointed you have to leave the kill to the big boys?"

Rosanna shrugged. "As long as he's nailed, what else matters? I'm happy with that."

"Oh he'll be nailed, all right. Crucified."

What else did matter? There was no need for guilt, but all the same Rosanna felt it. Not enough to change her course though. She'd written up her reports and every word of them was the truth. Just not the whole truth. Where was the dividing line between honesty and deception? Justice was truth, she'd said, and now her silence was a lie, so was it justice?

It hadn't been her job to check flights to Zurich. That had been Ben's doing and if he'd found precisely what they were looking for, why should she butt in and say that she'd found more? Because she'd been looking for it. Yes, Danielle Brightman had boarded the flight to Zurich. She'd passed through the security check-in at

11:45. Walking like a zombie. Three minutes later, Dr Madeleine Rackman had also passed through security. Someone called Danielle Brightman had boarded a flight to Cape Town on the second of March, but Rosanna was willing to swear it wasn't the same woman. CCTV might prove it if anyone chose to investigate, but no one had. Not yet, at least. How the passports had been managed, she didn't know, but if a woman could slice off her own finger, she was capable of anything.

Rosanna knew she should speak out, and yet she had no intention of doing so. *I do solemnly and sincerely declare and affirm that I will well and truly serve the Queen in the office of constable, with fairness, integrity, diligence and impartiality…* If she were willing to ignore her oath, how could she, in good conscience, remain in the police force?

She couldn't. But then, she realised, as she logged off and switched off her screen, she'd already reached that conclusion days ago.

14th March 2019

MH   This interview is being taped and may be given in evidence if your case is brought to trial. I am DCI Michael Hollingbrook. Please state your full name and date of birth for the tape.

SD   Simon Philip Delaney. Seventh of May, 1982. Can I have some water?

MH   Of course. Also present is…

KW   Kevin Peter Wicks, solicitor.

MH   Thank you. Now. Mr Delaney. You understand why you are here. We are looking into the disappearance and probable murder of your wife, Judith Theresa Delaney, in the early hours of the eighth of March, 2019. Are you still claiming that you have no idea where she is?

SD   How many times? I was in London the whole night, and if Mrs Hargreaves saw or heard someone entering my house and arguing with my wife, it wasn't me. A taxi driver. Have you thought of that? She told me she was going to call a taxi.

MH   To go to Bristol to see a cousin whose mother had been rushed into hospital.

SD   That's what she told me.

MH   This would be Adrian Merriman, who sold his house in Bristol and moved to Nerja in Spain on the fourth of January, where he was supervising renovations on his new property at the time of your wife's disappearance. The Adrian Merriman whose mother died two years ago.

SD   Okay, okay. So she must have been lying. What do you want me to say? I only know what she told me. I want you out there finding her, and finding the bastard who killed her. Her and my child! Find them, you hear!

MH   Calm down, Mr Delaney. I can assure you we are doing everything we can to find your wife, dead or alive. Now, I take it you have been shown the CCTV evidence that casts doubt on your claims that you were in London the entire night of your wife's disappearance.

KW   May I point out, Chief Inspector, that with regard to all the CCTV shots, both in Oxford and London, the man in question is not clearly identifiable as my client.

MH   That is correct, Mr Wicks. Let us say they feature a man of Mr Delaney's height and build, who takes great care, throughout, to conceal his features. Largely thanks to a distinctive wide-brimmed hat, identical to one belonging to Mr Delaney.

SD   I never wear the bloody thing! It's Jude's idea of a joke.

MH   A witness, Mrs Isaacs, tells us she saw you wearing it when you collected your wife from her reading group. Where is it now?

SD   I don't know! It stays in my car. If it's not there now, I don't know where it is. Whoever this guy was, and whatever he was wearing, he wasn't me.

MH   And yet he had the keys to your wife's car. We see him opening the door, starting the engine and driving off. Rather odd, don't you think, unless he had the car keys? Keys that were later found in your possession.

SD   It wasn't me! It wasn't me! Whoever it was, it wasn't me!

KW   My client has already made that clear, Chief Inspector, and you have no footage of this mysterious person entering or leaving my client's apartment in London. Merely in the vicinity, which means nothing.

MH   So, if you did not return to Oxford in the night, you could not have been the man seen parked in a layby on the bypass near Iffley, some time after two a.m. on the eighth? You'll appreciate why we instigated a search of the river.

KW   And you did not find my client's wife, Chief Inspector.

MH   Not yet. Just the ring finger, found by a fisherman at Sandford lock. DNA has confirmed the finger is your wife's, Mr Delaney. Like the blood soaked into the rug we retrieved. Like the traces of blood found in your house, despite attempts to clean it up. Perhaps her assailant was more anxious to dispose of your wife's body first. Perhaps he intended to return at leisure and do a more thorough cleaning job. No comment, Mr

Delaney? Please take a moment to compose yourself. Have another drink of water. Better?

KW My client understands perfectly well, Chief Inspector, that his wife has been attacked and brutally injured, but unless you find a body, we cannot know for certain that she is dead.

MH But since she has not responded to repeated appeals, and no one of her description has sought medical attention, we are surely justified in assuming the worst, don't you think, Mr Wicks? Mr Delaney?

SD I didn't do it! I wouldn't kill my wife. Why would I? I loved her. For Christ's sake, she was carrying my child!

MH Yes. Like your first wife, Mr Delaney. You claimed to have loved her, too.

SD I did!

MH She was also carrying your child. You told a guest at your wedding – your first wedding, that is – that you didn't want children. You didn't fancy a life of nappies and screaming brats.

SD That was then. That was before… It was different when Alison was pregnant.

MH But she died. While you were in London. You suggested at the time that she had committed suicide because she had found out about your affair with Danielle Brightman.

SD Yes.

MH Questions were raised, during that enquiry, about keys to the bedroom where she was found. It was suggested that you might have locked her in.

SD   No. No it didn't happen. It didn't happen.

MH   Why were there keys concealed in your safe, Mr Delaney?

SD   I never put any keys in my safe.

MH   You've stated that no one else knew the combination, so only you could have put them there, but you've forgotten why. Were they the keys mysteriously missing on the day of Alison Delaney's suicide?

KW   You tested them, I believe, Chief Inspector, and they did not fit any locks in the house.

MH   But of course we know that the locks to that room were changed after Mr Delaney moved on to his second wife. Who is now missing, presumed violently murdered. Two wives, Mr Delaney, and both of them quite a catch financially.

SD   For Christ's sake, I didn't marry them for their money!

MH   No, I'm sure you married for love. The sort of love that locks a pregnant woman in a bedroom.

KW   My client has already denied this unsubstantiated allegation, Chief Inspector, which was not pursued at the time of his first wife's death, so I suggest you move on.

MH   Very well, let us return to your second wife. Whom you also loved. Although several witnesses have suggested she seemed fearful of you. A Mrs Delia Philby, one of your clients, said that your wife was terrified you would be mad with her, when she was late serving tea.

SD   That. No, that was nothing. It was the pregnancy. Mood swings. She'd be laughing one minute, in tears the next.

MH   That must have been irritating.

SD   It's how women are when they're pregnant.

MH   And you know all about that, don't you? Two pregnant wives and a pregnant mistress. Danielle Brightman is also carrying your child.

SD   No! She's not my mistress. She's never been my mistress.

MH   If she's nothing to you, why have you been visiting her repeatedly since your marriage to Judith Granger? Witnesses in the same street have observed you furtively approaching the property. If not for a clandestine assignation, then why?

SD   I… no…it wasn't… I wasn't having an affair with Danny. I'm not the father of her child. It's just not possible!

MH   And yet she sent you proof, Mr Delaney, with the letter we found in your safe. A paternity test, confirming you as the father of her baby. "No point denying it now," that's what she wrote to you. "It's me and my baby, or her."

SD   No. No. No, no, no, no, no, no, no.

MH   Tell me about the phone that you kept locked away in the safe so your wife wouldn't find it.

SD   It wasn't mine. It was Jude's, I tell you. She ordered it for the office.

MH   So why do we find no fingerprints on it except yours? And text messages from Danielle Brightman that could only be to you.

Confirmation of everything else we found in that safe. Your clients' funds systematically transferred to a Swiss bank account in the name of Danielle Brightman. A bank account that was closed, all funds withdrawn, by Mrs Brightman on the first of March.

And shortly after, a text from her to you: "I've got it. Do it now. See you in SA." She sent you several more text messages. "Have you done it!" "You had better do it now or you'll be sorry." "Stop being a coward. Do it." "You'd better be here on Saturday, or else."

She's a demanding mistress, isn't she? A life sentence for murder might well be preferable to a painful and probably short life with Mrs Brightman. A life, alas, without the £6,049,652 she's currently holding for you. The South African police are still trying to track her down.

Was this the real subject of your wife's phone call to you on the night of the seventh? She hadn't just discovered your affair, she'd discovered your financial fraud. Was she threatening to come to us with the evidence?

Is that why you rushed home? To stop her? To stop her for good?

Was that how it was, Mr Delaney?

Silence.

Mr Delaney makes no reply. Perhaps it's time for a tea break. Before we go over the finer details.

PART FOUR
THE DEVIL

unredacted

1. Jude, Seoul, 17th June 2018

I was in a bathroom in a hotel in Seoul. It was no different to the bathroom I had showered in, that morning, in Paju. A hotel is a hotel is a hotel. Sometimes I forget which continent I'm in, let alone which city. But now I was in Seoul, a tourist as far as the hotel staff were concerned. It was early evening, too early to hit the town, with or without intent, so I'd been wallowing for an hour in the bath, flipping through transcripts and sipping a gin and tonic. Not shaken but stirred with a slice of lemon.

When my phone rang, I assumed it was Richard, asking for my report, so I ignored it. I was finally out, dripping on the bath mat, when it started to ring again. I wrapped a towel round me and fished it out of my jacket pocket, ready to growl a reply. Then I saw who it was.

"Danny?" I headed for the queen-size bed. "How are things in Oxford? Have you—"

"Jude." The word was strangled. I had a stupid image of someone struggling to squeeze the last trace of toothpaste from a tube. Why was I being so flippant? Couldn't I hear the desperation in her voice?

"Yes, I'm here."

There was a silence that swept away any trace of flippancy. It seemed to last eternity, but it was probably only a couple of seconds before I said "What is it, Danny?"

She was still struggling to speak. "Mum said I had to speak to you."

"What's happened?"

"Everything. I can't… I don't know where to begin."

"In that case go back to your day of birth if necessary." I was sounding far calmer than I felt. Danny's distress was setting off warning sirens. I wanted to scream at her "Tell me the worst," but she was already on the brink of incoherence, so I needed her to stop and get her thoughts into order. "Start at the beginning." I sat on the edge of my bed, tensed for action as if North Korean troops were about to come storming in.

Danny swallowed, audibly. "The concert, I suppose, then."

"Right. The concert. Which one?"

"You were there. St John's. You must remember."

"Of course I do. That was, what, three, four years ago? Alison played the Schumann. She was fantastic."

"Yes! She was!" Danny spat it out defiantly. "He was there and I saw him."

"Who did you see, Danny?"

"Simon." The name came out like a snake hiss.

"Yes of course he was there. I saw him too, totally out of his depth as usual."

"It wasn't just that, though. He was green, jealous. I saw the look in his face. I saw someone shake his hand and say something and he looked like he'd swallowed vinegar."

"Well, he's never going to grasp her talent. Is he still acting jealous when she plays?"

Danny gave a curdled laugh. "What do you mean? When she plays? She doesn't play!"

"Not at all? I know that record deal with Reynolds fell through—"

"It didn't just fall!"

There was a rap on my door. "Jude, any time you're ready, we'll be—"

"Sod off, Martin!"

"Sandy said if we could just—"

"Tell Sandy I'll be down when I'm fucking ready! I'm on the phone. Fuck off!" I paused to make sure he'd gone, then dropped the raging bull roar and reverted to calm quiet control. "Go on, Danny. What do you mean, it didn't just fall through."

She drew an audible breath. "It was him. He contacted Reynolds privately, told him Alison was drinking too much, and a deal would send her over the edge. So Reynolds backed out."

"I see." I kept my voice steady with an effort. "You know this for sure?"

"I didn't at first. I just assumed Reynold's offer had been a spur of the moment thing, and he hadn't really meant it. Alison was disappointed. She'd been practising non-stop. I went to see her. You'd gone off to… I don't know where. I never do. Where are you now?"

"South Korea. Annoying the Americans. Never mind. You went to see her. Was she drinking? I did notice she got through quite a few glasses when we met up Christmas before last."

"That's the point, don't you see? She never used to. It would be one small glass of white and then mineral water for the rest of the evening. She never touched spirits. But when I went, there was a bottle of gin. She played perfectly, but she had a sip first because she said it helped to steady her nerves. I said, 'But you don't have nerves, Alison. You're a natural.' And she said, 'But I can't afford to make mistakes, like at the concert.'"

"Did she make mistakes? If she did, I didn't catch them."

"Of course you didn't, because there weren't any. But she was convinced she'd made some. Or someone convinced her."

"I see."

"And the next time I saw her, it wasn't just a sip to steady her nerves. It wasn't just drink, either. She told me she had a prescription for panic attacks. Panic attacks!" Danny was fully in control now, spitting with rage. "Where did that come from? I said I'd heard talk of her taking part in something at the Sheldonian and she just shook her head and said 'I'm not up to it. I can't do it anymore.' I said of course she could, music was her whole life and she just burst into tears, babbling about being willing to give up everything if she could only have a baby."

I pushed my damp hair back, staring at the ceiling and remembering Alison as a serene swan, always slightly wistful, but never on edge, never wailing, never frenzied. It was Danny and I who'd mastered histrionics. "I know she was disappointed that Simon didn't want kids yet, but I hadn't realised it had got that bad."

"It had. And worse. It was more and more difficult meeting up with her. There was always something that got in the way. Then…" Danny's voice trailed off quite suddenly.

"You still there?"

"Yes." A small voice now.

"Go on, Danny. Tell me what happened."

"I can't."

"Yes, you can. Please. Tell me."

She was forcing herself again now. "January. At Merton. I saw Reynolds and I asked him what happened to Alison's record deal. He told me how Simon fucking Delaney had contacted him to warn his wife was a wreck, a total lush, and it would be much better if he just backed off, or she was likely to have a breakdown."

"The bastard."

"Yes. I was so angry. I…"

"You told Alison?"

"No. I was stupid. I wanted to challenge Simon, tell him I knew what he'd done, make him sort it out, go back to Reynolds and confess that he'd lied. But…"

"Go on. You talked to him?"

"I phoned him. I just said I'd spoken to Reynolds and he jumped in. 'Let's meet for dinner, I'm worried about Alison,' all that crap, and I thought, maybe it would be easier, face to face. He wouldn't be able to fob me off then."

"But?"

"When we met, he just kept going on and on about Alison, her insecurity, how she needed support, talking as if he'd summoned me, not letting me get a word in."

"Taking control, yes. And you wouldn't put up with that."

"I didn't. In the end I told him to shut up. I shouted it. I said, 'Why did you ruin Alison's career? Can't you handle her success?' Everyone in the restaurant was listening. He said, 'Come on, let's go and see Alison and we can talk it through.'"

Silence.

"And?"

Still silence.

"Danny. What happened?"

"I thought it meant he would have to tell the truth. He'd have to come clean with Alison. But we never got there."

"Go on."

"He stopped the car. It was somewhere in the middle of nowhere, dark, no other traffic around. He just slammed on the brakes and stopped. I hadn't realised how angry he was. He said, 'Listen to me you bitch, you shut your fucking mouth, you don't get in my way or I'll grind you into the dirt, you little piece of shit.' I tried to get out of the car and he was fighting me and… and…"

"And? What happened, Danny? Tell me. You've got to tell me."

"I can't."

"You must."

"I can't say it."

I could feel myself turning into a serpent of white ice, gathering itself to bite Simon Delaney's throat, to rip his heart out. But I kept my voice level. "Is your mother there, Danny?"

"No. I told her…" She was fighting back tears unsuccessfully. "I told her I couldn't talk to you if she was there. It's no good, I can't talk anyway. I shouldn't have—"

"Yes you should. Talk to me. Take a deep breath. Tell me."

She screamed it. "He raped me!"

"All right." Getting her to talk was one thing. Knowing what to reply was another.

"No, it's not all right! He raped me. He kept raping me. In every… he… I can't tell you what he did, how he… I can't!"

"All right, Danny. You don't have to—"

"He kept saying I was a piece of shit and I'd wish I'd never been born and it was true. I wished I was dead. I couldn't do anything. I was nothing but a filthy piece of meat. He used me and then he shoved me out and I just wanted to die in the ditch."

"But you didn't die, Danny. You reported him. Tell me you reported him to the police."

"What do you mean?" She was sobbing uncontrollably now. "I couldn't tell anyone! I couldn't look at anyone. I went home."

"You walked?"

"Yes. I suppose so. I don't remember. Just the car. I remember the car. His car, coming back, fast, afterwards, and I was so scared, I thought… I hid in the hedge and I thought he'd stop and I wouldn't be able to get away, but he just drove past."

"It was dark. He didn't see you." I could imagine it exactly. He was looking for her, realising, now that it was too late, that he'd made a big mistake in leaving her alive. I closed my eyes. "He didn't find you. You got home."

"I don't know how. But I must have done, because I was there and I realised my bag was in his car, with my keys, cards, everything. I found it the next day in our garden."

"Of course. He wouldn't want to hang on to any of it. Too incriminating."

"I suppose. I remember going to the back door, scrabbling for the key under the pot. Mum was at the hospital, night shift. I just locked myself in the bathroom and sat in the bath and scrubbed and scrubbed and wished I was dead."

"Dear God, Danny."

"In the morning, when Mum came home, I tried to pretend everything was normal."

"You didn't even tell her?"

"No. I couldn't, don't you see? I felt so filthy, so defiled. If I said it, it would be worse. She wanted to know how I'd got the cuts and bruises and I said I'd come off my bike. I hadn't told her I was meeting him. I just tried to shut it out. Only a week later, Alison phoned, wanting to meet me, and I thought I've got to tell her. She's got to know what she's married to. But when we met up, she was so happy, going on about how wonderful Simon was being, how affectionate – Oh God, I wanted to be sick!"

"Yes."

"She said he'd agreed at last that they should have a baby and he'd whisked her away to Paris for the weekend and there'd been nothing else for the last week but him all over her and she was sure she'd conceived. Jude! What could I do? What could I say?"

"Nothing. Of course, you couldn't. Oh, he's a clever bastard."

"I know." She sounded exhausted, wrung out.

"You never told me, either."

"Because I couldn't tell anyone."

"But now?"

"I told Mum. I had to tell her in the end. She's so upset."

"Are you surprised?"

"She wanted to go to the police but I said no point."

"No, not now. It's too late for that."

"She said I should at least tell you. So I have. I don't know what else to do."

"Good. Well, that's good. It's good that you've told me." I kept talking while my brain tried to compute. "Look, I've got a couple of things to clear up here, but then I'll come home. Alison will have to be told."

"How?"

"I don't know. But we'll find a way. She's got to know what he did to her and what he did to you. He can't be allowed to wreck two lives and sit back in triumph. She's got the only thing she ever really needed from him – the baby she's carrying. We'll get her out of there."

My cool determined tone must have settled her. She'd spewed up the poison now. She was ready to take control again. "Yes. We must. You're right. I'm glad it's …"

"I know."

"I'll go now. We'll talk when you get home."

As soon as she rang off, I called her mother.

Madeleine answered instantly. "Jude."

"Where are you?"

"In the conservatory. She thinks I've gone out, but I don't like to leave her at the moment. She told you?"

"Yes. Oh yes! God almighty, Maddy!"

"I know, I know. Why didn't she tell me before?"

"How are you coping?"

"Christ knows. If I'm holding it together, it's only for her sake. Jude, when will you be back in Britain?"

"I need three or four days to wrap things up here, but I'll make it as soon as I can. I'll book a flight now. Just hang on in there, Maddy."

I returned to my bathroom and stood under the shower. I was going to screw that bastard and make him choke on his own balls. I turned the water to ice cold. I was going to be ice cold from now on. I was a planner. I would plan.

* * *

Danny didn't plan. She never had. She was impetuous, rushing in without foreseeing the consequences. That was why she had phoned Simon, why she had gone to dinner with him and put herself at his mercy. It was why she was impetuous now, and for some reason, despite a career dependent in part on predicting what others would do, I hadn't predicted what Danny would do. I'd said Alison must be told, so she did it. She told her.

She was back on the phone to me two days later. Nine a.m. my time, so it must have been the early hours in Britain.

"Jude! I was trying to get hold of you."

"Sorry. I wasn't in my own room. Listen, I've got a flight booked on Friday and—"

"I told her, Jude."

"You've told Alison? I meant for you to wait until I got back and we could visit her together."

"I couldn't visit her. I couldn't go anywhere near where he might be. I phoned her. I told her."

"And did she believe you?"

"Stop interrupting me. You don't understand. I phoned her after I spoke to you. I told her everything and she kept saying, no, no, I must have it wrong. He couldn't do that. Why was I saying such terrible things? I couldn't get her to believe me."

"Oh Danny, of course she wouldn't, if you sprang it all on her like that? God, I had enough trouble getting my brain to cope with it, and I wasn't besotted with that lying fucking rapist. You were telling her the castle of her dreams was built on quicksand. No, built on slime."

"I know, I know, but she must have started to doubt, because she phoned me back. She wanted me to tell her again. I wanted to convince her of what he'd done to her, and all she could talk about was what he'd done to me. In the end, she said she couldn't stay there with him, not after that. She would have to leave him. I said to come to us now, Mum would come and pick her up, but she said no, she couldn't walk out without a word. She had to tell him face to face."

"Oh Jesus. Danny! Surely you knew that's exactly what Alison would do. She'd have to be fair and honourable and let him defend himself, and he'd lie and twist and persuade her black was white. He did, didn't he?"

"I don't know! She promised to phone us and Mum could come for her then. Only she didn't phone. We waited, and then Mum had to go to the hospital but she told me, if Alison called, to get her straight into a taxi. But she didn't call. I phoned her. I kept phoning and there was no reply. Nothing. In the end, the next day, Mum drove there, but no one answered the door. She went round the house and knocked and called, but there was no answer. And she still hasn't answered her phone. Jude, I don't know where she is and I don't know what he's done with her. I shouldn't have told her. It's my fault."

"No! Stop it, Danny. There's only one person to blame and it's Simon Delaney. Now listen. I'm coming home. I'll see if I can swap my flight for a stand-by. Keep trying her phone. If you find out anything, let me know. I'll be there as soon as I can."

I phoned one of my colleagues. "I've got to go home. Family emergency. My father's dying."

"Your father died four years ago."

"My mother then."

"What's going on, Judith?"

"I have to go. Don't be difficult, Sandy. Just take my word for it, it's important."

"What about the Americans?"

"You're the diplomat. Be diplomatic."

It took a fair bit of my own diplomacy but in the end I managed to get a standby ticket on a direct flight. Economy; beggars can't be choosers. Boarding the plane, I checked with Danny once more. "Still no word from her?"

"No! Mum's making calls. But he's killed her. I know he has."

"Danny! You don't know anything. He may be a bastard but he wouldn't be that stupid. She's probably taken herself off somewhere, to think. She may be fine. Just calm down and wait for me. I've got to switch my phone off now, but I'll see you at Heathrow."

She may be fine. Who was I kidding? I was fearing the worst just as much as Danny. I was going to have to go on fearing it for the next twelve hours.

2. Jude, Heathrow
20th June 2018

We were coming in over Kew. I could see it clearly. As the plane took another plunge, I was remembering our first meeting, in a greenhouse, with Alison, the sad little girl whose brothers had died and whose mother was now dead too. A bond had been made that day that nothing would ever break. We'd gone on to take different paths, Alison to the Royal College of Music, Danny following her father in Oxford, me to Cambridge, and then to careers and marriages, but we'd remained indivisible in ways other people would never understand. Except Maddy, perhaps, Mrs Doctor, who had mothered all three of us.

No more mothering now. We had grown up, passed some invisible threshold… My gut knew that today another threshold had been crossed from which there could be no turning back.

Hands were pressing against my seat. The passenger behind me was breathing heavily, shuddering with nerves. The ground came up to meet us and I usually enjoyed the thrill of danger but not today. All I felt was a sense of doom. I'd travelled in haste, but now I wanted to delay the end.

I sat motionless, refusing to stir until the hordes had finally shuffled to the doors. Once I'd passed the last stewardess, smiling her corporate smile and thanking me for flying with Korean Air, I fished out my phone and switched it on. Texts promptly piled up. There was only one I needed to read. I read it. The chill in my stomach gnawed its way into my heart. I pocketed my phone and marched towards Arrivals.

I saw them a few moments before they spotted me, their expressions confirming the brief blunt text. Madeleine, face lined by grief, and my Danny, drawn, gaunt, desolate, arms wrapped round herself until she saw me. Her mouth opened in a silent tormented greeting, her arms dropped and she ran towards me, embracing me in a wave of desperation. I embraced her back.

"Jude, thank God you came!" her broken voice whispered in my ear.

"I've been in the air for twelve hours. Only just got your text. Please tell me it's not true."

She gasped a strangled scream.

I pushed her back, holding her so that I could see her eyes. "Say it."

"Yes! It's true." Her face seemed to disintegrate before me. "I shouldn't have told her. But I did, I told her and because of that she's dead, Jude. Alison is dead."

I found myself swaying, still disorientated by being back on solid ground. Why did I need it spelling out again? I'd known what was coming before I'd even got on the plane. Over Danny's shoulder, Madeleine shook her head in confirmation.

"How?" I asked.

Danny hugged me again, tighter. "I don't care what they say about suicide. It was Simon, I know it. He killed her, Jude! I know he did! I told them but they wouldn't listen. They've let him just walk away. How could they? He killed her!"

I winced, imagining how her unrestrained grief would have gone down in a police station. I glanced at her mother again.

Madeleine smiled painfully. "Simon was in London, nowhere near, and plenty of alibis. Danny, my poor girl, can't accept that it was suicide. She accused him and they took him in for questioning, but of course they had nothing to hold him on."

"Poor Simon," I said.

Danny pushed herself away from me, staring at me with horror. "How can you say that?" She was beyond being capable of registering sarcasm.

I would have made the point clearer, but now that I could focus on her fully, I was filled with equal horror, taking in her skeletal frame, her hollow cheeks, her sunken eyes. "Danny! Are you…? Oh my God, it's back, isn't it?"

She looked away. I turned to her mother.

Madeleine swallowed. "Yes. It was too good to be true. The cancer's back. And it's spread."

"Jesus," I whispered. "Have you started treatment?"

Danny shook her head fiercely. "I don't want it."

"Danny…" I paused. There was too much pent-up emotion here on a Heathrow concourse. We needed privacy. "Come on. Let's get home. Where's your car? I'll drive."

"After that long flight?" asked Madeleine. She would always be concerned for us all.

"I got some sleep," I lied, taking the keys from her. I wanted mother and daughter sitting together, supporting each other, and giving me time to think. How had Danny seemed, the last time I saw her, which was more than three months ago? She'd been a little feverish, maybe, but she often came across that way. Or had I just grown complacent, thinking that the cancer was so far behind her we no longer needed to worry about it? I'd stopped looking for the signs. It was obvious now that things had progressed rapidly to crisis point for Danny as well as Alison.

We travelled mostly in silence, none of us ready to release the flood just yet. Danny began "Alison…" once or twice and then cracked up. I met Madeleine's agonised eyes in the mirror. At the Rackman's Oxford house, we hurried inside and while Danny went to collapse on the sofa, with Theodora to attend her, I managed to steer Madeleine into the kitchen.

"You said it's spread. How bad is it?"

"Bad. The worst. Inoperable." She could barely get the word out. "She must have known, but she never told me, missed her last check-up, as if… My darling girl, everything, what Simon did to her, the cancer and now Alison. It's destroyed her."

"There must be something that can be done. We can't let her just refuse treatment."

"She won't. She's adamant."

"I know it was awful last time but we have to talk her into it."

"Do you think I haven't tried? From the moment I realised... Oh, why didn't I see it sooner? But her damned independence. You know how we are."

Yes, I knew. Danny had been living back at 42A for the last six years, since the first bout of cancer and the break-up of her brief marriage. Laurence Brightman has been an academic like her. Not bad, just insufficient to the task of coping with sickness and chemotherapy. He'd envisaged marriage as coffee on the patio over erudite discussions of theoretical concepts. Danny had realised the match was doomed. With her blessing, he'd jumped at the offer of escape to an American university and she moved back home, where Madeleine could keep a professional eye on her. The back bedrooms at 42A were converted to an apartment for her, so that she could retain her sense of independence. It would have been easy for Danny to avoid Madeleine's scrutiny if she'd wanted to. And she clearly had, for several months.

"When she finally let me see how bad she was, I insisted she get herself referred to oncology, but I think she only agreed when she knew it was too late. She's put it off so long, I think there's nothing anyone can do now but offer palliative care and she's even resisting that. Jude, she's determined to die, that's the truth of it."

I hugged her, fighting for words. "Then at the very least we must get her out of this foul mess and into calm waters. Find her a hospice or something."

"I don't want a hospice." Danny had caught up with us, her eyes shining with fierce defiance. "You know what I want."

"No, Danny. Please, no."

"Yes! I joined Dignitas as soon as I was given the all-clear last time. I told you I was never going to go through that again. I've been ready for it ever since, but now… I can make the arrangements, I know what to do, but first, I want that bastard to pay."

I knew that anguish in her voice as if it were my own. It wasn't just her hatred of Simon driving her, but her guilt that her impulsiveness had led to Alison's death. I had to take it from her.

"Danny, that bastard will pay, but you've got to step back. Leave it to me. Please. Going to Switzerland doesn't have to be the answer."

Danny gripped the doorframe to support herself, her knuckles white. Her eyes were burning. "No, it doesn't. You're right. There's another solution if you prefer! Simon Delaney killed Alison. I don't know how but I know he did. And he killed me too that night when he… But they're letting him walk away from it, scot-free. So I tell you what. I won't go to Switzerland, I'll do it here. You do it with me. You drive a knife right through my heart and then you make sure Simon Delaney is framed for it. Let him go down for my murder. That's what I want. You can do it, Jude. I know you can figure out exactly how to do it."

I stared at her, then screamed at the ceiling. "Jesus!"

Madeleine's hands were outstretched, one on my arm, one on Danny's. "Danny, my love, how could you suggest that?"

"He has to go down for murder! He is a murderer, isn't he? He killed us both. He's got to pay!" Danny was swaying, close to collapse. We took her arms and guided her back to the living room where Thea was waiting, alert. As soon as we'd lowered Danny onto the sofa, Thea was up on her knee. Danny stroked her, instant calming therapy, but the determination was still there, etched into her face. "Make him pay, Jude."

I sank down on the adjoining chair. "He will pay, Danny. I promise you."

"Well then."

"But not that way. I'll make it happen, all right, but not that way. I don't want you involved."

"I am involved. I've already been to the police."

"To accuse him of murdering Alison. You didn't say anything about what he did to you?"

"No. I couldn't."

"They've spoken to him, so he'll have twisted things, making out you're just an ex-lover with a grudge."

"Ex-lover! There was no love in what he did to me!"

"I know." I reached out and patted Madeleine's hand because I could see she was near to collapse, herself. "But it will be his word against yours and it's too late for any physical evidence. So step back, for everyone's sake, but especially your own. Think about yourself and forget that bastard. Wipe him out of your mind and let me deal with Simon Delaney."

It was clear that the day had exhausted Danny. Her mother managed to persuade her to take a little soup, then we got her upstairs into bed. Back in the living room, all restraint gone, Maddy burst into tears as she hugged me. I had gone rigid, every muscle frozen.

"Sorry," I said. "It's taking some time to process all this. I was still dealing with everything Danny told me on the phone. Now Alison – do you know what happened?"

"It was suicide, apparently."

"No way! She was leaving him, yes. And she was pregnant. She would never have killed herself."

"I can't believe it myself. But he wasn't there and she was alone in the house. He must have imprisoned her there, you realise that?"

"Yes. Of course he must have, or she'd have run to you."

"He must have tormented her, bullied her, twisted her mind, making her believe there was only one way out for her."

"The child." I could see it all. "She must have been wild, fighting him. She'd been on medication. She'd been drinking too much. All he had to do was convince her that she was mad, everyone would see she was mad, she'd be certified. The courts would agree she wasn't fit to care for her own child, and the baby would be taken from her. Worse than that, given to its rapist father. She couldn't let that happen."

"I think you're right. What other explanation can there be?" Maddy moaned. "What makes it even worse is that I went there. Danny had waited all night, all morning for her to phone. She'd arranged that I'd go and collect Alison when she was ready, but in the end, I went to find her. There wasn't a sound from the house, nothing. I went round the back, rattled the door, called, but nothing. I thought the house must be empty, but all the time she was lying up there, maybe not dead yet, just unconscious. I could have—"

"No use thinking that, Maddy." I scooped up the cat and hugged it. "We can't save Alison now. We're five years too late. We should have saved her that day when she introduced him and it was so fucking obvious he was wrong for her, with his smarmy words and his red roses, straight out of a bloody Dummies Guide to Wooing Women. He could never have been her soulmate the way Tim might have been. Simon Delaney doesn't have a soul. I should have killed him then, instead of letting him take Alison from us."

"Jude…" Maddy took a startled Theodora from me, her face anxious. "Sometimes you frighten me. You're frightening the cat."

"Sorry. Sorry, Thea. None of that can be undone. We've got to think of Danny, now. Why, why, why didn't she tell us what he'd done?"

Madeleine sank onto a chair, clasping her hands, and bowed her head over her knees. "We know why. You understand it. I just wish… She only told me now because I insisted on knowing why she wouldn't even consider treatment. Even then I had to wring it out of her. Oh dear God, Jude, I want to kill that man. He's taken two of my girls from me. More than that! Everything. All that might have been. Daughters and grandchildren, Alison's baby – and Danny, no hope for her now. She had her eggs harvested before the chemo, you know, because she really hoped, one day… I'd hoped… Now it's all gone. She's lost that too, and all because that man… I can't even bring myself to say his name!"

"Yes. That man. Forget him. Leave him to me. I'll deal with it."

She looked up, alarmed. "When I said… you wouldn't… Jude, you're not actually planning to kill him?"

"Maddy, what do you think I am? Do you seriously think I go around with a Walther PPK strapped to my thigh? There are far better ways of dealing with people. I shall deal with Simon Delaney. I don't know how yet but I'll do it. Let me sleep on it."

* * *

Madeleine was in the kitchen early, making tea for Danny. "If I can get her to drink it."

"Do your best," I said, stabbing a loaf with the bread knife. "We've got to persuade her to fight this monster. If things work out, it might even give her the incentive to stay alive if she can."

"What things?" Danny had made it downstairs, so quietly we hadn't heard her. "Will you get him?"

"Yes, Danny. I'll get him. And when I've got him, we're both going to have to disappear."

"That's easy enough for me. That's exactly what I intend to do. I told you. I'm going to Switzerland—"

"Yes, Danny, maybe. But this is going to take time, so you must promise me you'll accept some treatment. Palliative care, anything to keep you going. Give me time and then, one way or another we are both going to vanish. You because you're his pregnant mistress and you've got his money—"

"No! Never. His mistress? Pregnant with his child? Never, never, never!" Danny was raging with indignation, while beside her Madeleine was wincing with grief for lost grandchildren.

"Hush." I took both their hands. "Danny, he's probably already told them that you had a fling, just to counteract your accusation and any others you might yet make. He raped you. Guilt is whispering in his ear. He's waiting for you to accuse him. Instead, let the lie run. Let people think it might be true, that you were, are involved."

"You're asking a lot," said Madeleine.

"Too much?"

There was a moment's hesitation then Danny shook her head. "Whatever it takes."

"All right. Deny nothing, that's all. I'll provide the proof that he's fathered a baby. I have friends… but leave that to me. When you disappear, the world will think that it's with his money and his child."

"And you?"

"I'll disappear too, because he'll have killed me. That will be after I've married him."

Danny looked horrified. "You can't!"

"You reckon I couldn't seduce that slimy toad?"

"I can't believe you'd let him touch you!"

"For Alison and for you, yes I would. I'll seduce him and I'll let him murder me. And then I'll come home with his head in a basket."

Madeleine, who had been shaking her head, aghast, broke into a bleak smile. "My Judith of Bethulia. Of course you will."

3. Jude, Bristol, 15th August 2018

"Jude. You're early." Tim Draycott, tall and rather saturnine, ushered me into their house. It was a subdued greeting, compared to his normal. Any jollity had seeped out of Tim when Alison had died. He'd loved her still, despite her marriage to Simon Delaney and his almost civil union with Ade. Of course he had attended the funeral and had seen me draped so lovingly on Simon's arm, so I wasn't surprised by the frost of his greeting.

"Hello, Tim."

No hearty kiss. Instead, he turned and led me down the passage to the Space.

"Ade. She's here."

Ade didn't know how to be frosty. "Hey Jude! How're you doing?"

"Oh, you know."

"Do we?" said Tim, waspish.

"Well, I'm worried about Danny, how about that? Just as you are, I imagine."

"Yes. No point in being worried about Alison anymore."

Ade looked pained. "He doesn't mean that. He's not stopped stressing about what happened. But yes, of course we're both worried about Danny. It cuts me up just thinking about it, so I'll do anything you like."

I smiled, cautiously. Ade knew about the cancer returning. I was fairly sure neither he nor Tim knew about the rape or the rest of it. They'd have been worse than frosty if they had. "All right, it's nothing too demanding. I'd just like you to come to Wales with me."

I assume they were expecting a rota of hospital visits or something. My proposal took them both by surprise.

"Wales?"

"Why?"

I gave them the guff about the need to find a quiet retreat where Danny could recuperate. They seemed to accept it.

"If it's for Danny," said Ade. "I'll do anything for her."

"Why do you need him with you?" asked Tim.

"Because I want a husband, okay?"

Tim snorted. "So I've heard." Ade just gaped at me, his grin widening.

I tried my best to make my explanation of Danny's need for privacy convincing. "Best if we can pass ourselves off as a couple looking for a holiday place. We can find the perfect place, sort out the purchase, get it all done quietly, and then Danny can move in without anyone noticing."

"Okay," said Tim, cautiously.

"I'll pack a bag, said Ade, bounding for the stairs.

* * *

So we drove over the bridge and across Wales and found our refuge. A bolt hole to vanish to, when the time came, but where I would already be established as a resident before I turned up in the wake of my own murder. Providing myself with an alternative husband, even if he later vanished, would make it less likely that anyone would equate me with the missing Mrs Delaney, should it make the national news.

There was a secondary purpose, much closer to the explanation I'd given Ade. If we could only persuade Danny to rediscover the will to live, to keep going for a little longer, then it could serve as a bolt hole for her too. I would take care of her there, while Madeleine remained behind in Oxford, fending off enquiries until the interest died down. No hope of quiet recuperation maybe, but at least a place to go in peace when the time came.

So I wanted a peaceful place, but also one sufficiently difficult for Simon or the police to find, just in case things didn't go entirely to plan. A place with more than one exit, if possible, but not accessible to random passing traffic. The Boat Shed fitted the bill perfectly. Even the satnav had trouble pinpointing it. It was invisible from the road but giving ample advance warning of anyone approaching, and with an escape route via the river if required.

We made ourselves known to neighbours and to the nearest pub. Ade certainly made an impression. He never could take his drink. How he thought he would manage running a bar in Spain, which was their joint ambition, I didn't know. Tim would have to be forever reining him in.

Now, at the pub, a couple of glasses were enough for him to embrace the role of fond husband, describing our wedding, the cake, the bridesmaids, our honeymoon, our pets and, of course, the children we were planning.

I had to get him out before he said something really unfortunate. Safely in the car though, it occurred to me that there had been more than a little wishful thinking in his flight of fantasy. I prompted him before he could slump asleep in the passenger seat.

"Are you getting broody, Ade?"

He managed a somnolent chuckle. "Wouldn't mind there being a mini-me out there somewhere. Always fancied being a dad. In an abstract sort of way."

"Very abstract. Not hands on?"

He grimaced. "Distant patriarchal oversight, maybe. Not the nappies bit."

"Of course not." I let him settle back while I sent a text to Madeleine. "I've found our Bethulia." Then I started the engine.

Ade shifted to get more comfortable. "You wouldn't marry Simon, would you? Tim would throw a fit."

His snoring saved me the trouble of an immediate answer. No one could sleep as solidly as Ade. Apart from surfacing with an urgent need to pee at Cardiff, he was dead to the world the whole way, leaving me free to consider a new possibility, another thread to weave in to the noose I had planned for Simon Delaney. By the time we turned into Lemmingford Road, I'd made my mind up. It was never wise to bring too many in on a conspiracy, but sometimes a few extras could make all the difference.

I pulled up in front of Ade's home and nudged him awake.

"Come on. There's a light on. Tim's still awake. Let's get you in."

"Uh? Are we there?"

"Yes. Move."

Tim opened the door for us.

"I'm glad you're still up," I said.

"Had to make sure you didn't abduct him too, didn't I?"

I followed him through to the Space where he had coffee brewing, before I responded. Ade had blinked himself more fully awake.

"Okay, start again. I'm glad you're still up, Tim, because I want to talk to both of you. I've been thinking about things Ade has said today, and I know that you think I'm a callous cow, out to snatch up my best friend's widower, which I don't deserve. I wasn't going to say anything, but I've decided to clear the air and explain exactly how it is."

"I think we have a fair idea…" Tim began.

"Shut up, Tim. Sit down and listen. I am seeing Simon Delaney. I am seeing a great deal of him. I don't know for sure if it will play out as I intend, but assuming he asks me to marry him, I shall say yes. Don't look like that. I need you both to accept it, because you are not going to make me change my mind. This is all part of the plan."

They stared at each other for a moment. Then Tim said "Plan?"

"What did you think I was doing? Falling for a prick like Simon Delaney? The man who destroyed Alison's career and drove her to suicide? The man who also destroyed Danny."

They were both quiet now, holding their breath, their eyes fixed on me, waiting for me to explain. So I did. Everything about Alison that I knew or guessed and enough about Danny to have Ade looking nauseous and Tim white with anger.

"So you're going to kill him?" suggested Ade, hopefully.

"No. Better than that. He's going to kill me."

"Ugh?"

"Tim gets it, I'm sure. And Tim's going to help me. Aren't you, Tim?"

"Count me in," said Tim, without hesitation.

"What about me?" asked Ade.

"You can carry on being my husband for now, over in Wales. Better than that. You have this craving to be a father, don't you? I'm going to carry your child."

"Ugh?" Ade repeated, his expression priceless.

"Don't worry, I'll keep my hands off you. But you needn't keep your hands off yourself. It will be yours and Danny's child. Maddy and I did toy with the idea of me somehow being a surrogate mother for Danny. You're the perfect candidate."

"But he's her cousin," said Tim.

"Ah." Ade pulled a face. "Well yes and no. I was adopted."

"You were? You never told me! Why didn't you tell me?"

"Because, you know, it never mattered. Mum and Dad were my Mum and Dad. It wasn't something I ever thought about. They told me when I was about twelve, but then it was forgotten."

"Right. I see. Anything else you forgot to tell me?"

"Unlikely," I said, trying to get them back on topic. "Ade can never keep his mouth shut about anything."

"No. You're right," said Tim. "Okay. We should have guessed you were all cooking something up. That performance at the funeral. It was so OTT." He glanced at Adrian. "Maybe you were sobbing so hard, you didn't notice Jude all over that bastard. I couldn't believe it. I shouldn't have believed it."

"Ye of little faith," I said. "I was making the web tight, that's all."

"Yes, of course. So, let me get this straight. The plan now is for you to carry a child for Danny?"

"I never pictured you as a mother, Jude," said Ade.

"Neither did I. But what the hell. What wouldn't I do for my sisters and for Maddy? I'm sure she can make the arrangements, do whatever's necessary through the clinic. I don't know that it will work, but it's worth a try… if only for the pleasure of depriving Simon of another child that he thinks will be his. He already has one on the way, though he doesn't know it."

"You're pregnant?"

"Good God no, you don't think I'd let him impregnate me, do you? I couldn't carry Danny's if I were. No, I have a couple of friends, Lucy and Brenda, keen to have a baby. We came to an arrangement. My first date with Simon, I got him blind drunk, slipped in a little pharmaceutical aid, and I milked him like a cow. While he was snoring, I drove his Porsche to a rendezvous with Brenda on the outskirts of Swindon. I handed over the goods and left them to provide the turkey baster. He was still snoring when I got back. I enjoyed the look on his face when I told him I'd been at the wheel of his pride and joy."

"God, Judith, I never want you as an enemy. Anything else you have planned for him?"

"This and that. The deal, with Lucy and Brenda, is that they get a kosher paternity test done, but in Danny's name. Something to convince the police he's been having an affair with her all the time, and something to convince Simon that there's yet another child out there he'll never get to see. That's something I want to rub his nose in. He got unpleasantly possessive about the child Alison was carrying. The child she took from him. So I want it to happen again. And again. And I want him to weep."

* * *

We all wanted Simon Delaney to weep. Tim was in the plot now and I knew I could trust him to do what was required when the time came. Meanwhile, Ade was happy to do his part, Madeleine handled the business, and it worked. First time, no complications, far quicker than we'd expected. I can't say I enjoyed the experience, but it could have been worse.

I was convinced almost at once that the embryo had taken – maybe my maternal instincts kicking in at last – so I didn't wait for official confirmation that I was pregnant. I decided it was time to marry. Simon was obviously up for it but he was dilatory about popping the question, so I took charge. We were ready to shock the world at the inquest.

Everything seemed to be on course. There were hiccups, naturally. I'd schooled Danny in what to do and say, but she still found it unbearably painful, just being in his company, even with me between them, and Madeleine was fighting to stop herself leaping forward to scratch his eyes out.

And then, of course, there was the girl detective. That was a complication I hadn't foreseen at all.

4. Dr Madeleine Rackham

I don't know why I let Jude talk me into it. It went against all my instincts, and yet, and yet… I had lost Alison to that man and now I was losing Danny in the cruellest possible way because of him. I couldn't bear to think what he'd done to her, physically, but even worse, emotionally. He had to be made to pay, but what could the law do? "Nothing," said Jude, the expert on what improbable things could be done, officially and unofficially. "We do it ourselves."

Then, once we'd started, once Jude had begun to tie him in her Gordian knot, there was really no going back. Sometimes I would lie in bed, the mother in me screaming to see him burn in Hell. The next night, I would be set tossing and turning with guilt at what we were doing. It wasn't how things should be. But then, nothing that he had done was how it should have been, so I left Jude to savage him. My God, she was savage too. Just saying his name, I thought she would spit fire. If she had turned up on my doorstep with his head in a basket, I wouldn't have been at all surprised. Sometimes, as I nursed my beloved Danny and watched her sicken and sink, I wished Jude would.

There was a moment when guilt nearly got the better of me and I meant to call a halt, before it went too far and got out of hand. But Jude returned from her first trip to Wales with Adrian and told us how she'd brought the boys on board, with a new twist to her scheme. A child. Danny's child. How could my heart not leap at the thought? This was something at last that I could help with. Something positive and good, in amongst all the negative evil. I no longer had to stand passively on the side-lines, watching with constant jabs of guilt.

Best of all, the possibility of a child gave Danny something more to strive for, something to keep a small flame burning in her will to live. If she could only survive long enough to see her child born… It wasn't to be. I blame Simon Delaney even for that. He started haunting us. Our adversary the devil, walking about like a roaring lion in our night. It began after their confrontation at Alison's inquest. Danny knew Simon's car all too well and she swore she'd glimpsed it in our street. Then she insisted that she'd seen him in our garden. I tried to set her mind at rest by keeping all the doors and windows locked, but I stopped putting it down to her paranoia when I too caught sight of him, lurking. I called Jude and she took over in ways only Jude would. We soon had alarms, CCTV and panic buttons. I turned down the offer of a handgun, but she installed a couple of friends in a flat across the road, ready to spring to our defence whenever we felt threatened. Jude never did anything by halves.

Despite our precautions, Danny was all nerves and her distress was dragging her down. Jude might keep us safe from Simon, but she couldn't keep Death at bay forever. We both realised it when the terrier girl detective came calling again, undeterred by snow and ice.

How she got to us, I don't know. The roads were impassable. I was at home, preparing some brunch to tempt Danny into eating something. I carried a tray up and found her on her feet, half dressed, supporting herself on the banister.

"I don't want you having to wait on me," she said.

"Oh Danny! That's what I'm here—"

There was a knock at the door, and Danny started. I put the tray down hurriedly, to peer down the stairs. Only an indistinct silhouette was visible through the coloured glass of the door. Danny had picked up the cricket bat, always propped ready, and was gripping it so hard I thought the knuckle bones would break through the skin.

"It's all right," I said. "It's not him."

"You don't know that!" It was too much, on top of everything else she was going through, that she was being driven frantic with terror of that man. There was no chance that he'd get in, but the mere thought of him possibly prowling outside was enough to send Danny demented.

"It's definitely not Simon," I insisted, as she made to follow me downstairs, the bat raised as high as she could manage. "Not nearly tall enough. It will be a delivery or something."

"I'll come down with you."

"No, you stay." I shooed her away and went to the door, assuming that the figure on the doorstep, in the inflated jacket and knitted bobble-cap, would hand over a parcel. Then I recognised her. The police woman who had called before. I'd invited her in that time and talked freely about Alison because Jude had said it would help to set the scene. But I couldn't talk to her again, not now.

"DC Quillan." I said it aloud, hoping Danny, if she were still hovering on the stairs, would get the message. I held the door half-shut just in case. "I wasn't expecting to see you back again."

"I'm hoping to speak to your daughter, Mrs Brightman," said the DC. "I've left five or six messages but no one's got back to me so I thought I'd better try calling in person again."

"Well, you've had a wasted journey, I'm afraid. My daughter…" How I longed to say "My daughter is too ill to see anyone." But that wasn't the game we were playing. I was supposed to be a mother disgusted by my daughter's improper behaviour. Easier said than done. "She was working all night so she'll be in bed and I don't want her woken."

The poor girl looked frozen. I really wanted to invite her in, make her tea and warm her up. There was so much I wanted to do and couldn't. "I'm sorry," I said and started to shut the door.

She almost pushed her way in. "I am not here to threaten your daughter. She's not in trouble. I just wish to discover what really happened to Alison Delaney, your daughter's friend, and I think Mrs Brightman knows more than we were able to establish at the time."

The desire to tell her everything was almost overwhelming. Oh, to have this whole thing over with. To let her see Danny and hear the truth from her own lips. But no, if Danny did speak to her, she would have to lie. Could I at least get that part of the charade out of the way? Danny wasn't up to it. Not today. "No, I'm sorry. As I told you, my daughter is asleep and she doesn't like being disturbed. Sorry."

I managed to shut the door, took a moment to recover my composure, then I hurried back upstairs. Danny was in my bedroom at the front, peeping out through the curtains.

"She's still there."

I joined her and peeked out. Yes, the detective was still there in the snow, like an orphan. She looked up at us and we hurriedly stepped back from the window.

"I have to speak to her," said Danny, sinking onto my bed.

"You're not up to it."

"I have to be."

She was going to insist, so I put it off. "Let me speak to Jude."

"What if Simon's there?"

"I'll have to chance it."

I got her back to her bed, then I phoned Jude. "Can I speak to Mrs Brooks?" I asked, when she answered.

"It's okay, he's not here. What's up?"

"She's here. The detective woman, again. At the door, not just phoning. I put her off, but I'm not sure I can keep getting away with it if she comes back."

"Oh hell. What's she doing out and about in this?"

"She looks as if she dressed for the South Pole. I felt quite sorry for her. She went away, but she could be lurking round a corner. It's bad enough worrying that Simon might be creeping around out there."

"Has he been back?"

"Last week. I thought I saw his Porsche this morning, but I'm probably beginning to imagine it. He's driving us both paranoid."

"If it's any consolation, you're doing the same to him. The texts are sending him crazy. You are remembering to make sure all the doors and windows are totally secure? Especially when you go out?"

"Yes, I haven't been taking any chances. And Danny's got the alarm you gave her, keeps it on her at all times."

"She mustn't hesitate to use it. Remember, you've got guardians just across the way, and they'll be on him before he knows what hit him."

"I know, and I'm very grateful. But what about the detective? What do we do?"

"Right. Well." I could hear a pen scratching. Jude was doodling, as she always did when she was marshalling thoughts. "Ideally, Danny should speak to her at some point."

"But she's not up to it, Jude. She's not good."

"We should have sorted this before. It's not going to get any better, is it?"

"No. It's only morphine and grit keeping her alive." The blunt reality of the situation hit me with agonising force. "She wants to go, Jude, and it's reached the stage where I want her to, as well. I can't bear seeing her struggle against it."

"Let me speak to her."

"All right, but don't put pressure on her."

"Promise."

I took the phone through to Danny. "Are you up to speaking to Jude?"

"Of course." She took the phone from me. "Hello, Jude."

I could hear Jude's reply. "How are you doing, girl?"

"Oh, you know. Some days are better than others."

"And today?"

"Not such a good one. But I know what you want. The Quillan woman. I have to see her, don't I?"

"Only if you're up to it."

"I'm as up as I'm ever going to be. Mind you, one look at me and she's never going to believe I'm a pregnant femme fatale."

"All right. We'll see what we can do. I'll come over now."

I grabbed the phone back. "Jude, the roads are terrible. You'd be better off—"

She laughed. "I can drive anything anywhere, Maddy. I packed Simon off this morning by suggesting the roads were too dangerous. His masculine ego immediately took the bait, so now I have to go one better, don't I? I'll be there ASAP."

She arrived half an hour later, parking up at the gate. I came out to greet her. "Is it wise, leaving it there?"

"The only bloody place in the street. I don't have time to walk a mile. The good news is, no sign of Simon's Porsche. If he was here, he's gone now. Right, hello Thea." She picked up the wet cat and followed me into the house. "Where is she, then?"

Danny was downstairs to the living room, and Jude burst in on her, then stopped dead, in shock. She gently put the cat down.

"Hello Jude," said Danny. "If *you* look at me like that, it's not very hopeful, is it?"

For me, living with Danny, the changes were imperceptible day by day, but Jude hadn't seen her for nearly three weeks. I looked at my daughter with fresh eyes, seeing what Jude saw. Danny was dying in front of us. Thea had jumped up on her lap and Danny's fingers were stroking her, but God knows how she found the strength to move them.

Jude recovered herself quickly. "Nonsense. It will be fine. We'll do this, and then you can forget all about her."

"I hope so, Jude, because, to be honest, I can't hold on much longer."

Jude met my eyes with that blaze that was a mixture of tears, anger and fire. Then she looked around the room. "Okay, so we get the lighting right, a bit of makeup... Let's see what you've got in your wardrobe. Then we'll go over exactly what you have to say."

I left the transformation to Jude, while I stood guard at the window. A figure appeared at the gate. "She's back," I whispered, turning to see my daughter transformed from "skeletal" into "Goth." I winced. "She's coming up the path."

"We're not ready," said Jude steadily, working on eyeliner. "Ignore her."

"But we want her here."

"When we're ready and not before. She's alone, isn't she? She can't force her way in."

So we crouched, motionless, waiting for her to go. The lights were out and the window was too high off the ground for her to come and peer in, but Jude was taking no chances. Thea was the only one breathing normally. Then Danny began to shake, sick, I thought, until I realised she was giggling.

I peered out cautiously. "She's going. No, looking back. No, she's gone. What if she really has gone this time?"

"As soon as we're ready, we summon her back. You've still got her card, haven't you? Now, Danny, let's hear you damn me to hell."

There were clothes to be arranged, padding to be slipped into place. Not that much was needed. Danny's stomach was swollen anyway. Then Jude was grilling her on what to say and how to look.

"It's going to be too much for her," I said, painfully aware what a strain it was for Danny.

Jude immediately sat back, but Danny was fired up by my words. "No! I'm fine. I'll do this. I want to. Just give me a dose to get me through it."

"You rest for a bit now," ordered Jude and beckoned me out of the room. Once out of Danny's sight, Jude's self-control sagged. For a second she looked almost as bad as Danny.

"I didn't realise how much she'd gone downhill."

"I know. She can't hang on much longer, Jude."

"I see that. I've still got things to do. If she can just keep going a little longer… Oh shit, I shouldn't have waited this long. It's just…" She laid a hand on her stomach. "I thought the idea of her baby might keep her going long enough to…"

"I know. She's tried. But she can't try much longer."

"No. She can't. So – you've got Tintinette's number? Let's make the call."

Just as Jude had predicted, DC Quillan was only too happy to come back. I rushed her in, because I knew time was limited. Jude was ensconced upstairs, listening on a baby monitor. I hovered in the hall, ready to intervene if necessary.

I couldn't hear much, certainly not enough to tell how the interview was going. I paced, until I heard Danny's voice, loud and clear, saying "Is that all?" The pre-arranged signal warning me that she couldn't take any more.

I made short work of bustling DC Quillan out into the snow. Fortunately, this time, she didn't linger. Jude came hurrying down and we went in to Danny.

She had collapsed. "Was it enough?"

"Bloody brilliant. Oscar performance," said Jude, helping me get her to her feet.

"I went to pieces a bit about Alison."

"But you drowned me in delicious vitriol. Couldn't have done it better. Now come on. Let's get you cleaned up and back to your bed."

We carried her up, between us, and I let Jude hold her, sooth her, sort her out. Loving sister. It must have been so painful for Jude to have to sit this out with Simon and see so little of Danny.

She came down with me to the kitchen once Danny had drifted into a doze.

"Thank God that's over."

"How did it go, really?" I asked. "Because there isn't going to be a second run."

"It was fine – assuming Miss Marple was more interested in words said than intonation. I don't know what to think about that woman. A detective permanently worrying at Simon's role in Alison's death. It's not something I reckoned on. I'm still not sure if she's a help or a hindrance."

"Can she mess things up?"

"Possibly. All we can do is trust. I expect she'll come and nag at me at Summervale. I'll have to decide then."

"Soon, Jude? It has to be soon."

Jude hugged me. "I know. I need a little more time to get everything lined up, but I promise you, no more prevarication. If she can just hold out a little longer, then we can let Danny go."

* * *

It was a month she needed. A trip to Bethulia to make it ready. Endless financial shenanigans and computer trickery. She'd taken charge of Danny's phone months ago and had been entertaining us with details of the texts she'd been sending Simon. That was Jude. For months I had gone along with her byzantine planning, an academic chess game with an infinite number of pieces that only she could have dreamed up. The part of it that had been truly in my hands, the creation of Danny's child in Jude's womb, had been the one gleam of joy in any of it, but none of it, even that, had seemed quite real. Until now. Now everything had become stark, cold, real and terrible.

Finally, Jude phoned me. Her voice was steady, but I could tell the effort involved. "Time for the end game, Maddy."

"Thank God." I looked at Danny, who shut her eyes in relief. "Thank you, Jude."

Arrangements were already in place. It was just a question of determining the time. Jude met us at Beaconsfield. She and Danny hugged. They both cried. I don't think they actually said a word. Then Jude hugged me and we parted.

Getting on the plane was a trial. Danny had to get herself through security, in case she was captured on CCTV. Once I'd followed her through, I thought, to hell with it. We'd have to trust to luck from then on. I got her into a wheelchair and held her tight throughout the flight. Adrian, thank God, was there to meet us in Zurich. He was the one in tears, though he did a masterful job of supporting her at the bank, before driving us on to the clinic. He couldn't stay for the end – not just because of Jude's instructions but because he'd never have been able to cope with it. Instead, Tim took over, handling everything from now on, ready to come back to Britain with me, while Ade returned to Spain to establish his alibi.

Jude was able to make one brief phone call, to tell me she'd had her scan and now she wanted to cut Simon's throat.

I sat with Danny. "You're going to have a son, and all is well with the baby."

She smiled and lay back, happy at last.

I held my daughter as she died.

PART FIVE
THE HANGED MAN

"Hello, son. Are you keeping okay?"

Simon's lip curled. "What do you think?"

"No. Well. It must be hard."

"Really? You've figured that out, have you."

Philip Delaney sighed, started again. "Your mother sends her love."

"Oh, sure."

"She'll come next time. But I wanted a chance to speak to you alone."

"Right. You'd best speak then."

"I suppose this is what it takes for me to have a chat with you. Prison. You've acted as if we didn't exist from the moment you went off to university."

"Have you actually got something to say, or can we just settle for goodbye?"

"Look, son, I know I've always been a disappointment to you. I was never the father you wanted. Never rich enough, never wise enough, never felt the drive that you have or—"

Simon yawned, pointedly. Would he never go?

"All right," said Philip. "I couldn't help it that you despised me, but I've always tried to be proud of you, of what you've achieved for yourself. I thought 'at least he's honest in what he wants.'"

"Finished yet?"

"I just want you to be honest now. With me, and with the lawyers, too. I spoke to a solicitor and he said it would go better for you, for the sentence, if you told the truth. It's not too late."

"I have told the truth. I've told everyone. I didn't kill her. Got that? I didn't kill her."

"Which one, son?"

"What?"

"Two wives and you never even told us you were remarrying. Didn't invite us to the wedding. We wouldn't have known about the first if that lovely girl Alison hadn't contacted us and asked us to be there. I really was proud of you when we met her. She was a wonderful girl, such a talented pianist, too."

"What would you know about it?"

"We heard her play. She sent us an invitation to a concert. I don't suppose you noticed us there."

Dear God, not that concert again. Of course he hadn't noticed his parents. He'd spent his life trying not to notice them. Hopeless fucking losers.

"She was brilliant," Philip said. "Everyone thought so. They showed it. That was the problem, wasn't it? I saw your face that night, that expression, the same one on your face when your brother won a school prize and you didn't. You couldn't bear her to be a success, with you stuck at the side applauding." He leaned forward, his voice low. "Did you kill her, too?"

"What? What?" Simon was half out of his chair in rage. "It was suicide, you stupid idiot. I wasn't fucking there, was I?"

"Yes, but did you drive her to it?"

Simon stared at him, trying to block out the memories of that day as they came hurtling at him, battering his defences. "You don't know what you're talking about," he said, his voice breaking.

"Oh my son. She was a gift from Heaven, that one. You should have been at that girl's feet, not destroying her. And the second one, Judith. What did you do to her?"

"Nothing! Do you understand? Nothing! It's what she's done to me. She was the gift from Hell. Can't you see that? Can't anyone see?"

"She was an interesting girl, though I only met her briefly. At your first wedding. We talked about Persian poetry. Did you know she spoke Persian?"

So? Big deal. She'd been a translator; it was her job. How was he supposed to know what languages she spoke? "Your point?"

"She was smart."

"Oh, don't I know it!"

Philip sat back, shaking his head. "If it's really true that she put you here—"

"She did!"

"Then maybe it's no more than you deserve."

"Right!" Simon sprang up, guards immediately stepping forward. "Get out. Go on. Go to Hell. Visit over!"

Back in his cell, he watched the sun creep across his window. It was all he would see now, day after day after day, time moving on without him, all his minutely devised plans for his life reduced to smoke, blown away on the wind. But this would never be solitary confinement for him. He could feel them standing behind him, where they would always be. Alison, her fingers on his neck. Danny's nails raking his cheeks. Jude's whisper in his ear. "Got you, you bastard."

PART SIX
WHEEL OF FORTUNE

"Now are you sure you'll be all right with that?" Mr Davis rubbed his chin as he watched Rosanna push off from the bank and manoeuvre out onto the water.

"I'll take great care," she promised, dipping her oar confidently.

"Watch the tide, mind. Don't get swept out and don't get stuck in the mud."

"I won't. I promise."

Mr and Mrs Davis ran a B&B on the estuary. They were a middle-aged couple whose children had flown, so they'd decided to search for new chicks to fill their empty nest. A small matter of a pandemic had thrown their plans into confusion, but now that life was returning to normal, they were determined to be up and running again, observing all the proper precautions of course, but still eager to ply their guests with mountainous breakfasts, biscuits galore and advice on where to go, what to see and what the weather was going to do. There were only two other guests, and they had set off for a serious coast path hike before eight, leaving the Drakes to give their full attention to Rosanna.

Rosanna had chosen Awel Deg because its garden dipped down to the river, giving her a clear sight of the opposite bank. The discovery that the Davises kept a couple of kayaks for their guests was a bonus prize. Her quarry was visible, a little upstream on the other side of the estuary, a tedious long drive via the nearest bridge, but hardly any distance at all across the water. So close.

On her arrival in the area, she'd driven that way, before returning to book in at Awel Deg. She stopped by a house called Curlew Cottage, and ventured down a lane between straggling hedgerows, confident that she was concealed from view. But then the hedges had given out and she had a clear uninterrupted view of the converted boathouse. Which meant anyone in it would also have a clear uninterrupted view of her as she approached. No chance of concealment. A kayak, however, was another matter.

Rosanna wasn't a novice on the water. She'd spent a holiday with the Barlows in the Lake District, where she and Shelley had become reasonably proficient in kayaks. Derwent Water was one thing. Tidal estuaries were a different matter, but Rosanna reckoned that she could easily manage it.

The tide had come in enough to film over the last mud flats. Time to go. At water level, the river appeared much wider than it had seemed from the sloping garden, and Rosanna could immediately feel the current pushing her kayak upstream. It was going to sweep her far beyond her target if she didn't take care. Her arms were beginning to ache with the strain of fighting against the flow. At last, within an oar's reach of the far bank, she allowed herself to drift unresisting on the incoming waters, until her goal came in sight – a jetty with a motorboat moored to it.

She edged up to the piles, fending off with her oar to avoid crashing noisily into the wood, then tied up and climbed, as quietly as possible, onto the jetty. A path opened between a wedge of sloe and hawthorn, to a rough lawn dissected by the remains of a slip-way, where an inscrutable tabby cat sat on an old weathered bench, watching her arrival without stirring a whisker.

"Hello Thea," she mouthed, before slipping between a ceanothus and a hydrangea to a short flight of steps leading up to a railed patio.

Two steps up, she stopped to survey the scene.

The woman was sitting on a canvas chair, laptop on her knees, one hand occasionally reaching down to stroke the head of the dark-haired toddler who was playing with a stuffed elephant on a rug. Her hair, cropped short, was darker than it had been. More chestnut than Pre-Raphaelite auburn. Without makeup, in a pair of faded jeans and a baggy sweatshirt, she bore very little resemblance to the glamorous photograph from Simon Delaney's desk that had been released to the press. Most people wouldn't equate the two. But Rosanna did.

Rosanna craned her neck to catch sight of the fingers busily tapping on the keyboard. Yes, one missing on the left hand. The movement of her head, though slight, was enough to catch the woman's attention. She looked up sharply, stared for a moment as Rosanna climbed into full view, then said calmly, "We appear to have a visitor, Danno. Shall we give her ten out of ten for stealth?" She raised her voice. "Maddy!"

A glass door opened and Dr Rackman appeared, wet mug in one hand, tea towel in the other. "Is it time for…" She stopped, seeing Rosanna.

"Would you mind looking after Danno for a bit, while DC Quillan and I have a little talk?"

"Yes. Of course." The doctor kept her eye cautiously on Rosanna as she placed the mug down, picked up the toddler and gave him a protective cuddle. "Will you be all right?"

"I'll be fine, Maddy," said Jude. She shut the laptop and set it on the ground, then strode over to join Rosanna. "Let's go down. After you."

It was easier than Rosanna had expected. No panic, no indignant denials, no aggression or attempted flight. Very civilised. She led the way back down, confident that Judith Delaney was following. Theodora jumped down from the bench as they reached the grass, politely making room for them. Rosanna started to turn, to ask if they were to sit, only to find herself thrown to the ground, pinioned, with hands searching her, head to foot, more thoroughly than the average suspect at the police station.

"Just checking to see if you're wired," said Jude.

"I'm not," said Rosanna. She decided it was futile to struggle.

"I agree. That's something. Let's go out on the boat. I always enjoy a day on the water. Easier to talk than sitting here, with me constantly wondering whether you have a companion stashed in the bushes."

Easier for Rosanna to be accidentally knocked overboard too. But it was too late to worry. If it came to a physical fight, on the water or on dry land, she would lose. So she shrugged and made her way down to the jetty, lowering herself into the motor boat when Jude nudged her. She fancied that Jude might be holding a gun, but she wasn't going to look round to see.

"Canoe! Very good. I didn't hear a thing." Jude jumped in after her and started the motor. No gun after all. She cast off and guided the boat out onto open water. "Let's head for the sea."

"Whatever you say. You're in charge."

"I always am. So, DC Quillan, all on your own or is a contingent of the Dyfed Powys Constabulary lining the banks?"

"I'm on holiday, that's all. And I'm no longer with the police."

"No? I'm surprised. You would have gone far."

"I don't think so. I didn't have the right commitment to the rules."

"A bit selective in what you chose to reveal? I've seen a transcript of the evidence you gave at Simon's trial. Enough to nail him but there could have been a lot more, couldn't there? Enough to get him off, even."

"I was only a DC. I'm sure the major crime unit dug up all the evidence required."

Jude was steering the boat effortlessly towards the churning foam of a sandbank, unaffected by the push of the tide. Awel Deg was already behind them. "So you stayed to see him being sent down and then you left the police."

"Eventually. I handed in my notice as soon as he was sentenced, but then it was Covid 19 and we were in lock-down and it didn't seem right to quit while the crisis was on, so I stayed on, in uniform, until things seemed to be settling."

"And now you're on your own private crusade. How long did it take you to find me?"

"Not long. There aren't that many properties called Bethulia." Rosanna smiled at Judith's raised eyebrow. "You came here with Adrian Merriman, the cousin Simon thought you'd gone to see in Bristol. He sent a postcard to his partner and a neighbour picked it up. She said it was of an otter statue. I googled it. Obviously not Bideford, since the card mentioned Wales, so it must have been Cardigan."

Jude gave an exasperated laugh. "Trust Ade to do something so silly. And the idiot mentioned Bethulia, too?"

"His neighbour thought he'd written a woman's name on the card. Beth Julia. I thought Bethulia might be more significant."

They were curving round the sandbank into the open sea. "The name means something to you, does it?"

"My father didn't like to have us under his feet in the house. I was packed off to Sunday School each week."

"It must have been a very thorough one, if you studied the Apocrypha."

"Not really, but one of our teachers, Miss Clarke, brought in a book of paintings inspired by the Bible. I think she was more interested in art than in religion. That was probably why she didn't last long. There were several pictures – Botticelli, Caravaggio, Cranach I think

– of a woman cutting off a man's head. It… made an impact."

"Personally, I prefer the Gentileschi version. Takes a woman to depict a woman really being strong. And a man being destroyed by her, instead of the other way round. Yes, that would impress you."

"I asked Miss Clarke about them, so she told me all about Judith of Bethulia, the beautiful widow who entered the enemy's camp, seduced the commander, Holofernes, and when he was drunk, cut off his head to carry home in a basket."

"It was a mistake to rename the house, wasn't it?"

"Possibly."

"My little joke. Misplaced. So you deduced that I wasn't a rotting corpse somewhere in the Thames. And you've hunted me down. To what end?"

"Just to get all the answers, I suppose. I could figure out what you'd done. All that evidence planted in the safe. Were those keys really the ones missing from the room where Alison died?"

"He wasn't stupid enough to keep the originals, but who could tell once the locks had been changed? Which I encouraged him to do. Poor Simon was convinced he was the only one who knew the combination to the safe. I love safes. One of the first tricks I learned. From a friend. His passwords were simple too. He's terribly easy to predict. All his confidential business was an open book to me."

"He didn't really fiddle the finances, did he?"

"God, no. He was tediously honest in business. Yes, that was me, with a little help, from other friends. I have a lot of friends. Colleagues. Contacts. Some on this side of the law, some on the other. They know better than to ask what I'm about or why."

"So you are now six million pounds richer."

"For a short while. I gave a lump sum to Ade and Tim to stop them going under in the pandemic. Most of the rest has been returned, by various means, to his more deserving clients. But I reckoned it would be perfectly proper to hold on to the money I'd invested in him, as well as Alison's fortune. He still has her house, theoretically. I am considering what to do about that."

"It's not ended yet, then?"

"Does anything ever end? Certainly not this. I have Danno out of it, and he'll go on for Danny's sake."

"Simon's son."

"No, though it was agreeable letting him think it was. Daniel Adrian. I promised him the boy would be named after his mother and father."

"The paternity test was just a forgery?"

"Absolutely genuine. A child that Simon knows nothing about, since he was unconscious when he made his contribution."

"Not borne by Danielle Brightman though."

"Good God no! He raped her. Do you imagine she'd be willing to have his seed inside her? That boy, called Noah, poor thing, is with a couple of friends."

"More friends willing to do you a favour."

"I was doing them one. They wanted a child; they needed a donor. Simon provided the means. If I'd known they were going to burden the mite with a name like Noah, I might have thought twice. That was the only child in my initial plan. Danno was a later addition, a little gleam of hope for those who most deserved it. Carried by me, but Danny's child."

"I saw her. You know that, of course. You were there, weren't you?"

"Upstairs, listening. How did you know?"

"You'd left your car outside."

"And you recognised it."

"Only later, when I saw it in your garage. The day when I called on you and I knew for certain everything was wrong. Your Stepford wife act was so at odds with that photo Dr Rackman showed me of you in the black basque."

"I overdid it, didn't I? I did feel a bit like Freddie Mercury with a hoover. So the car was a give-away."

"Same numberplate."

"Have you ever thought of taking up train spotting?"

"No. I didn't know you were there when I spoke to Danielle. I suspected someone else was in the house, but I thought it might be Delaney."

"He'd have been a dead man before he got in."

"When I saw Danielle, I realised I was supposed to think she was pregnant but it was obvious to me she was ill. Dying."

"I was afraid a cushion and dim light wouldn't be enough. It's an occasion I recall with acute pain. That interview nearly finished Danny."

"I'm sorry."

"Don't be. It had to be done. We needed it to happen. I just wish we hadn't left it so long. Maddy was in agonies."

"Was it Dr Rackman who amputated your finger? Or did you do it yourself?"

"I threatened to. Maddy wasn't keen at all, but in the end I twisted her arm. She's done a bit of emergency surgery. She was very good, although it was a struggle to stop her staunching the blood flow too soon. We needed a good amount."

"You were really prepared to sacrifice a finger?"

From being suspiciously affable, Jude was suddenly fierce. "I'd have sacrificed every last drop of my blood for my sisters."

"Lucky that a fisherman found it, then."

"Yes, wasn't it?"

"Another friend?"

"One on the wrong side of the law, in that case."

Rosanna gripped the side of the boat. Waves were rising and falling under them now as they headed further out, the boat speeding away from wide beach and cliffs. "Who are you, really?"

Jude laughed. "Who do you think I am?"

"I know who you are supposed to be. Judith Cartwright, daughter of Ronald and Eileen of Doncaster, born 1983, parents and younger brother died in 1988. Married in the USA to Edward Granger – and widowed shortly afterwards? Translator for a business advice company in London, and then secretary for an electronics company in Cheltenham. The boss, Mr Harper, told the police he had an idea Simon Delaney had pressurised you to leave your job with him."

"Yes, I must thank Mike some time."

"Not really your boss?"

"A friend. Works for us now and again."

"You built up a complete fake identity. Is any of it real?"

"Enough of it is. Judith Cartwright, bless her sweet memory, was real. I've used her as a handy spare for years. The name's similar enough to put any confusion down to mishearing or bad handwriting. She was born a few years before me. Actually died with her parents in '88. Car crash."

"Her death isn't registered."

"It was, at the time. Still listed on paper, I'm sure, but everyone relies on on-line records these days."

"And you have friends who can doctor on-line databases."

"I have friends."

They were out on the deep now, the wind rising. Rosanna had to raise her voice. "And your fake first husband, Edward Granger?"

"Oh, nothing fake about Eddie. He was quite real. I was in California for a while. He was a marine. I was using my Judith Carter ID when we had a naughty week in Reno, got very very wild, very very drunk and found ourselves very very married. Horribly embarrassed about it when we sobered up, so we agreed to keep quiet and pretend it hadn't happened. We went our separate ways, and a few months later he was killed – accidental firearms-related incident, so American. A pity. He was a nice guy. But it did give me a perfectly legitimate alternative identity, which is always useful."

"I'll remember that."

"I think you remember everything. Just as you notice everything."

"So who are you, when all the lies are stripped away?"

"Judith Francesca Carr. I didn't exactly lie when I listed my father as a civil servant. Okay, maybe not civil service exactly, but employed by the government. Lieutenant Colonel to be precise. Defence attaché at various embassies through my childhood."

"And you? What service were you in? MI5? MI6? GCHQ?"

"Whatever service you suppose me to be in, who said I'm not still in it?"

"Out here?"

"Maybe I took a sabbatical. Maybe I'm working again. Don't we all work from home these days? I can translate anywhere."

"You really are a translator?"

"Amongst other things. I was born in Germany, my mother's Italian, I spent my early years in Egypt and Jordan. Not Iraq; I was sent to stay with Maddy when my father was there. Then later in Japan and Korea. I picked up a lot of languages, so it was an obvious course to take. I specialised in Arabic and Farsi at Cambridge. Polished my Korean later."

"And you were willing to take a sabbatical from all that in order to destroy Simon Delaney."

"What would you do for your dead mother? He killed my sisters."

"Not your real sisters."

"Real in every way that counts. Judith of Bethulia. He's lucky I didn't go the whole hog and cut his head off. Many nights I was sorely tempted. But a life sentence is almost as good." The waves were bigger now, the shoreline a distant grey fringe far behind them. Jude gazed out to the horizon. "We brought their ashes out here. I reclaimed Alison's from the crematorium where he'd dumped them. I like to think of them both, Danny and Alison, indivisible, one with the ocean, encircling the entire globe, while Simon Delaney remains trapped in a tiny cell. Discovering what it's like to be locked in, held prisoner."

"I was right, wasn't I? That's what he did with Alison?"

"Oh yes. She told him she knew what he'd done, to her and worse, to Danny, and that she was going to leave him. That would be quite enough to trigger a melt-down in Simon. He locked her up to stop her. He must have known, the moment he turned the key, that he'd never get away with it, but he couldn't undo it either, so he had to go on. He tried to frighten her, to convince her that he'd keep her there till she gave birth. Then he'd get custody of the child because she was insane.

"It wasn't the first time she'd fallen victim to his gaslighting techniques. She was too frantic for logical thought or she'd have realised he'd simply trapped himself in a cul-de-sac. He was probably more demented than she was, but she couldn't see it. She was driven to desperation and the drink and the pills were there. He'd got her onto them, you know. Of course you guessed that. Then he got her off them again when he realised he'd turned her into a useless zombie, instead of the trophy wife he thought he'd bought. Never realised that she'd hidden a stash just in case she couldn't cope. The irony of it, eh? He'd locked her in with them. I think she was probably in such a state she took some just to try and get a grip, but it wasn't enough. She felt her only option was to finish it properly. The only way to rescue her child from his grasp. He'd transformed himself from angel to demon and she could no longer see him in any other light. It destroyed her."

"You can prove all this?"

"Of course not. But I know what he did, because he has a very uneasy conscience and he talks in his sleep. If they've given him a cell mate, the prison authorities probably know the full story by now. I know what Alison did because I know – knew – Alison as well as I knew Danny, as well as I know myself. She was always grasping at dreams. She genuinely thought she'd found one in him; he turned it into a nightmare and that broke her. There was a moment, when she decided to finish it, when she wrote on the bathroom mirror. An apology to her baby. 'I can't leave you.' It was too late then to change her mind."

Jude's jaw was set. "That is what Simon Delaney did to her. I won't speak of what he did to Danny. He broke both of them, so I broke him. So easy. I was his nightmare. Weak men are always petrified there's a woman waiting to emasculate them. It's what drives most serial rapists or misogynistic violence, I suppose: terrified weakness, living in dread of the strong woman with the snippers. And Simon is so weak. That's why he couldn't cope unless he destroyed Alison and Danny."

"But he wasn't on trial for them. He was on trial for you, your murder. His lawyer's lodged another appeal. Your body was never found, and corpses don't usually go missing forever in a river."

Jude glanced over the side of the boat into the opaque green with a sinister smile. "Not like the ocean, eh?"

"No. You probably could lose a body in an ocean. You might have to lose a lot of bodies. Other people might join the dots like I did, and you can't drown them all. He could still get off."

"That's true. It would be annoying, but maybe I don't care that much. He's finished, whatever happens. Just as long as he doesn't come looking for me and his son down here – because then I really would have to kill him."

"Would you do it?"

"To keep Danno safe from him, oh yes. What would you have done to protect your mother?"

Rosanna took a deep breath. "I did nothing for her. I said nothing – until it was too late and nobody would believe me."

"Your father got away with it, so you worked out your guilt by going after Simon Delaney instead."

"What would you know? You don't know anything about me."

"Oh, but I do. I made it my business, when you started getting too close. I could never be quite sure what sort of a threat you were. So I know how your mother committed suicide. Mandy Quillan, hopeless alcoholic according to most of her neighbours, but driven to suicide by her husband according to daughter Rosanna. The daughter who saved herself by leaving home to live with friends who supported her into a better life. And a budding career in the police, which you have now thrown away in order to crush Simon Delaney."

Jude sat back, folding her arms, letting the boat drift. "It wasn't the same, you know. I've seen all the files, so I know what sort of a man your father is. A back-slapping charmer to outsiders and a merciless psychological tormentor at home. You assume Simon's the same but he isn't. Just inadequate.

"His father's a poet. Fancy that. Published even. Poems in a couple of notable anthologies. But poetry doesn't earn a living. You do that by slaving on an assembly line or a cheese counter, to get by, day after tedious day. Philip Delaney's talents were far beyond Simon. Beyond his understanding, so he fixed on the talents that he did have, grabbing at the little ambitions that he could reach, the Porsche, the gorgeous wife, the office in Docklands. Unable to look higher. And anally obsessed with planning his life to the nth degree. He falls apart if one little piece doesn't slot into its proper place. I think I might actually have felt sorry for him if his falling apart hadn't killed my sisters. But he did kill them. And for that he had to pay."

"Are you satisfied, or do you want more?"

"A good question. What I want is not in anyone's gift. Alison and Danny are still dead, and nothing anyone does to Simon will bring them back. But at least I have Danno."

"And you're safe here. Does anyone else know who or where you are? Apart from me and Adrian Merriman. And his partner Timothy Draycott. I assume he was the mystery man on the night."

"Timothy? Mystery man? I don't know who you mean. I had no accomplice. It was all my own work."

"Someone played the part of Simon Delaney for the benefit of CCTV cameras and nosey Mrs Hargreaves. Someone with the hat and the car keys."

"If you say so. I have no recall of any such person."

"Then let's hope the police don't decide to check Mr Draycott's alibi as well as Mr Merriman's."

"Yes, let's hope so. He doesn't deserve the hassle. So in answer to your question, no, no one who didn't need to has any idea what I've been up to. My family's unaware anything has changed in my life. They never know where I am from one moment to the next anyway. My father died a few years back, heart-attack in a hotel in Tokyo. They were very discreet about the details, so I'm guessing he wasn't alone and over-exerted himself. My mother lives in Greece with her latest, Yiorgos, and I don't suppose the mysterious death of a businessman's wife back in Britain would have impinged on her consciousness. Same with my brother David, who's an art dealer in New York. We phone occasionally. He doesn't know that I married or that I died. My… company officially regards me as still on the books. Life goes on. For some of us.

"So, Miss Quillan, in your turn, do you take satisfaction in what you helped to do to Simon Delaney? Has it paid for your failure to protect your mother?"

307

Rosanna flinched, despite herself. "Same answer as yours. No. She's still dead."

"No closure then?"

"Not from that, no."

"But?"

"I've been contacted by the police back home. My stepmother Debbie left him, or he threw her out. Seems she's a homeless alcoholic now. He took up with another woman. He hit her and she went straight to the police. Wants him prosecuted. Now they've dug out my statement from when my mother died."

"So justice might yet be done."

"If there is such a thing."

"A good question. But I have a more pressing one to think about, first. What, I wonder, am I going to do with you now?"

Rosanna looked round, as they rose on the swell. "We're far enough out, if you're planning to dispose of me."

"We are, aren't we? But I don't think I will. You'd only turn up on a beach in Anglesey and questions would be asked. Besides, there's been enough waste already. What have you been doing since leaving the police?"

"This and that. At the moment, I'm working in a supermarket."

"On the tills? No, I think not. Ex-detective; you're probably employed to lurk among the trolleys and pounce on shoplifters."

"Beggars can't be choosers."

"But hardly the best use of your talents. I'm sure we could find you something better."

"Are you offering me a job?"

"Why? Do you fancy being a nanny?"

"Not really my thing."

"I could make enquiries. Suggestions. Because…"

"You have friends."

"Precisely." Jude began to turn the boat, heading back for the estuary. "Time to go back to Maddy and Danno, I think. Catch the tide and move on."

Printed in Great Britain
by Amazon